FAUN

FAUN

❖

A contemporary retelling of
Nathaniel Hawthorne's fable,
"The Marble Faun"

Martha Horton

This is a work of fiction. Names, characters, places and incidents either are the product of the author's imagination or are used fictitiously, and any resemblance to any actual persons, living or dead, events, or locales is entirely coincidental.

This book was printed in the United States of America.

To order additional copies of this book, contact:
Xlibris Corporation
1-888-795-4274
www.Xlibris.com
Orders@Xlibris.com

42008

For Marianna and John

In some long-past age, he must really have existed.
Nature needed, and still needs, this beautiful creature.

Nathaniel Hawthorne, *"The Marble Faun"*

PREFACE

I was in a ship's cabin, seasick and seven months pregnant, somewhere in the middle of the Atlantic Ocean. I was going home to Pennsylvania to have the baby. My Roman husband, a cinema stuntman, was to follow as soon as he finished a stint in the Italian air force.

My one-year-old daughter's bed was sliding from one side of the room to the other as the USS United States pitched and rolled. It was January, 1965; there was a storm at sea; and the ship had made no progress toward New York for 48 hours.

Marianna would chirp delightedly each time the ship tilted enough to send her crib on a roller coaster ride around the cabin. She was not sick, only hungry.

A stewardess knocked and brought in some jars of baby food. The ship lurched, the door swung and hit her arm. A jar fell and shattered, scattering glass shards and spewing pureed peas over the floor. The stewardess smiled gamely and said something along the line of "Oops!" I replied with a groan from my bunk.

The next day, the storm abated. I was able to feed and cuddle my daughter to sleep; clean the room and myself. The stewardess brought me a sandwich and some tea. I picked up the book I had selected for the trip at an English bookstore in Milan.

The title and cover illustration had caught my eye: "The Marble Faun," with an artist's rendering of a classical sculpture. The description on the back cover told me:

'This was the last major work by Nathaniel Hawthorne . . . Hawthorne tells a romantic story for the purpose of bringing out the inner complexity of man's soul and the effects of sin on human character. In 'The Marble Faun,' the sin is murder, the place is Rome, and the major characters are an American sculptor, two American women studying art and an amoral Italian count, Donatello, who strongly resembles the famous Faun of Praxiteles."

Fascinated by the classical, intrigued with mysteries, infatuated with Italy, and married to a bona fide Roman, I expected the book to entertain or, at the least, distract me during the remaining days of the crossing.

"The Marble Faun," however, was not an easy read. I grew impatient with the many pages of exposition and outdated travelogue. I was annoyed with evidences of what appeared to be the author's smug provincialism and anti-Catholic prejudice. I was out of sympathy with his characters, frozen in their 1860s social milieu. Motivations were left unexplored, plot twists unexplained. The ending actually made me angry.

But I was in love with the book. I thought "The Marble Faun" would make a marvelous movie. I could picture dramatic camera angles, imagine the haunting background music. From time to time, I would pick it up and reread certain sections, hoping to find some important information I had missed before which would tie up the loose ends. I even did a bit of research, only to find that readers in Hawthorne's day, too, were puzzled with aspects of the plot and unsatisfied with the conclusion.

Some twenty years later, my husband (successor to the Roman, who had not transplanted at all well), took me to see Andrew Lloyd Weber's "The Phantom of the Opera" in New York City. The scenes of the Phantom's black lair under the Paris Opera House brought back to mind the eerie episode in "The Marble Faun" when Miriam disappears during a visit to the dark and dismal catacombs of Rome and encounters her nemesis.

Yes! "The Marble Faun" as a Broadway musical! Marianna, now a beautiful singer with theatrical aspirations, was attending Oberlin Conservatory, and we were both entranced with musical theater. Again I picked up Hawthorne's tale.

There were many marvelous opportunities in the "script" for musical numbers: Hilda in her tower, singing to the doves; Miriam and Hilda, musing over Beatrice Cenci's fate; Miriam and the enamored count in the Villa Borghese park . . . but the plot! Today's audience—whether for a book, a movie or a musical—would demand reasons, answers.

If a similar story were told today, could rationales for the action be supplied?

I decided to try.

Not many weeks into the project, I realized that I couldn't rely on my memories of Italy from the 1960s—I had to go back. I needed to experience Italy again, and there were some specific things I wanted to investigate.

First was the faun himself, who is still in the Capitoline Museum where Hawthorne first saw him. Hawthorne wrote in his Italian notebook about visiting the Sculpture Gallery of the Capitol "*. . . where I looked at the faun of Praxiteles, and was sensible of a peculiar charm in it; a sylvan beauty and homeliness,* *friendly and wild at once. Its lengthened, but not preposterous ears, and the little tail which we infer, behind, have an exquisite effect, and make the spectator smile in his very heart. This race of fauns was the most delightful of all that antiquity imagined. It seems to me that a story, with all sorts of fun and pathos in it, might be contrived on the idea of their species having become intermingled with the human race; a family with the faun-blood in them, having prolonged itself from the classic era till our own days . . ."*

Hawthorne also gave several pages in "The Marble Faun" to a similar description of this statue, and young Italian count Donatello's resemblance to it.

I found the statue, but not its magic; the charisma was created by Hawthorne.

Donatello's villa at Monte Beni is described in the novel in a chapter entitled "A Tower among the Apennines:" *"About thirty yards within the gateway rose a square tower, lofty enough to be a very prominent object in the landscape . . . its antiquity was evidently such that, in a climate of more abundant moisture, the ivy would have mantled it from head to feet . . . . Connected with the tower, and extending behind it, there seemed to be a very spacious residence, chiefly of more modern date. It perhaps owed much of its fresher appearance however, to a coat of stucco and yellow wash . . ."*

He also described portions of the interior: *"It was constructed in a most ponderous style, with a stone floor on which heavy pilasters were planted against the wall, supporting arches that crossed one another in the vaulted ceiling. The walls were . . . completely covered with frescoes which doubtless had been brilliant when first executed . . . the designs were of a festive and joyous character, representing Arcadian scenes where nymphs, fauns and satyrs disported themselves among mortal youths and maidens . . ."*

I learned that Hawthorne and his family, while visiting Italy, had lived in a villa outside Florence which Hawthorne described in the Notebooks:

August 2, 1858: The villa is on a hill called Bellosguardo, about a mile beyond the Porta Romana: and we found it a hot, disagreeable walk through narrow, dusty lanes which climb the hillside between the high garden walls of the many villas hereabouts. Less than half an hour's walk, however, brought us to the iron gate of our villa . . . About thirty yards from the gate rises an old square tower, machiolated and battlemented . . . which dates, no doubt, from the middle ages and looks as old as the Palazzo Vecchio itself. The tower is gray and mossy with age . . . but the main body of the villa, appended to it, is covered with fresh modern stucco . . ."

Hawthorne disclosed in a letter to his friend Fielding: "I hire this villa, tower and all, at 28 dollars a month; but I mean to take it away bodily and clap it into a Romance which I have in my head ready to be written out."

I wondered if the tower and villa still existed. My travel agent put me in touch with a professor at SUNY Geneseo who takes students on seminar trips to that part of Italy. He didn't know anything about the villa, but referred me to a fellow professor who is a member of the Nathaniel Hawthorne Society. She referred me to Frederick Newberry, a professor at Dusquesne University and then editor of *The Nathaniel Hawthorne Society Journal*. Professor Newberry told me the journal had recently published an article by Fabrizio Barbolani di Montauto, whose family had owned the villa at the time Hawthorne rented it; in fact, this venerable gentleman grew up in the villa. I wrote to him and asked if I could see the villa when I came to Italy. He wrote back explaining that he had recently sold it, but would arrange with the new owners for me to visit.

Fabrizio Barbolani did more, escorting me personally to the villa where artists were busy restoring the frescoes which Hawthorne had described in "The Marble Faun." also showed me an alabaster skull which was mentioned in the book, and a photograph of his grandfather as a young man. Fabrizio pointed out his ancestor's elongated ears, speculating that Hawthorne used his grandfather as a model for the faunlike character in the novel.

There's another tower in "The Marble Faun:" the residence of the character Hilda. Hawthorne describes a small piazza with a bakery, a cigar shop, a fruit stand, a church with stone angels blowing trumpets decorating the facade, and *". . . a shabby palace . . . distinguished by a feature not very common in the architecture of Roman edifices; a medieval tower . . . At one of the angles of the battlements stood a shrine of the Virgin, such as everywhere at the street corners of Rome . . . for centuries a lamp has been burning before the Virgin's image."* The Hawthorne journal editor referred me to a manuscript he had just received from Professor Alma Amoia in Rome, entitled "Hawthorne's Rome: Then and Now." Dr. Amoia had done my research for me: she placed the tower at Via dei Portoghesi, across from the Portuguese church, Sant' Antonio dei Portoghesi. I was thrilled to find it, with the Virgin's shrine Hawthorne described still intact (although now embellished with corroded electric lighting).

Fabrizio di Montauto wrote in his article: "Old Tonino, whom I met in the 1920s when he must have been about 80 years old, still remembered the American writer who often came to their home to drink a glass of wine, a truly excellent wine that was produced until about thirty years ago, made with the grapes of local vines with a good alcohol content and an exceptional bouquet." This wine must have made quite an impression on Hawthorne because he takes a page to describe it in "The Marble Faun." It is the Monte Beni wine which Donatello produces at his estate and calls "Sunshine:"

"Taste it," said Donatello, filling his friend's glass, "But first smell its fragrance; for the wine is very lavish of it, and will scatter it all abroad."

"Ah how exquisite!" said Kenyon. "No other wine has a bouquet like this" . . .
and he goes on to describe it with a pale golden hue, delicate piquancy . . .
"sipping, the guest longed to sip again, there was a deliciousness in it that
eluded analysis." I was curious about this white wine, produced in the
Chianti region which is extolled for its red. I asked Elmira, NY restauranteur
Joseph Pierce, Jr. for guidance, and he referred me to a distributor in
Manhattan who suggested I look for Pomino, a white produced near
Florence, as the closest to what Hawthorne might have drunk.

Colleen Pisaneschi, who lives on a hilltop outside the Siena, was at the
time a translator for the Enoteca Nazionale, a library of wines. She took me
to Pietrafitta, a picturesque winery and vineyard near San Gimigniano which
dates back to the 12th century. Dante Alighieri doted on the Vernaccia wine
of Pietrafitta, and it's still quite good—better than the Pomino I found in
a Florentine wine shop. But Donatello's "Sunshine" eludes me.

My research trip was a delight, as visits to Italy generally are—even
armchair visits. I hope that readers will enjoy "Faun," and perhaps be
encouraged to read "The Marble Faun" as well. Hawthorne's fable continues
to fascinate.

Martha Horton
Elmira, New York
July 2007

PROLOGUE

Imagine, now, a real being, similar to this mythic Faun: how happy, how genial, how satisfactory would be his life, enjoying the warm sensuous, earthy side of Nature, reveling in the merriment of woods and streams . . . as mankind did in its innocent childhood, before sin, sorrow or morality itself, had ever been thought of!

Nathaniel Hawthorne, "The Marble Faun"

With an almost imperceptible rustling of leaves the only overture, the creature leaps, laughing, from the branches overhead.

He rises up before them, beautiful, human in form but with an animal's seamless grace. He is lithe-muscled and golden, his head covered with thick curls through which protrude the tapered points of his ears, lightly furred and fern-tinged. An almost supernatural energy surrounds him, benign but powerful, as if he is closer to his creator than the young shepherds who have come to the forest hoping to encounter him.

"*Il fauno!*" they call.

The faun!

He beckons the shepherds to follow him into a deep sun-dappled glade, a place uncommonly beguiling and verdant. Some trees are in pale bud or early blossom; others bear full-blown foliage and fruit; a few are aflame with autumn scarlet. Spring and summer vines and flowers intertwine, blooming together in capricious disregard of season. A waterfall, emanating from the gnarled trunk of an ancient evergreen, shimmers down into an emerald pool.

Here the golden-eyed faun pauses, reclining against a tree trunk. His lips are upturned in an anticipatory smile. He draws a reed pipe from under his cape and begins to play a simple tune. Soon, as if by magic, lissome, long-limbed nymphs emerge from the greenery.

The faun ornaments his melody with trills and triplets. The glade fills with the sound of invisible woodwinds and stringed instruments. The nymphs draw the shepherds into a lively dance.

Music saturates the air; the sky deepens to twilight lavender. The dancing grows warmer and wilder until at last the faun puts away his pipe. As the dancers fall exhausted to the forest floor, he reaches up into the foliage and brings down bunches of purple grapes which he places into a large earthen flask. The fruit is instantly transformed into sweet red wine to refresh the flushed and breathless dancers.

The moon rises, full as a ripe peach. Two by two, the shepherds and nymphs find secluded nooks where they murmur and nestle and twine. The most enchanting of the nymphs, with hair silver and flowing like the waterfall, smiles at the faun and leads him into the blackness of the forest.

The moon fades; the music fades.

The tall young man in a linen jacket who has been watching from behind the director's chair shakes his head, rolls his eyes, and scribbles a few lines on his note pad.

PART ONE

ROME

Trees, grass, flowers, woodland streamlets,
cattle, deer, and unsophisticated man.
The essence of all these was compressed long ago,
and still exists, within that discolored marble surface
of the Faun of Praxiteles.

Nathaniel Hawthorne, "The Marble Faun"

CHAPTER ONE

Nathan Kendall's Narrative

So full of animal life as he was, so joyous in his deportment, so handsome, so physically well-developed . . . There was an indefinable characteristic about Donatello that set him outside of rules."

Nathaniel Hawthorne, "The Marble Faun"

This time, I am not writing for publication.

Before more details fade from memory, I must set down what happened for my own clarification and to fulfill a promise to my wife.

I am forwarding a copy to you and a few other friends who have expressed an interest in what I might entitle "The Fable of the Faun." As you read my narrative, along with pertinent entries from Hannah's journal, you will probably have questions for which no answers are provided. I ask you to remember that this is not fiction, in which the author can neatly tie up all the loose ends in the final chapter. It is life, with all its inconsistencies and uncertainties, imperfectly recalled.

As a journalist, my accustomed role has been that of observer and investigator. In this instance I was a participant and, perhaps, the catalyst. Does the whole strange story hinge on my catching the gleam of sunlight on copper-colored hair? Was the bizarre chain of events set in motion because I saw something familiar in the way a woman walked?

I would like to believe that nothing I did—or left undone—contributed to the fall of the faun. Perhaps another motive for writing this account to exonerate myself.

The story begins in that year I surprised everyone by leaving Business News Network. It was, I admit, a radical departure from my career path. Since I graduated from Cornell, my career had progressed nicely from an assistant editor spot at a Gannett weekly in Westchester County to one of the chain's Midwestern dailies. There, in addition to general reporting, I developed a column of commentary on business, politics, travel, entertainment—whatever provided a subject for what I deemed my discriminating analysis and witty reflection. On the basis of the column's success, I was hired by Business News Network, beginning in their London bureau. I shaved my beard and made an effort to polish my image, cultivating the TV anchorman look: earnest countenance, wry smile, smoothly styled hair (the receding hairline was not intentional).

My transformation to foreign correspondent was a success, and my next move was to the number two spot at BNN-Milan. After a year there I was tapped for bureau chief in Brussels. I didn't want to go.

Twenty-nine may be early for a mid-life crisis, but rising through the ranks of a large publishing corporation no longer fulfilled me. My life was certainly interesting, even exciting at times, but never fully engaging. Perhaps it had been too easy, with few struggles and no real sacrifices, no "dark night of the soul," as Fitzgerald put it. I wanted to pause, breath deeply, really taste my time and place, savor it. I wanted to stay in Italy.

I'm half Italian, as you probably know. My mother went to Rome for three years with the U.S. Information Service in the Sixties and came back to the States with an Italian husband. The marriage lasted long enough to produce my two sisters and me; then my father tired of married life and disappeared into the Australian outback. My mother didn't seem to miss him much, and she quickly resumed her maiden name, Kendall. We did not see or hear from my father again. Perhaps I fancied that by living in Italy I could put myself into the skin of the adventuresome young man my father had been, understand him better. And myself.

I also wanted to begin work on a semi-autobiographical novel based on my experiences as a foreign correspondent.

When I told my family about my intention to leave BNN and try my hand at freelancing in Italy, Mom was all for it. She, of all people, understood the seductiveness of the country, the lure of sharing geography with generations dating as far back as history itself. Whether or not she suspected my need to establish a closer kinship with my father, she didn't say. She merely cautioned me, "Don't get lost," leaving me to interpret the advice as I chose.

My sister Tina, by then a fast-tracking sales director for a hotel chain, scolded me for making a stupid career move but wished me well. Daniella, cozily wed to a banker and mother of two bright and beautiful boys, worried that there was some problem in my personal life. Well, there had been, but it was over.

So now I had no ties, no responsibilities except to myself. I turned in my resignation and began to reinvent my life.

I decided to make my headquarters in Rome. As if it were a sign from the patron saint of freelance writers, I found a small apartment on the Via Tiburtina beside the old Aurelian wall, just a few blocks from where I got off the train from Milan.

The neighborhood was not stylish but had the distinct advantage of low rentals. My building was a boring five-story stucco. One entered through a vestibule with a black and white checkered tile floor. Next was a high-ceilinged hall with dingy dark blue wallpaper. At the end of the hall was a rickety cage-style elevator (or murky stairway, take your choice). Apartment number twelve was furnished with threadbare oriental carpets and massive mystery-wood furniture, dulled black with age. But included was a partners' desk which provided more working space than I had ever enjoyed in a modern office and a wall of shelves which could accommodate my major possessions—books and CDs. There was a tiny kitchen, a gaudy pink bathroom, an alcove with a sofa bed. From the window over the desk, I could see the sun set behind the dome of Santa Maria Maggiore. Perfection!

I set up my computer on the desk and went to work. Years of networking on both sides of the Atlantic began to pay off for me. I contracted to write a weekly column for the international edition of an English-language newspaper and signed on as a stringer for a couple of trade publications. I established contacts with editors at travel magazines. I joined Stampa Estera, the foreign press club in Rome, renewing acquaintance with colleagues I had encountered during the Milan stint. After a few months of hustling, I found I was able make ends meet and still smell the roses. It was with a modest degree of smugness, I admit, that I congratulated myself on achieving the sort of lifestyle which eluded my hard-driving, stressed-out peers. I was ready for whatever self-revelatory insights and adventures might follow.

Rome had a wealth of raw material for articles which interested me and my editors. One of my favorite sources was the film industry. While Rome is no longer the motion picture mecca it was in the days of Fellini and DeSica, there is still enough activity to generate news items and an occasional feature. When I learned about an upcoming British-Italian production being filmed at Cinecittà, the government-subsidized studio complex on the outskirts of the city. I queried an entertainment magazine and got the go-ahead to do a story.

I had some doubts that the film, based on the life of the Greek sculptor Praxiteles, would rate four stars. But an eminent American actor was playing the title role and his co-star was being touted as the new Sophia Loren. The British director's most recent film had been, if not a blockbuster, an award-winning artistic success. I was eager to visit the set and interview the principals.

Before heading for Cinecittà, I surfed the Internet for some background. Praxiteles, I discovered, was a ground-breaking artist much revered in his own time (fourth century B.C.). He was socially prominent in Athens and made enough money selling his works so that he wasn't dependent upon commissions from the government or affluent patrons, as were the more familiar Renaissance sculptors of Italy.

Praxiteles is recognized, according to one art encyclopedia, for introducing the undraped female form to Greek sculpture, with the purpose of enhancing the popular appeal of the state-approved goddesses. He also displayed "a predilection for the playful activities of adolescent gods." Many of his works were removed from Greece to Rome where numerous copies were made, including a famous faun (a copy of his "Resting Satyr") now displayed in Rome's Capitoline Museum.

More significant, at least in terms of a story line, was Praxiteles' relationship with his favorite model, the courtesan Phryne. He once promised Phryne his most valuable masterpiece in exchange for her services as a model. A woman of discernment and considerable street smarts, Phryne suspected that he might pawn off one of his lesser efforts and devised a plan to ensure this didn't happen. She had a fire set in his studio and observed which piece he rescued first from the flames. It was, of course, his best work, a statue of Eros, and that is the piece she insisted upon having as her reward. I began to see possibilities for the film.

Thus informed, I caught the Metro for Cinecittà. I was met at the studio by Raffaella Bianco, a member of the production company's public relations staff and a new friend. I had made a lasting impression on Raffaella at our first meeting by impulsively inviting her to dinner before I learned she was married to an Italian soccer star.

"Are you free for dinner tonight?" she greeted me with our standing joke.

"No, I'm married to an Olympic gymnast from Romania," I replied.

"What happened to the Polynesian pearl diver?"

"She got tangled up in some seaweed and drowned . . ." I wiped away a mock tear.

"You're incorrigible!" Raffaella chided, showing off her English vocabulary.

Raffaella still attracted me. She had a perfect oval face, small shapely lips, slightly prominent but perfectly straight nose, smoky blue eyes and golden hair—a Botticelli beauty. She put too much makeup on the face and pulled the hair back so tightly in a bun that only a few tendrils escaped around her ears. I felt the urge, not for the first time, to loosen that lustrous hair, pull her into the shower with me, and wash her beautiful face.

"When are you going to quit this racket?" I asked, as she handed me a hefty press kit.

"When Bruno quits soccer," she replied grimly.

Raffaella hated her job and the whole cinema scenario. But, she had confided to me once over a cappuccino, she was not going to stay home and have *bambini* while her husband cheated on her, the fate of so many other soccer wives. So long as she had a high-profile position, Raffaella theorized, she had Bruno's respect. If her formidable husband, a national sports icon in his azure Lazio uniform, might be tempted to stray by his adoring female fans . . . well, she, Raffaella, was pursued by famous actors and wealthy producers.

So she dieted her way to a size nothing, wore classy little designer suits, and cultivated a cordial but perfectly correct persona. She wore immense gold-rimmed glasses, and rumor had it that the tinted lenses occasionally served to hide evidence of Bruno's jealous tantrums. Theirs was not an ideal marriage.

Paging through the press kit, I noted the film's title, "The Marble and the Muse," and rolled my eyes.

"I know. They had a barn storming session, and that was the director's boyfriend's suggestion," Raffi explained.

"Brainstorming. Barnstorming is buzzing around the country making political pitches."

"Whatever." Then Raffaella gave me the bad news. The shooting schedule had been changed and neither the director nor the lead actors were on the set today.

"I'm so sorry, *caro*, I tried your cell and left a message." (I hadn't checked it—damn.) Noting my dismay, she quickly improvised: "Your trip isn't wasted—I have something very special for you. We're shooting a dance scene . . ."

"You're kidding!"

"No, really, Kendall. You see, Praxiteles dreams about the mythological characters who are the subjects for his sculpture. There are several of these dreams in the film—this one is about the Faun. And the set is spectacular."

"It sounds to me like Praxiteles was smoking something," I grumbled. "I can't do a whole story about a fancy set and some tap-dancing satyrs, Raffi."

"Don't be such a grooch. You can do a story on the faun. He's an aristocrat, a count, Donatello di Monte Beni. Come on."

"You mean grouch. Or maybe Grinch." I followed, deciding to make the best of it. The piece would bring only a modest sum; it wasn't worth a second trip to Cinecittà.

As Raffaella escorted me to the set, she told me that the production company's choreographer had spotted a young man running in the Villa Borghese park who looked a lot like Praxiteles' faun.

"He asked Donatello if he'd like to be in the movie, and 'Tello just laughed. I guess it took quite a bit of persuasion. But he's a perfect faun—you'll see." Her enthusiasm went beyond mere hype, and my interest was aroused.

The set Raffaella had described as spectacular looked like a Disney World version of Arcadia—the designer evidently couldn't say no to anything that bloomed, twined or trickled. There were dozens of people milling about amid cables and dollies and pulleys and props. Bored dancers, done up like Greek shepherd lads with short skirts and leather laces wound around their calves, were adjusting their costumes and blotting perspiration from their faces. Their feminine counterparts, admittedly an eyeful in their diaphanous draperies, alternately giggled and whined in several languages.

My enthusiasm for the project waned through the tedium of the highly involved set-up process, and after about twenty minutes I asked Raffaella if I could interview the faun now, before the shoot.

"Okay. I'll see if I can break him loose." She made her way through the maze of cameras and lights, ferns and fountains and eventually returned, leading by the hand a bizarre figure dusted from head to toe with greenish-gold powder. A faun or satyr, according to my research on Greek sculpture, was customarily portrayed with pointed ears, horns, a tail and sometimes goat legs, often carrying a reed pipe, a shepherd's crook, a branch of pine or crown of leaves. This fellow, fortunately was not encumbered with all these accouterments; he was reassuringly human except for the alien ears, and carried only the reed pipe.

"This is Conte Donatello di Monte Beni. He owns a vineyard near Florence. He's doing us a big favor by being in this film, *c'e va'*, 'Tello? Maybe he'll decide to be an actor and give up the wine business now," Raffaella blithered, a thing I'd never heard her do before.

The young man laughed and shook his head. "No, never. You know I cannot act, *Signora*." Then he leaned forward to shake my hand. "*Molto piacere*. I'm happy to meet you." There was genuine cordiality in his face and in his grip.

I had been prepared not to like him; he was just too good-looking. Although nearly naked except for a fig leaf thong, a fake animal skin cape and elf ears, he managed to look at ease, perhaps because he had the body to carry it off—well-muscled but lithe. He had thick curly hair. His eyes were an unusual amber color. His smile was warm and wide, revealing perfect teeth.

And the young count didn't display the expected swagger of the Italian film *fusto*, I noted approvingly. He carried himself with unselfconscious grace and energy. It would be difficult not to respond favorably to so engaging an individual.

I introduced myself (since the distracted Raffaella had neglected to do so) and took a few photos of Donatello with the bogus grove behind him; another with the make-up woman dusting him iridescent green.

We spoke briefly. His English flowed easily although he occasionally reverted to Italian to express himself more precisely. When he was called to the set, we made an appointment to continue the interview the following Monday over lunch, at Doney's on the Via Veneto.

Now the crew was ready to film Praxiteles' dream of the demi-god he would sculpt in marble. Raffaella found me a vantage point right behind the assistant director. The sequence began with the shepherds prancing into the forest where the faun hosted a sort of bacchanalia, with considerable assistance from the long-legged, long-haired nymphs. Perhaps on the screen it would appear a charming fantasy (film editors work magic) but to me, in spite of the intense preparation and fancy paraphernalia, the scene fell flat—neither ballet nor folk dance, and too tame for an orgy.

The entrance of Donatello, however, with a leap from the foliage of a prop tree, was impressive. He had, in addition to great looks and agility, a certain other-worldly quality which captured the imagination. He capered through some choreography with the shepherds and then settled against a tree trunk in a pose which, Raffaella whispered, duplicated that of Praxiteles' statue of the faun. Even with the nymphs to distract me, he held my attention. I sensed the indefinable aura that must have attracted the choreographer—charisma is an over-used word, but the only one applicable.

Unfortunately, one of the shepherds had stomped on a nymph's gauzy skirt, nearly disrobing her, and the scene had to be shot again.

I'd seen enough. I thanked Raffaella with a kiss on her silken cheekbone and took the Metro back to Rome. As I reviewed my notes, I jotted down a memo to myself to photograph Donatello beside the faun statue in the Capitoline Museum. It would be an interesting accompaniment for my story and I was frankly curious to see whether the resemblance was as striking as the choreographer thought.

I looked forward to continuing the interview and getting better acquainted with the faun-like count.

I liked him.

CHAPTER TWO

Nathan Kendall's Narrative

Here . . . are scenes as well worth gazing at, both in themselves and for their historic interest, as any that the sun ever rose and set upon.

Nathaniel Hawthorne, "The Marble Faun"

The Via Veneto was once the most glamorous quarter-mile in Europe: high fashion boutiques and jewelry stores, international banking houses and airline companies, turn-of-the century hotels festooned with flowers. In the Sixties, according to my mother, you would find seated under Via Veneto's rainbow of café umbrellas some of the world's great film directors and their stars, top designers and their mannequins, leaders of finance and industry, diplomats and nobility, elegant prostitutes of three sexes, and resident expatriates, some of whom were undoubtedly spies.

The mix now includes fewer genuine celebrities, regular working people like myself, and a residue of Eurotrash. You have a hard time distinguishing the tourists from the natives because they all wear Benetton, L.L. Bean and Tommy Hilfiger. But the Via Veneto remains a pleasant place to sit, sip an *aperitivo* and people-watch.

On the day of the appointment with Donatello, I left my apartment early to enjoy the walk at a leisurely pace. When I first came to Rome I bought a bicycle which, along with the Metro and the bus, met most of my in-town transportation needs. But that day I didn't want to worry about parking the bike at Doney's. Or perhaps I was avoiding comparison with Donatello, who was apt to come zooming up on a motorcycle, the preferred mode of transportation for young Italian males. I can admit it now: I was afraid to ride anything mechanized in the city's vicious traffic. Perhaps being tall was part of it—my vulnerable kneecaps seemed to extend beyond the protective parameters of the vehicle. Riding a bicycle put me out of the competition for speed, space, and machismo. I did bring my *telefonino*, the other necessity for making a *bella figura* in Rome.

I strolled along the old wall to busy Via Marsala, cut through the station and past the Baths of Diocletian to the shaded arcades of Piazza della Repubblica. There I stopped for a cup of espresso, a growing addiction ever since the first clammy winter in Milan. Once I caught a whiff of the bracing aroma, I had to have it whatever the weather.

By now the sun was high and the July morning heating up. I chose the shady side of Via Quattro Fontane; then crossed for a glance at the gardens of Palazzo Barberini, one of Rome's grandest art museums. There was a woman in a green dress emerging from the shadows of palazzo—she stopped to put on sunglasses. She was quite attractive—curvaceous and compact, and somehow familiar. Her hair, very shiny, medium length and unabashedly straight, was a particular shade of auburn that stirred my memory.

She began walking toward me: fast-paced, chin high, arms swinging, coppery hair bouncing.

"Hannah!"

She stopped, turned and, skipping only a beat or two, gave me a wide smile.

"Nathan Kendall!"

I would have hugged any other Cornell classmate I encountered in a foreign city, but Hannah and I had not progressed from acquaintance to friendship. I was never sure that she liked me, or even that I liked her. But here we were, and I was grinning foolishly, delighted to see her. I held out my hand; she accepted it with a firm grip. I think we both said something like what are you doing in Rome?

"I'm freelancing now, mostly travel stuff," I told her, "and I'm a permanent resident of the Eternal City."

"That's wonderful! Come to think of it, I might have seen your byline on a piece in the *New York Times*. Something about Hadrian's Villa?"

"Yes, something," I replied shortly. I was proud of that story. I'd put considerable passion into it and it made the front page of the Sunday Travel section. "And are you here to see the sights? *Turista?*"

"Oh, no. I'm working on an opera." After graduation, Hannah told me as we fell into step, she had gone home to Buffalo and earned her master's degree at the university there. Then she took a graduate assistantship at Yale while she completed a doctorate in composition. She was collaborating on an opera now, "an amazing opportunity," she said. "The libretto's based on the 16th century Cenci murder. I'm here for a few months to visit the

Cenci sites and sort of immerse myself in the ambience of evil old Rome while I finish the score."

Not a tourist.

I felt she had slighted my *New York Times* piece, and I'd quickly responded with the *turista* put-down. It had either gone over her head or, more likely, she had kindly chosen to disregard the jibe. I was suitably chagrined, and decided to make it up to her with a lunch invitation. For one thing, the opera project was a good story possibility for me; for another, I liked having her walk beside me. I'd forgotten she was small. The top of her head would fit under my chin.

"Dr. Ingram, would you like to join me for lunch and meet an Italian count who's working in a new movie?"

How could she refuse?

CHAPTER THREE

Nathan Kendall's Narrative

His usual modes of demonstration were by the natural language of gesture, the instinctive movement of his agile frame, and the unconscious play of his features, which, within a limited range of thought and emotion, would speak volumes in a moment.

Nathaniel Hawthorne, "The Marble Faun"

As Hannah and I walked down to Piazza Barberini, I told her about my visit to Cinecittà and how Donatello had been discovered in the park. I gave her a witty replay of the forest scene, describing it as a Dionysian disco.

"Sounds like just another Satyrday night to me," she quipped, topping me.

We stopped to admire the Triton Fountain with Bernini's muscular sea god, and I explained that it was one of the works which inspired Resphigi's orchestral suite "The Fountains of Rome." But of course she already knew that.

When we reached the foot of Via Veneto, I pointed out the Fontana delle Api, a drinking fountain with a bee motif, and explained that the bee is the emblem of the Barberini family.

"It's so whimsical . . . also Bernini's work, isn't it?" Hannah asked, all innocence.

"Yes." I had been about to launch into a dissertation on Via Veneto when something in Hannah's amused expression signaled a warning. I had attempted to be cordial, a seasoned resident sharing choice Roman insider anecdotes with a newly-arrived compatriot. Now I began to remember incidents from the Cornell days which made me suspect I was coming across as a patronizing bore.

I'd first encountered Hannah Ingram in an American Lit class when I was a junior and she a freshman. For me the course was a prerequisite; for her, a music major, an elective for general liberal arts credit. Perhaps that was why I, already editor of the campus literary publication, was annoyed with her penchant for holding forth in class as if her opinions were of comparable value.

We clashed directly more than once, but most memorably in a discussion of Hawthorne's *The Scarlet Letter*. Hannah said that Hester, the fallen woman sentenced to display her shame by wearing a scarlet letter A for adulteress, was not noble in refusing to name her partner in crime, the oh-so-spiritual preacher Dimmesdale: "Hawthorne made her a hypocrite. By suffering in silence she tacitly accepted a double standard."

I thought her premise was off the wall and said so. In the course of our ensuing argument, I realized (belatedly) that she had come up with a cogent point. The professor thought so, too, and affirmed her reasoning. The incident didn't exactly endear us to one another, and I summarily classified Hannah as a "brain" rather than dating material.

I couldn't completely dismiss her, however, because I sat right behind her in class. I was always staring at her hair, like fine strands of spun copper, wondering what would happen if I touched it. I imagined her shrieking, slamming me with the weighty Lit textbook, and filing a sexual harassment complaint.

The following year Hannah showed up with David Lin at one of our fraternity parties. Dave, a Chinese-American unique in that he was majoring in psychology instead of some cutting-edge technology, was a good friend. We were both on the tennis team. I was dating Barbara Something that semester, a honey-blonde pre-med major who gave soft kisses and hard massages. She and Hannah were sorority sisters, and the four of us spent the evening together, discussing all the universal themes college students love to ponder and carefully avoiding anything to do with American literature.

Dave was serious about Hannah, he admitted to me, but she had her career goals and was not about to let him sidetrack her. He kept trying. When Hannah was to sing in a Renaissance music recital, Dave wanted to attend and begged me to join him. I reluctantly agreed.

Hannah had a solo, an Italian art song which I might have heard before but never like that. Her voice was strong, clear, warm and dark. She wore a period costume, crimson brocade sprinkled with pearls, cut low in the bodice, which gave me a whole new image of her. I noticed for the first time that Hannah had breasts. Her copper hair was pulled up on top of her head with wisps escaping around her cheeks and the back of her neck.

The whole effect was disturbing; Dave's desire was obvious. It pained me that he had seen this romantic, sensual side of Hannah while I, in class with her a whole semester, had missed it.

When we went to congratulate Hannah at a reception after the recital, I became uncharacteristically tongue-tied but managed to mouth some compliment or other. It made her sea-green eyes crinkle and she laughed. Eventually she and Dave went off on their own, leaving me to my punch and cookies.

I remember seeing Hannah only once more at Cornell. She and Barb turned up at a tennis match in which Dave and I were playing. I can't remember who won; it was a hot day and I was gasping by the time we finished. After Dave and I showered, we joined the women and headed across campus to get something cold to drink at a student hangout in Willard Straight Hall. I recall that we teased Hannah because we had to walk so fast to keep up with her.

"What's the rush?" I complained, and Barb commented, "That woman doesn't waste any time getting where she wants to go."

Dave added wistfully, "I think she's trying to get away from me."

They broke up before we graduated.

Hannah, now, had the same keen vitality I remembered, but with less of an edge. Perhaps it was because she had already completed some major steps toward her career goal; perhaps it was because of her obvious delight with being in Rome. I decided, whatever our past history, I liked the present Hannah very much indeed. I hoped we wouldn't snipe.

As we turned up Via Veneto toward Doney's, I asked about the opera. "Why the old Cenci story, Hannah? Hasn't that been done to death? I remember something by Shelley . . ."

"Yes, a lot's been written and there was even an opera or two about Beatrice Cenci. But I didn't get to choose the subject. Evan Comstock—he's the librettist and an attorney, as well—thought he could give the story a new twist, make it like a courtroom thriller."

"Courtroom? Don't you mean torture chamber? As I recall, the papal court got its evidence courtesy of the rack."

"Well, yes, but we're skipping that part, I'm happy to say. Evan is concentrating on the lawyer's use of the incest story as a defense for Beatrice. It parallels what's happening today in a lot of domestic violence cases."

"Are you for or against the defendant, then?

"We're being purposely ambiguous, maintaining the paradox of a victim/murderer. And, of course, we don't really know the whole truth about Beatrice." Hannah said. "I hope I can come to understand her better here in Rome."

"Good luck with that—the whole city is a paradox," I said, not very helpfully. I couldn't see the musty old Cenci story as a modern opera any more than I could imagine a Greek sculptor and his statuesque fantasies as a movie.

Donatello was waiting at Doney's where he had saved us a table. We didn't see him immediately; he materialized from the deep shade of an umbrella, much like a faun from a thicket, I thought, amused with my simile. The Praxiteles dream scene had left more of an impression than I'd realized.

The count wore the obligatory sunglasses and a white silk shirt open at the throat, his hair longer than fashionable and curled over his ears. He looked every inch a movie star/playboy count, and I wondered how Hannah would react. Would I be totally eclipsed? They exchanged a few sentences and I saw that she responded to his unexpectedly modest charm and infectious energy much as I had, with interest and approval, but with none of Raffaella's flutterings.

When our waiter arrived, I ordered a Campari and soda, which Hannah seconded, but Donatello asked for mineral water. He also declined the wine I ordered to accompany our lunch: "I drink only my own wine."

He told us about the small vineyard which had been in his family for centuries. Hannah and I, both from upstate New York near the Finger Lakes wine region, wanted to hear more.

"Are you located in the Chianti district?' I asked.

"Monte Beni is close to the Chianti vineyards, but we produce only white wine," Donatello said. "My family has been growing grapes and making wine for nine hundred years."

"Makes our wine industry seem almost new," I observed, and we compared the similarities and differences of our native vineyards.

"Do you export your wine, Donatello? Can we get it in the States?' Hannah asked.

Donatello explained that most of the Monte Beni label was sold within a 100-mile radius of his home in Tuscany, "but I supply it to a few special hotels and restaurants here in Rome, in Milano, Genova, Venezia. I like very much to visit those cities."

"Have you traveled outside Italy? England, perhaps? Your English is very good," I said.

"You are kind. I studied English in school, of course, and I talk with English and American people when I have opportunity."

"But have you ever been to England," Hannah asked, "or the United States?"

"No, I'm sorry. I would like very much, of course. But I have not seen many countries—only France, Switzerland."

"You would love the Finger Lakes, I hope you can visit some day," Hannah said. "The vines grow on steep hills around the lakes . . ." She went on to describe our exceedingly beautiful part of the world with enthusiasm, then caught herself short. "But I sound like a travel agent. I'm sure Monte Beni is just as beautiful."

"I think my home is the most beautiful place in the world," he said with conviction, "but I hope some day to travel more."

Hannah said that she had always yearned to travel, particularly to Italy where so many great composers had found their inspiration.

I responded with my story of giving up a nice promotion just to stay and work in Italy. "I don't want to get stuck covering some EC financial crisis when the Palio's running in Siena. And I'd rather investigate the Etruscan tombs in Tarquinia than industrial waste in Germany."

"Why do you like Italy so much?" Donatello wanted to know.

"For one thing, my father was Italian, from Rome," I said.

"He's no longer living?" Hannah noted the past tense.

"I don't really know. He didn't stay with the family, didn't stay in touch. I scarcely remember him."

Hannah turned thoughtful. "How sad," she said, with real concern. "For your mother, too." I wondered if her parents had given her the "beware of Italian men" lecture that my mother had ignored.

"Although my mother was disenchanted with him, she never fell out of love with Italy," I went on. "Italian music, Italian art, Italian food, Italian wine, even the language, which she insisted my sisters and I learn."

"You speak Italian very well," Donatello commented.

"Thanks. When my sisters graduated from high school, my mother took them on a package tour of Europe which included five days in Italy. Dani bought a lot of shoes in Florence and Tina did some serious flirting with a waiter in Venice, but neither of them really shared Mom's infatuation with things Italian."

"She obviously succeeded with you," Hannah said.

"She did. When my turn came, she was determined to create a fellow Italophile. We spent three weeks in April touring on our own. I remember Easter morning in Florence," and I described the scene as Hannah's eyes widened: drums marking cadence for men in Medieval costume; the fantastic green and pink marble facade of the duomo gleaming in the sun, bells clanging, doves swooping up past Giotto's bell tower to a sky the same intense blue as an Easter egg.

"*Esatto!*" Donatello exclaimed. "It is just like that, the *Pasqua* celebration. So beautiful, with the birds flying up to the *cielo* . . . heaven?" He raised his arms over his head and fluttered his fingers. "I see it every year, since I was a little boy."

Hannah smiled, enjoying his enthusiasm as much as my story. "I'll bet you were a very happy little boy, Donatello."

"Oh, so happy, yes. Until my parents, they were killed in an automobile accident. Very young."

Hannah was all sympathy. "I'm so sorry. That must have been a tragedy for you."

"But it was long ago. Do not be sad for me, Signorina Hannah," said Donatello.

"So you are the last of the Monte Beni dynasty?" I speculated. "That must be a big responsibility."

"Yes, but it is not so hard," he said, "My job is to run the wine business and to fill the palazzo with bambini."

"All by yourself?" Hannah laughed. "Have you found a collaborator for this endeavor?"

Donatello blushed. "No, not yet, Signorina Hannah. But I enjoy looking."

"There are certainly plenty of pretty women to choose from at Cinecittà," I pointed out.

"Signora Raffaella? But she is married."

"No, no. I was referring to the delightful dancing nymphs."

"Oh yes, I know them, they are very beautiful. But not so intelligent and simpatica, like your Hannah."

Now Hannah blushed, but she replied smoothly, "Thank you for the lovely compliment."

I was unexpectedly pleased that Donatello had called her "my" Hannah, however premature and problematic that possessive pronoun might be.

"Your turn, Hannah. Tell us about your family," I said, really wanting to know.

She shook her head. "I'm not nearly so interesting, I'm afraid." She turned to Donatello. "We have something in common. My mother died very young, when I was only four."

"I am sorry for you," he reciprocated her concern.

"When I try to remember my mother, I hear music. She was a pianist. Perhaps that why I chose music—or it chose me."

"You play piano?" Donatello asked, rippling his fingertips across the tablecloth.

"Yes, and sing and compose."

"You write music? Brava!"

"It was my father who raised me," Hannah continued. "He's an engineer and a partner in a big architectural firm. He always hoped I'd follow in his footsteps, break the glass ceiling at some big corporation."

That explained a lot, I thought.

As Hannah explained the "glass ceiling" metaphor to Donatello, I checked my watch. It was after four; we had finished lunch an hour ago. We should be leaving, but I was enjoying Hannah's company too much to break up the party now. On impulse, I offered, "Look, if you aren't busy, you might like to come with me to an opening at an art gallery. It's not far from here. I don't know know much about the artist, but he's done a series of glass pieces based on Dante's *Inferno*. And the gallery owner is a minor celebrity—Lili Castelli."

"That sounds interesting. I'd love to come," Hannah said with no hesitation.

I brought out the cell phone. "I'll just call ahead to let the gallery know I'm bringing guests." Fortunately I still had the invitation with the phone number in my pocket diary.

While I was fiddling with the cell, Donatello, whom I hadn't really expected would care to accompany us to a cultural event, jumped to his feet. He preempted me by tucking a wad of *lire* under his plate to pay for lunch and whisked Hannah out of her chair with a breezy *"Andiamo!"*

I'd been upstaged.

CHAPTER FOUR

Nathan Kendall's Narrative

She resembled one of those images of light, which conjurers evoke and cause to shine before us, in apparent tangibility, only an arm's length beyond our grasp: we make a step in advance, expecting to seize the illusion, but find it still precisely so far out of our reach.

Nathaniel Hawthorne, "The Marble Faun"

The invitation to Galleria Castelli was one of many such sent to members of the Stampa Estera and was, as I well understood, a polite request for press coverage. I had not planned to attend until the event became an opportunity to prolong the day with Hannah. Also, there was a possibility that I could meet Lili Castelli, a favorite with the fashion magazines, and arrange an interview. It might interest *Vogue* or *Elle*.

With Donatello leading us on a shortcut around Trinitá dei Monte church, I told my companions as much as I knew about Lili Castelli. A vivid personality with a vague resumè, she had come to Rome about a year ago. She had opened the gallery in a choice location on Via Gregoriana, sparing no expense to make the building a showplace of taste and imagination. With considerable skill and discernment, she established herself as a patron of rising young artists whose work might be controversial but of sufficient merit to garner serious media attention.

Castelli was herself an artist. Her work was often critiqued as being too ephemeral, but could be found, like Donatello's wine, in some prestigious establishments and private collections. She also dealt in art objects and antiques, and there was speculation that her far-flung sources included some who were only quasi-legitimate.

At Trinitá dei Monte, Hannah got her first excited glimpse of the Spanish Steps before we turned down Via Gregoriana. When we arrived at the ornate wrought iron gate of Galleria Castelli, I presented my press card to a uniformed doorman. He checked his invitation list, nodded, and escorted us through a garden courtyard to a glittering reception hall.

As I had anticipated, the Galleria Castelli was the epitome of elegance, almost but not quite a parody. The walls were hung with ornate tapestries; the carpets were cushy Chinese and Persian. Chandeliers sparkled beneath a vaulted ceiling. Marble-topped tables held huge vases of exotic flowers, elaborate ice carvings, and silver trays laden with every edible from artichokes to ziti.

A waiter found us and offered slender flutes of champagne. Donatello declined, but Hannah took a glass and raised it to me.

"This is a marvelous treat, Kendall. I'm so glad we ran into each other."

I beamed.

A minion tapped me on the shoulder and invited us to view the *Inferno* exhibition. It was set in a vast "black box" room where dramatic lighting showed the pieces to their best advantage. I've seen outstanding glass art creations at the Corning Museum of Glass near my home town, and these were comparable. There were a dozen large pieces, standing about seven feet high. Each was composed of many layers of colored, carved and faceted glass depicting the topography and denizens of the Circles of Hell.

At first glance, the pieces appeared to hold delicate, almost ethereal images, like the doomed lovers, Paolo and Francesca. But as one gazed at a seemingly tranquil scene, the lighting evolved from soft blue to fiery red and the piece would erupt with a representation of one of the terrible creatures who tortured the damned souls in Dante's masterpiece.

As a molten medium, glass is particularly appropriate to the subject of the Inferno, and its malleability works well in illustrating the ripping and rending of flesh. I found the works both brilliant and appalling, and totally incompatible with calamari canapes.

If the three of us had viewed the exhibition in the context of a warning and had departed the gallery for some more mundane amusement, we might have avoided our own inferno.

CHAPTER FIVE

Journal of Dr. Hannah Ingram

A height of some fifty feet above the roofs of Rome gives me all the advantages . . . The air so exhilarates my sprits that sometimes I feel half inclined to attempt a fight from the top of my tower.

Nathaniel Hawthorne, "The Marble Faun"

July 11, 1997

I'm writing this in the heart of Old Rome, just a few blocks from the Tiber—no, Tevere—and around the corner from Piazza Navona.

I think my whole life has been leading up to this summer—seeing, sensing, assimilating bits of history and translating them into music. I want my work to transport people to times and places and emotions they never knew before.

"Dream big, Hannah," Dad always told me. Of course, he wasn't thinking about music, and I'm afraid he'll never understand the satisfaction I find in composing. But now that I have my first major commission, I can make a name for myself and Dad will be proud.

Mille grazie to Evan Comstock for this opportunity, and for all his practical help, as well—like lining up this apartment for me. It belongs to a cousin of Evan's who is spending the summer in Scotland. He even had his secretary make my travel arrangements.

On the flight from JFK, my seat mates entertained each other with complaints about the food, the service, the movie, the lines for the restrooms. But I found it all exhilarating—the sunrise filling the sky over the Atlantic; my first green glimpse of Italy beneath the wings.

After I cleared customs at Fiumicino, I followed Evan's secretary's instructions and took the train to Termini station in Rome—no minor accomplishment with all the luggage I brought. Some friendly German teenagers gave me a hand with it, and directed me to the taxi stand at the station when we arrived.

The traffic here is incredible, with motor bikes weaving in and out of the lanes and everyone honking their horns. And there's so much to see, I could hardly take it all in. Piazza Venezia and the Victor Emmanuele monument (called "the wedding cake," the cab driver told me, a perfect description). Remains of ancient Roman temples rising right in the center of a busy square. Churches, museums, shops, restaurants—like a travel video running on fast forward.

Then the driver left the main street and did a quick series of twists and turns, totally disorienting me. He maneuvered the cab into a dark, dingy little alley. I was beginning to wonder what sort of tenement Evan had consigned me to when the driver braked in front of a venerable old building with a square tower—Number 18, Via dei Portoghesi.

How to describe it? Crumbling pinkish brick and yellow stucco, columns flanking a dark, shadowed entranceway, green shutters closed over narrow windows, a balcony overflowing with ferns. And a tower—mine!

The building manager (*custode?*) was expecting me; Evan's cousin had left the keys and a nice welcome note with her. Signora Neri is friendly enough, even speaks a little English, but she left me to wrangle my luggage up the stairs by myself. A daunting proposition, and I've got some nice bruises on my shins to show for it.

The first room in my apartment is a studio, furnished in rattan and wrought iron and Dhurie rugs. There's also a mini-kitchen in one corner, hidden behind a bamboo screen. A free-standing spiral stairway—very Sixties—goes up to the bedroom and bath, and from there pull-down steps open to a small square patio on top of the tower.

First thing I did was check the view from up there. I can look down into the cobbled streets and across to other rooftops and terraces—some with palms and frangipani in terra cotta pots and elegant patio furniture; others with tricycles, TV aerials and laundry hung out to dry. Almost in my face are some fellow musicians—big Baroque stone angels blowing horns, figures on the facade of a church across the street. Doves circled overhead, then swooped down past the angels to find tidbits on the cobblestones below.

Unpacked and headed for the shower (no stall, just a circular curtain and a drain in the floor, but the floor is marble and the water pressure's impressive). Then I went out to see Rome.

I followed the foot traffic in the street to find Piazza Navona—mobbed with tourists, and no wonder. It's pure theater, a set for an opera, a huge oval "stage" with the surrounding churches, *palazzi* and sidewalk cafés as scrims. The stage is set with flamboyant fountains and horse-drawn carriages; the chorus is composed of artists and peddlers, a wedding party posing for a camcorder, mimes in full make-up and living statues posing for pictures, a tarot reader wrapped with strings of crystal beads, a snowy-haired couple in Lederhosen seated by a fountain with their arms around each other. There were couples everywhere with their arms around each other.

It's just like the books, just like the movies, just how Kim and Margaret described it when they took me out for a buon viaggio dinner. They gave me a detailed replay of their two-week vacation in Italy, including some close encounters with Italian men who never answered their letters. Of course, I'm not in Rome for a vacation, but getting to know the city is definitely on my agenda. I circled Piazza Navona a couple of times with a silly grin on my face, just savoring the scene and thinking "I'm here!"

I would have stayed longer if I could have found a seat at one of the cafés, but they were all occupied, with people waiting. I got out my guidebook and plotted a course for the Trevi Fountain. After a few misguided meanderings, I found it, exactly as it looked in "Three Coins in a Fountain" and "La Dolce Vita." The fountain is wonderful to see, of course, but part of the appeal on a sultry day like this must be the sound of the rushing water. I lingered awhile with a gelato from a street vendor (strawberry, luscious) until I began to get really drowsy—jet lag? After a few unplanned detours, I found my way back to the apartment.

There are some interesting shops close by—a tobacco store, tabaccheria, where you buy postage stamps and bus tickets. A panetterria—the smell of baking bread is almost irresistible. A fresh fruit and vegetable place, wine shop, newsstand, even a flower shop. Bought an Italian magazine to help brush up on the language but fell asleep looking at the pictures.

Evan's cousin must spend every summer away—there's no air conditioning and the bedroom is stifling (get a box fan) but I didn't wake up until after seven. Showered again, and chose a nearby place to eat from the guidebook—Ristorante Da Nonno. Brick walls, hanging lamps, white tablecloths, little bouquets of fresh herbs. And a friendly waiter who didn't flirt. I give it four stars.

I ordered all my favorite Italian things: prosciutto e melone, fettuccini with porcini mushrooms and cream sauce, sliced tomatoes with fresh mozzarella and basil. A carafe of Brunello. The waiter talked me into trying veal scallopine with artichokes—fabulous! An hour and a half later I polished it off with a cup of espresso (skip a few courses next time).

July 12

Went down to the corner bar for a cappuccino, a brioche and a tall glass of red orange juice—a wonderful Roman way to start the day.

Set up the computer and the Yamaha and reviewed Evan's libretto. Evan's not a professional dramatist—he's a very successful attorney, part-time poet and avid opera buff. I suspect that the Three Cities Opera Company decided to produce "The Cenci Case" with some expectation that Evan's high-profile career as a criminal defense lawyer will be a box office draw (that and his long-time financial support of the company), but he's a brilliant writer, as well.

Evan has taken the medieval murder and contrived an ingenious courtroom drama that's chillingly contemporary. As we have often discussed, the music must provide the pathos and poignancy, the menace, the terror. Evan chose me as composer, he said, on the basis of my requiem and oratorio and some glowing recommendations (from whom, he declines to say).

Not surprisingly, the major character in the opera is the Cenci's defense attorney, Avvocato Farinaccio. The female lead is Beatrice Cenci, the lovely young victim/murderess. There's her stepmother, Lucrezia, frivolous, frail, but ultimately valiant (a meaty mezzo role I wouldn't mind singing myself), and Beatrice's sleazy big brother Giacomo. These three are involved in a plot to murder Beatrice's beastly father, the Roman aristocrat Francesco Cenci.

Evan kills him off before the opera begins. "Who would take the part?" he argued. "At least Scarpia and Don Juan and some of the other opera villains have a macabre appeal. Cenci was just a brute, terrorizing his family and anyone else he could get his hands on." Exit Francesco.

But we have plenty of characters without him. There's the judge, the Pope, and a younger brother, Bernardo, pardoned for his peripheral complicity at the last moment. The actual killer is Olimpio, dashing *castellano* of La Petrella castle where the murder was committed. Olimpio is Beatrice's lover, by whom she has a child.

Beatrice is most often portrayed in literature as a pure and innocent young girl who becomes the victim of her father's abuse and incest. She plots his death only after all other attempts to escape have proven futile. Or, as other writers maintain, Beatrice seduces Olimpio with the sole intention of inciting him to kill her father; the incest allegation is merely Farinaccio's desperate eleventh-hour ploy to save Beatrice from the axe. Evan's libretto neither condemns nor exonerates her, leaving the audience to sort out conflicting opinions and emotions.

I've set my basic motifs, the recurring themes for the major characters (except Beatrice). I've completed an ensemble for the four Cenci—a lot of close harmony with some interesting runs and slides—and the big aria for Farinaccio.

Beatrice is my great challenge—two arias, and duets with Olimpio, Lucrezia and the lawyer. She is innocent, abused, trapped, rebellious, calculating, passionate, arrogant and finally penitent. Evan has provided the words for this progression, but the music must make the audience feel what Beatrice feels. To find an authentic voice for Beatrice is my major task here in Rome. I began my on-site research today.

First I went to the Cenci palace, where all the family members lived at one time or another. After the killing of Francesco at La Petrella in the Appenine mountains where he had sequestered them, Beatrice and Lucrezia returned to Palazzo Cenci and resumed an apparently normal life—with Olimpio, the former servant, seated at the head of the table.

Finding Palazzo Cenci was no problem—it's pictured in my guidebook with a full description. But when I came to the cheerful buttercup yellow facade, "embellished with heraldic elements and pretty balconies," it conveyed no hint of dark deeds within. It's an upscale apartment building now, with elegant shops and offices and even a bar in the basement. No help.

I came across a reference in an old travel book to a building which had been part of the Corte de Savella where Beatrice was imprisoned. According to the book, one can still see the barred windows of her cell. I started out in the Campo dei Fiori—"the field of flowers"—as the book suggested. The big square bloomed with colorful market stalls and crowds of shoppers. I bought some peaches to eat along the way.

From there I found Via dei Cappellari, one of Rome's many dark side streets which look forbidding but turn out to be fascinating. Along this one, furniture restorers, wood carvers and other artisans were at work in front of their shops. I soon came to a stone arch with a plaque referring to the poet Metastasio; from there I would glimpse, according to the book, a courtyard with an old gnarled fig tree and a covered passageway.

Because the book was old I wasn't too discouraged when I couldn't spot the tree. There was a little courtyard with passageway—the courtyard was piled with pungent garbage, and a couple of unsavory-looking characters were hanging out in the passageway. They looked me up and down and muttered something I couldn't translate (a blessing, no doubt).

I was beginning to notice, as I had not on my first ecstatic day in Rome, the same unpleasant attributes of urban life that plague big cities in the States. Somehow, it's even more offensive here, where nearly every street or building has some great historical significance. And what might be merely annoying back home—like a couple of rude young men—seemed menacing here. Perhaps that's the case in any foreign city, or perhaps it has to do with Rome's particularly bloody past.

I kept on walking, went around the block and found the opposite end of the passageway—the men were gone. I took a deep breath and entered: there were some dirt-encrusted windows with rusty bars in the evil-smelling murk, but which window had been Beatrice's? Another dead end.

I had one more site on my list. Beatrice, Lucrezia and Giacomo had been severely punished for their patricide: a public beheading in Piazza di Ponte Sant'Angelo. (The unfortunate Giacomo was flayed first and quartered after.) Surely standing on the very spot of the grisly execution would resurrect for me the terror of Beatrice's final moments.

I headed toward the river and strolled along it, grateful for the shade of the overhanging trees. I could admire the view across the Tevere even if my search for the soul of Beatrice Cenci was not progressing as planned. I passed the Mazzini bridge, the Prince of Savoia bridge, the Victor Emmanuele bridge.

Finally I reached the Sant'Angelo bridge and the square which had been the execution place of Beatrice and her accomplices. Tourists swarmed across the bridge, which was crawling with street vendors and littered with their unappealing wares. In the square itself were a small parking area, a church, a bookstore, a bar with booming heavy metal music—and absolutely no lingering miasma of violent death. If blood had been spilled here it was now buried under layers of earth and asphalt and the sands of time.

I sat down and ate a peach. Now what?

I trudged back to the apartment and fell into bed, exhausted. Still jet lag? The heat? Frustration?

I woke up at three, decided to bid addio to Beatrice and just be a tourist for the rest of the afternoon. Hiked across Victor Emanuele bridge to St. Peter's, which I won't even try to describe. I was awed by the whole, enchanted by the details—the folds in the marble cloak of a pope's statue, the angle of light through a stained glass window. Here I experienced the heady sensations I had hoped to find at the Cenci sites; here, of course, nothing much has changed for centuries and the present does not impinge on the past.

When I walked out into the sunlight again, I was surprised to find I had been in the basilica only thirty minutes—it had seemed like hours of repose, an effect similar to that of deep meditation.

According to my guidebook, the Vatican Museum was nearby and this late in the afternoon, the line should not be long. Still serene from my St. Peter's interlude, I began the journey through gallery after gallery: Etruscan, Egyptian, Greek, Roman; familiar sculptures like the heartbreakingly beautiful Apollo Belvedere and the struggling, straining Laocoon, but literally hundreds equally enthralling. And paintings—rooms full of Raphaels! A long hall was hung with amazing tapestries; another with historic maps.

I had an inspiration in the Gallery of Maps. Neither Evan nor I had been able to unearth much information about the castle at Petrella, the Cenci murder site. I studied the huge antique maps hung on the walls of the gallery and was thrilled to find Castello de Petrella on one of them, between L'Aquila and Rieti, northeast of Rome. I made a sketch of the location. Perhaps I will be able to find the castle, if it still exists.

On through the seemingly endless corridors of art and historical treasures I went; everything was becoming a blur. It was almost like a dream or, rather, a recurring nightmare of mine—progressing from hallway to hallway without ever reaching the final destination.

I stopped trying to pay attention and just went with the flow, finding myself at last in the Sistine Chapel, where all eyes turned up to Michelangelo's magnificent ceiling. I felt only claustrophobia and as politely as possible elbowed my way through.

It was another ten minutes before I escaped the Vatican Museum, almost faint with relief.

The long walk home was refreshing—I even remembered to buy a fan on the way. I visited the neighborhood shops for bread, cheese, cherry tomatoes, Perugina chocolates and a bottle of Frascati. Took it all up to the roof for a solitary picnic and assessed my progress. Disappointing. But the sunset was a crimson glory, and I have the whole summer ahead of me. I left some crumbs for the doves.

July 13

Raining—very unusual for July, Signora Neri says—so I ate picnic leftovers for breakfast and settled down for some serious work at the keyboard. Although I hadn't had my Pope character in mind when I went to St. Peter's, I found a voice for him now: majestic, lots of horns, parallel sevenths. Not afraid to wield his power but carefully controlled. Good. I worked till midday, and then sloshed out to "my" ristorante where I managed to exchange a few complaints about the weather in Italian with the waiter. Bruschetta with black olives, ribollito (a hearty bean soup, fine rainy day fare), salad, espresso, home.

I sat at the keyboard but yearned for the bed. What's the matter with me? I made myself go out and buy an umbrella. The rain had settled into a steady drizzle punctuated with occasional gusts of wind—even Piazza Navona was deserted. I wandered around, feeling as gray as the weather, and eventually took cover in Feltrinelli's book store, a cheerful emporium where I found three British mysteries—in English, grazie infinite. Picked up a few choice Italian toiletries to try from the farmacia. Stopped at a bar for coffee. Bought panini and almond cookies to take home for supper.

Four o'clock on my third day in Rome and I was bored, with nowhere to go and nothing to do. Except work.

My feet were soaked by the time I got home. Hopped into the shower with my new Italian bath gel—Terra Rossa (red earth), warm, bitterweet, sensual. It made me feel like I was getting ready for a date instead of dinner at my desk and a good book.

By now, according to Kim and Margaret, any number of attractive men should have offered to show me around the town. But why am I even thinking about men? A lot of women come to Rome hoping for a romantic adventure—I'm not one of them.

Still, there's no denying that this city just pulsates with sensuality (now where did that come from? Anne Rivers Siddons?). The sinuous marble men in the Vatican Museum, the couples embracing in Piazza Navona, the sunset and the scent of Terra Rossa—everything here conspires to make a person uncommonly . . . receptive. Even the thought of Beatrice and her Olimpio, furtively mating in some murky corner of the old Palazzo Cenci . . .

Time for a cup of tea and P. D. James.

CHAPTER SIX

Journal of Dr. Hannah Ingram

". . . if I could only get within her consciousness! If I could but clasp Beatrice Cenci's ghost and draw it into myself!"

Nathaniel Hawthorne, "The Marble Faun"

July 14

The fresh, clear morning was a good portent. I woke up energized and determined to set aside my various frustrations and get to work.

Leftovers for breakfast again—dry cheese, dry bread, gummy cookies and tea (get espresso maker). After some housekeeping chores I was ready to confront Beatrice Cenci face to face.

Hanging in the National Gallery of Art in Palazzo Barberini is a famous portrait of Beatrice by Guido Reni. Legend has it that Guido painted her in prison while she was awaiting execution, but now art historians say Guido was not the painter and that the subject might not even be Beatrice. Nonetheless, I was determined to take a look.

The Palazzo Barberini is a beauty, with a long oval staircase leading up to the galleries. The purported Cenci portrait hangs in a corner of a corridor, protectively roped off from curious visitors (like me) who are motivated by Beatrice's notoriety rather than by appreciation of fine art.

I studied the image of a sad-eyed girl who looks wistfully over her shoulder at the artist (hold that pose for any length of time and beheading might come as a relief!). She is sweet and pretty and quite unremarkable. I can believe she was an abused child; I cannot imagine her planning a murder or defying a papal court—although many contemporary killers look equally innocuous.

Before I left the gallery, I viewed many other portraits, powerful images that could easily inspire a poem or a story or a piece of music. Only Beatrice eluded me. Authentic or otherwise, her portrait brought me no closer to knowing her. How was I ever to isolate this individual, her time and place, from the layers and layers of history coexisting here?

I was pondering Beatrice, and wondering what to do about lunch, when I heard someone call my name. I turned and there stood Nathan Kendall, an old Cornell classmate!

He's a freelance writer now and lives here in Rome. And he actually seemed glad to see me. As I recall, Kendall made a point of ignoring me at Cornell. He had a good mind, but was decidedly pompous in his opinions. I recall putting him in his place in Lit class a few times—I was more than a little opinionated myself. Anyway, he was certainly friendly today (except for a crack about my being a tourist) and even invited me to lunch on Via Veneto.

Kendall looks good. He's lost some hair but he has a lot more character in his face. The horn rims make him look sort of scholarly and distinguished (he used to squint a lot in college) and I like the little laugh lines around his eyes. His voice is deeper than I remembered, more of a bass-baritone now, and I'd forgotten how tall he is. I like walking beside him.

At lunch he introduced me to Donatello di Monte Beni, who has a part in a movie about Praxiteles. Donatello plays a faun—he certainly has the prerequisite animal magnetism, and he's genuinely nice, too. He owns a vineyard in Tuscany—seems very young to be running a winery, but he grew up learning the family business. Kendall's doing a story about him.

Via Veneto is another of those places I remember seeing in movies. Being there today at the café with Kendall and Donatello made me feel for the first time that I belong in Rome, that I'm taking part in the life of the city, not just sightseeing. I was hoping the feeling would last longer than the lunch—and then, right on cue, Kendall invited us to an opening at Galleria Castelli.

On the way we passed Trinità dei Monti church and the Spanish Steps—a fabulous view across the city to St. Peter's. The gallery is close to the Steps and very impressive, beautifully restored. The courtyard was a delight, with orange trees and orchids and a harpist playing beside the fountain. And the reception was absolutely lavish. White-gloved waiters passing champagne, masses of fresh flowers—the buffet table was a work of art in itself.

I met some fascinating people there—artists, writers, diplomats, Italians with the same names as the streets, "Commendatore" this and "Contessa" that. My Italian is shaky; Kendall's is fairly fluent, but it was Donatello who really introduced us around—the giornalista (Kendall), the musicista (me). Donatello is a count, Kendall told me, so it's no surprise that he's at ease in these exalted social circles.

The exhibition was a glass art ensemble on the theme of Dante's Inferno—very impressive, although some of the effects were gratuitously gory, I thought (shiny pink shredded tendons). In spite of the genius of the artist and the dramatic power of the presentation, there was something repulsive about the exhibition. It made me uneasy in the same way as seeing decaying garbage or a dead animal on an otherwise beautiful street. I was relieved when we left the Inferno to explore the rest of the gallery.

We climbed a marble staircase to the second floor, which had a series of smaller salons—a wonderland of gargoyles and garden statuary, lamps and love seats. There was even a room filled with ornately framed and frosted mirrors. We stopped to admire a huge oval cheval mirror—the glass must have been slightly flawed, because our reflections were so odd that we were startled for a moment. Then, like kids in a carnival fun house, we magnified the distortion by making faces and wound up laughing at ourselves.

At the end of the corridor was the studio of the gallery owner, Lili Castelli. Here I felt as if I had wandered into someone's dream and was sharing subconscious fantasies. Castelli's work, like the glass art, is surrealistic and multi-faceted, but soft rather than hard. Her medium is chiffon, stretched and mounted in layers and back lighted so that the images, limned in with airbrush and paint and ink, shimmer with life.

There were many faces, with eyes which seemed to shift their gaze as I passed. Images appeared to move and change—a tree, depicted as a stark wintry skeleton, bore fruit or blossoms, depending on the angle from which you viewed it. Disquieting, but these works beguiled where the Dante pieces had repelled.

The subject matter, heavy with symbolism, appealed to me—mythological, religious, astrological, environmentalist, feminist. I was curious to hear my companions' reactions. Kendall said he admired Castelli's creativity and craftsmanship but found her work too fanciful for his taste. Donatello, however, was as intrigued as I. His favorite was a tangle of grapevines which surrounds the gnarled trunk of a tree and binds its branches; the tree trunk in turn imprisons a nymph. "We used to grow the old grapes like that, on olive trees," he told me.

We studied the paintings at length and discovered a recurring figure—dark, shadowy, vaguely menacing—which emerged from the background of even the most lyrical work. I wondered if it could be the personification of death, which is always with us, or guilt, or fear.

Donatello nodded. "I think there is something in her life that she must resolve, this Lili Castelli. She seems . . . *inquieto*."

The comment surprised me. I didn't expect Donatello to have this sort of insight. He hadn't had much to say about the Inferno pieces except that he had read a lot of Dante in school and didn't like it. He had seemed even more uncomfortable than I with the macabre images.

After seeing her work, I was eager to meet Lili Castelli, and Kendall wanted to arrange an interview with her. We went back downstairs hoping to find her, but no one was able to tell us the whereabouts of our hostess. We were ready to give up and leave when Kendall spotted a woman coming from the office area at the rear of the building. She was followed by a tall, dark bearded man who was obviously agitated—scowling and muttering under his breath. She sent him on his way with a dismissive wave and an emphatic "Non mi turbare più, vai!." Something like "go away and don't bother me."

The man bowed low, making the gesture a mockery, and departed at an insultingly measured pace.

As soon as she noticed us, Lili Castelli composed a welcoming smile and came forward.

I don't think I've ever seen anyone more striking. Her skin is an almond color, with a sheen about it—she is luminous. Her hair is black, pulled back tight like a ballerina's; her eyes are warm brown, mahogany. She might be Eurasian, Middle Eastern or Italian, part Oriental or part African. The deep crimson of her silk shantung suit accentuated her exotic appearance. Around her neck were several long strands of pearls and garnets, probably real.

"I regret that little disturbance," she said, in unaccented English. "A buyer's agent who thinks our long-time association entitles him to be annoyingly persistent.

"But welcome to our gathering. I am Lili Castelli." She extended her hand first to me, and after identifying myself, I introduced Kendall.

"I'm delighted that you could join us, Mr. Kendall." Her voice has an interesting timbre and cadence which I can't categorize—she sounds the way my Terra Rossa smells. "I will be happy to introduce you to the artist and answer any questions you have about the gallery."

She turned to Donatello. "And this is.?"

Donatello stepped forward, bowed, took Lili's hand and brought it to his lips. "Donatello, Conte di Monte Beni, Signorina. Sono molto onorato di fare la sua conoscenza."

"La ringrazia, Conte. Lei e veramente troppo gentile," she replied. Even without much experience in speaking Italian, I could recognize Donatello's salutation as overblown and old-fashioned; Lili's reply was in like manner, as though she were playing a part on stage.

To me she said, "You are a fortunate woman, to have two such courtly companions."

Kendall asked if he might take some photos and set up a later time for an interview with her. She agreed, and offered to give us a personal tour of the gallery. By then we had seen enough—I was beginning to feel the same satiety I had experienced at the Vatican Museum. But we all wanted to see more of Lili, so we followed.

Her commentary was so knowledgeable and entertaining that I found a new fascination with the gallery. For example, there was an emerald ring, purportedly given to Lucrezia Borgia by her father, Pope Alexander.

"Lucrezia was not the monster legend would have us believe. There is no evidence that she ever poisoned anyone. More likely, she was abused by her father, who certainly manipulated her shamelessly. But she was kind to the common people and they adored her.

"Of course," Lili smiled, "there are in Italy perhaps five hundred rings with secret compartments for poison which people would like to believe belonged to Lucrezia."

I couldn't resist asking, "Do you have anything here pertaining to Beatrice Cenci?"

"Poor Beatrice . . . another mistreated daughter. No, I'm afraid not. Why do you ask?"

I told Lili about the opera and about my frustrating search for some sense of Beatrice's passion and despair.

"You have a challenging project, Hannah. I am so interested . . . perhaps I can help. I will try to think of places which might be evocative of Beatrice."

Throughout the tour, Kendall asked questions, took notes, snapped photos. Donatello, obviously entranced by Lili, was uncharacteristically quiet. He looked at her rather than at the things she showed us and hovered close, insinuating himself between her and anyone who tried to approach. I hope he wasn't bothering her.

At one point, when a waiter came with champagne, Donatello did speak, to tell Lili, as he had told us at lunch, that he drank only the wine from his own vineyard.

"It is like liquid sunlight, Signorina."

"I would like to try it sometime," Lili said politely.

"It will be my pleasure to bring you a case."

Lili's eyes widened and she laughed. "That's a very generous sample indeed!"

He was being a bit presumptuous, I think, but she handled it gently.

Lili excused herself to talk with some other guests and Kendall arranged to meet her on Monday for lunch and an interview at the Tre Scalini in Piazza Navona.

"Be sure to include Doctor Ingram," Lili suggested, and told me "I will have some suggestions for you by then."

We left the gallery and walked back toward Trinità dei Monti. The sun had set and both sky and city were swathed in a violet haze.

"It looks like one of Lili's paintings," I said.

Kendall nodded agreement. "Indeed so, and there's the obligatory dark menacing figure."

At the corner of Via Gregoriana stood the disgruntled buyer's agent, motionless, glaring in the direction of the Galleria. Was he waiting to apprehend Lili and continue his tirade? It might be an unpleasant encounter. I felt a shiver of apprehension.

"He's a sinister sort of character—I'd cast him as Mephistopheles in 'Faust'." My Inferno-induced uneasiness was back, and I was grateful that Kendall and Donatello were walking home with me.

We went down the Spanish Steps, threading our way around the crowd of people who congregated there, seated and standing, alone or in groups, contemplative or animated. I felt the descent, like the luncheon at Doney's, was a kind of informal initiation ceremony into Roman residency.

As we strolled, Kendall asked, "What do you think of la bella Castelli?"

"I think she's exceptional," I replied. "Glamorous, talented, successful and she still took the time to show us around. I really like her."

"She's certainly charming," Kendall concurred, "and she seems quite candid. But I'm curious to see how much of her past she'll be willing to reveal in the interview."

"*Non importa*," declared Donatello. "Who cares about the past? Look at what she is now."

"Yes, but what is she now? She could be some sort of spy, or an art smuggler, or a gangster's girlfriend," Kendall teased him. "I've heard all sorts of rumors about her."

Donatello frowned, the first time I had seen him with anything but a pleasant look on his face. "People are jealous and will say anything," he said, his lip curling and his face reddening. "But they will not say it to me!" His expression was so fierce and his anger so sudden that I was alarmed.

Donatello was obviously bewitched by Lili—we all were, to some extent—but the vehemence of his reaction seemed out of proportion. Love at first sight? Is such a thing possible in this day and age?

Kendall said something conciliatory in Italian to defuse the faun's fury and by the time we arrived at my apartment, Donatello had calmed down and was his sunny self again. When I told the men that I lived in the tower rooms, Donatello said he lived in a tower, too, in his family palazzo—explaining that a palazzo is simply a large building, not necessarily a palace.

Kendall was very impressed with my location. "What a great place! How did you ever find it?" he wanted to know. I told him about Evan's cousin and described the apartment, wondering if Kendall was expecting to be invited in.

"It's still a mess," I demurred, "and I'm afraid I'm not prepared for company . . ."

"And I have an appointment for dinner. I must go now," said Donatello, being tactful.

Kendall took Donatello's cell number and said he would contact him when the photos were developed and give him a set of prints. We said goodbye with many smiles and handshakes.

"He's certainly not what I expected," I told Kendall. "He's charming, genuine. Was your father like that?

"I don't remember, but my mother says he was good-looking and high-spirited—he and Donatello have that much in common. He was a Roman. Mom worked at the embassy, he was with a hotel that catered parties there."

"Very romantic."

"Maybe. I can't help but think he was a bit of an opportunist."

"Aren't we all? You can't blame him for wanting to get ahead."

Kendall frowned, and I realized I'd said too much.

"I'm sorry. It's none my business, Kendall. I didn't mean to . . ."

"And I don't know why I'm still so sensitive about it. I'd like to believe he was a better man. Sorry, Hannah."

I changed the subject. "I'm a little worried about Donatello. Does he imagine Lili Castelli could ever be interested in him romantically?"

"And why not?" Kendall laughed. "An older, more sophisticated woman might find a such a handsome young stallion quite agreeable . . ."

"Or maybe she would prefer a distinguished-looking journalist," I said. "She certainly was quick to grant you an interview."

"She was, wasn't she? And thank you for the compliment. If you really think I'm distinguished-looking maybe you'll agree to be seen with me again. Dinner tomorrow?"

"I'd like that very much."

"Did you know you're just a block or so away from the oldest restaurant in Rome?" Kendall asked. "The Hostaria dell'Orso. It was an inn in the time of the Cenci."

"Really? Will we go there tomorrow?"

"Oh no, not until my next big check arrives. It's also one of the most expensive restaurants in Rome. But I know a great little Sicilian place."

He'll call for me tomorrow at eight.

CHAPTER SEVEN

Nathan Kendall's Narrative

*. . . every few minutes, this pretty and girlish face grew beautiful and
striking, as some inward thought brightened, rose to the surface . . .*

Nathaniel Hawthorne, "The Marble Faun"

Inviting Hannah to lunch that day, however impulsive, turned out
to be a smart move. The interview with Donatello di Monte Beni went
better, I'm sure, than it would have without her company. She has an air
of lively appreciation that's disarming. People respond by opening up to
her—Donatello, certainly, and even I found myself wanting to tell her how I
had come to be the person I was. As we sat leisurely soaking in the ambience
of Via Veneto, I began to feel that we were old friends, Hannah and I, and
Donatello a new friend rather than just the subject of an interview.

Much as I relished going it alone professionally in Rome, I missed
the camaraderie of close companions. My Stampa Estera colleagues and
others I made contact with through my work, like Raffaella Bianco, were
not people I spent time with socially; in fact, I had had no social life in
Rome at all until that afternoon. I could be aggressive—perhaps too much
so—as journalist; I was less sure of myself, or possibly lazy, when it came
to personal matters.

I think I got the interview with Lili Castelli partly because of Hannah,
as well. There had been almost instantaneous respect and admiration
between the two women. Still, I couldn't help but wonder if Lili's inclusion
of Hannah in the interview arrangements was a defensive maneuver (she
might be thinking I would not press her too hard with Hannah present).

I could not quite accept Lili at face value, no matter how beautiful the face. There were many layers to the woman and many shadows around her, just as there were in her paintings. Even Donatello had noticed something in her art which made him sense that she was troubled or afraid. Hannah assumed he was just infatuated, but I think Donatello attached himself to Lili because he felt that she needed protection. She had sent the so-called buyer's agent away, told him not to come back, but he had merely moved to the nearest street corner to watch the gallery like a detective on a stake-out. Who was he, really?

Hannah commented that Lili had been surprisingly cordial to us; I conjectured that she may merely have wanted us close around her to keep the bad guy at bay.

But the Lili Castelli mystery was not my priority at that time—Hannah was. I was enjoying her company mightily and a little unsure of how to proceed. She had been unexpectedly pleasant to me, and I didn't want to give her a reason or an opportunity to put me down the way she'd done in college.

Our first dinner date went well. For one thing, Hannah was ready and waiting at the door of her building at eight sharp (I had frequently questioned whether my former lady friend knew how to tell time). She looked fantastic in a short black dress and high-heeled sandals, showing exceptionally neat ankles and pretty feet. She opted to walk a mile to the Sicilian place (at her accustomed brisk pace, over basalt cobbles), and there ate with hearty enjoyment.

We drank the red Sicilian house wine and reminisced: Hannah told me that Dave Lin, the tennis pal whom I had admired for his sensitivity, had joined the Marines; my old flame Barbara had become a veterinarian and married a horse trainer. Our Lit prof had taken early retirement and was mountain climbing in Nepal.

I told her about Brigid (an expurgated version), surprised to find a lump in my throat. Perhaps I had not completely resolved that situation, after all.

"She was Irish, a model. Part erotic, part neurotic. I met her when I was with BNN in London."

"A model! Was she very beautiful?" Hannah asked.

"Right out of a Celtic legend. Slender, ivory skin, black hair, dancing blue eyes. I'm afraid she made me look quite shabby in comparison."

"Never!" Hannah objected. "You have a very commanding presence."

I laughed at the outright flattery, but it was sweet of her to try.

"I was quite taken with her, as you might imagine."

"So what ended the idyll?"

"I was about to propose a permanent arrangement when Brigid told me that she intended never to have children." How she could deliver that pronouncement so casually still astounded me.

"Hannah, I've watched my sister Dani and her husband with their sons. I want to have that experience, to know that part of life. If I didn't have much of a father, at least I can be one." I startled myself with that disclosure; I'd never put those feelings into words before, not even with Brigid.

Hannah wisely said nothing, allowing me my thoughts. But a certain softness about her mouth, usually brightly smiling or forming words with animated precision, suggested empathy.

"How about you? Any serious entanglements after Dave?" I asked.

"Only one." Hannah told me about a liaison she'd had with a professor at Buffalo: "I guess we used each other. I took care of his clothes, his appointments, his apartment, and entertained his colleagues. He helped me make some important professional contacts and get some grants. I'm not proud of it, but I grew up a lot." A wry, self-deprecating smile, accompanied by deep breath, told me she was over it, but just.

We had Sambuca with our espresso and talked until midnight: environmentalists versus industrialists, philosophy versus religion, dogs versus cats (at least we agreed on that one). Astrological signs (hers Leo, mine Sagittarius), favorite colors (red for her, green for me). When it became obvious that the waiter was eager to close, we walked back to Via dei Portoghesi. Thanks perhaps to the Sambuca, I was able to slow Hannah down to a stroll, put my arm around her shoulders and pull her close from time to time. She didn't resist; but I still had that nagging suspicion that she might haul off and swat me if I did anything so explicit as to kiss her.

"Thank you for a wonderful evening, and for the great dinner," she said. She did not suggest that I come up and see her tower.

"I enjoyed it, too. Don't forget lunch Monday—one o'clock at Tre Scalini. It's in Piazza Navona," I reminded her.

"I know" she said, with a playful but solid fist to my biceps. "I live here, remember?"

"So you do." I grasped her shoulders, bent down and planted a kiss on her forehead. "See you then."

I really wanted to call Hannah on Sunday. I had nothing pressing in the way of work, and I could take her to Tivoli to see the fountains at Villa d'Este and my beloved Hadrian's Villa. But my breezy parting words had been "See you then," meaning Monday.

I assembled a sandwich and brought it to the desk with a Diet Pepsi, my alternate source of caffeine. I rifled through the pile of writing projects, all in various stages of completion, but I couldn't concentrate on any of them. My mind wandered to my mother, working in Rome thirty-odd years ago. I wondered if she'd had trouble concentrating on her press releases . . . I switched from Word to the Internet and sent her a long-overdue email:

"Hi, Mom! Guess who I ran into the other day? A girl I knew at Cornell . . ."

CHAPTER EIGHT

Journal of Dr. Hannah Ingram

. . . she found both congeniality and variety of taste, and likenesses and differences of character, these being essential to any poignancy of mutual emotion.

Nathaniel Hawthorne, "The Marble Faun"

July 15

I got absolutely no work done today. I tried to develop a half-dozen different Beatrice themes but scrapped them all as too banal. My mind kept returning to yesterday's events and my dinner date with Kendall tonight.

By mid-afternoon I gave up trying to work and went shopping. A glance at my closet had convinced me that I had nothing to wear that didn't look . . . professorish. Fashion is not a big priority with me, but everyone here dresses so elegantly, and the women at the Galleria opening reception were wearing their skirts mid-thigh, even women in their fifties. Why not?

I went to Rinascente, a department store I'd noticed while getting lost on the way to Trevi Fountain. I bought a black knit dress, very well made, a good basic wardrobe item. And close fitted, skirt well above the knees. As I was trying things on, I got to thinking about how Donatello had been immediately entranced by Lili, who is probably ten-fifteen?—years older than he is. He certainly didn't respond to me that way. Was it because he assumed I was Kendall's companion, or am I simply not so appealing on a sensual level? A few days ago I wouldn't have cared.

As it turned out, I could have worn my jeans. The Sicilian restaurant was not exactly fancy—the cliché "hole-in-the wall" comes to mind. Evidently Kendall is a regular there—the waiters gave him a noisy welcome when we arrived and they presented me with a pink carnation. Kendall suggested we let the chef choose our menu, and the food more than made up for the plastic tablecloths. Fusilli and eggplant in a sauce rich with garlic and sun-dried tomatoes—it smelled tantalizing and more than lived up to its aromatic promise. Pan-fried fish, crisp and flaky and fragrant with lime. Later, the owner sent a special dessert to the table for us to sample, a swirl of fresh raspberries and chocolate and mascarpone. I think I ate enough to last all week.

Between courses, Kendall told me about his job with Business News Network—interviewing heads of state, executives and entrepreneurs; investigating industrial espionage and fraud—he plans to write a novel based on his experiences. He was nominated for a Pulitzer for his series on international arms dealers—strange that he should drop out now, no matter how much he enjoys Italy.

He also told me about an Irish woman he'd been thinking of marrying. He broke it off, he said, because she didn't want to have children. It must have been traumatic for him—Kendall obviously adores his family, really enjoys his nephews. He'll be a wonderful father some day, I think, when he finally decides what to do with his life.

And I told Kendall about Peter. Not everything of course, but more than I've told anyone before. I've always felt humiliated about my relationship with Peter. I was the typical starry-eyed grad student, thrilled to pieces that the distinguished Professor Peter Van Houghten had singled me out for special attention. It took him only a couple of weeks to get me right where he wanted me—in his apartment where I could brew his special tea and wash his special socks.

During those first weeks he told me I was brilliant and beautiful and he couldn't keep his hands off me. Within a month we had settled into a routine in which we were "intellectual companions" and he declared that "sex wasn't really required in a mature relationship." And I so wanted to be considered mature . . .

But it wasn't until Peter told me he was leaving to spend the summer in Portugal and expected me to take good care of his special cats while he was away that I really matured. I calmly, efficiently packed my stuff, told him precisely what to do with the cats, and walked out. He sent a little note from Lisbon, to let me know he had "no hard feelings and many nice memories."

"How about you?" Kendall asked. "Hard feelings or nice memories?"

"Now that you mention it . . . I guess the hard feelings are gone and I do have a few nice memories." Telling Kendall about my misadventure must have been therapeutic. Somewhere along the way he's become a really good listener—perhaps it comes from interviewing people. I even admitted to him that it was probably a recommendation from the esteemed Dr. Van Houghten that secured me the opera commission. All's well that ends well, and it is well ended with Peter.

I felt very close to Kendall as we walked back to my apartment . . . even physically close. I liked the warmth and the weight of his arm around my shoulder. He smells good. I was looking forward to being kissed goodnight, and he did kiss me—on the forehead. Said he'd see me at lunch on Monday. Is he still mooning over the Irish model? Or do I have some sort of pheromone deficiency?

Maybe I've been avoiding emotional entanglements for so long that men sense it. In high school, I didn't date much and didn't care. When I did go to a party or a dance, the boys were so clumsy and sweaty and immature that I couldn't wait to get away from them. I entered college a virgin and hearing my sorority sisters discuss their sexual encounters in embarrassing anatomical detail didn't encourage me to change my status.

Then I met David, who was different. Intelligent, intuitive, insightful, a gentle man. At last there was someone I could trust to initiate me into the mysteries of sex, and I was not disappointed. But even with David, I held something back. I knew that our relationship would not outlast our college days. My heart and mind were set on making a career in music, and there was no room for David in my plans.

Is there room, now, for Kendall? Or is it just this sensuous city affecting me? All I'm sure of is that I'd better get busy and write.

(Kiss on the forehead, indeed.)

CHAPTER NINE

Nathan Kendall's Narrative

*. . . the world did not permit her to hide her ante-cedents without making
her the subject of a good deal of conjecture . . .*

Nathaniel Hawthorne, The Marble Faun

On Monday I picked up my prints: Donatello at Cinecittà, Lili at
the Galleria, and a few of Hannah I'd managed to snap unobtrusively at
Doney's. I knew the women would enjoy seeing them. And I stopped off
at the Stamp Estera to see if I could unearth more background on Lili
Castelli before the interview.

I parked my bike outside the building on Via della Mercede, entered
and checked my box for messages. There was a fax from an engineering
publication asking me to cover a media briefing that afternoon about a
new bridge design. I had been hoping to take Hannah sightseeing after
lunch, but it would have to wait.

On the second floor is a reading room where members often touch base.
I was looking for Paolo Cavaluzzi. Under the alias Il Calabrone (The Hornet),
he had written a sharp-tongued society column for one of the Rome papers
for many years. He was retired now and lived in a villa in the high-rent
Parioli district, but he still stopped at the club regularly to swap stories.

I eventually found Paolo having his ritual Punt e Mes and a cigarillo
at the bar.

"Come va, Paolo?"

"Va bene, except for growing old. And how are you doing, young stud?"
His handsome, tanned face was becoming heavily lined, but there was still
an evil sparkle in his eyes.

"I'm doing my best," I replied, "which doesn't approach your best."
We chuckled. "I need a little help, Paolo. What can you tell me about
Lili Castelli?"

He snorted. "Oho! Way out of your league, youngster."

"No, really. I'm interviewing her today. All I have on her is hearsay. If
anyone can give me the lowdown, it's you."

"I love flattery, but it won't get you much." His heavy-lidded eyes
narrowed conspiratorially as though he were about to impart a state
secret. "Castelli is her own invention, and that's not her real name, of
course. Father's family are big industrialists, part of the Pirelli clan. Molto
denaro."

"She's in a high-overhead business; I suppose her father is bankrolling
her?"

"Not likely! She doesn't get along with dear Papa. Sided with her mother
in the divorce, grew up radical in Paris and got involved in some naughty
political pranks."

"Merely naughty?"

"Nothing so dreadful her old man couldn't get her off, but it made her
very unpopular with the aristocratic side of the family."

"Paolo, you've got to stop smoking those things," I interrupted as he
blew a huge puff in my face. "Any history of drugs? Lili, I mean—I assume
you confine your addictions to nicotine."

"I have addictions you've never even dreamed of, ragazzo mio," Paolo
growled wickedly. He liked to call me "boy" as a sort of affectionate put-
down. "The lady's cash doesn't come from the drug trade, if that's what
you're getting at. Her gallery seems to be legitimate, although she may do
a few favors for friends—business which doesn't show up on the books.
She's very good at what she does. Not a bad artist, either."

I tried another angle. "How about her love life?"

"You've probably heard the Saudi prince story . . . or was it an Iranian?
They were students together at the Sorbonne. If they ever married, it was
done secretly. Papa would surely have seen to an annulment, anyway."

"More recently?"

Paolo shrugged. "A lot of high profile escorts—a Russian ballerino,
an Israeli general, a Turkish merchant prince. The lady is gorgeous, she
travels a lot, moves in exalted circles. Her picture is all over the rag mags
and scandal sheets, but seldom with the same man."

I sighed. "You're slipping, Paolo. Now, how about the Monte Beni family?"

"Old Tuscan aristocrats living off the land. They make a decent wine,
or used to . . . you have to go big to make money with wine these days.
Only one son remaining. A nice kid, from what I hear, probably too nice
for his own good."

"Yes, I've met Donatello. I like him." I wondered aloud, "What sort of future can there be for someone like him?"

"He has a shot at the films. Other than that . . . maybe he can marry well. In fact, you ought to try it, Kendall." Paolo let me have another faceful of smoke before grinding his cigarillo into the ashtray. "You can't peddle stories forever."

"Thanks for the advice, Paolo." The Hornet had made a fortune with his column, selling mentions to eager social climbers and doing political favors. Then he had married a famous fashion designer with an even larger fortune.

With more sincerity I added, "And thanks for the information."

"I'll try to do better next time, my friend. Good luck with the interview." Paolo applied his slim, probably platinum, lighter to another cigarillo.

CHAPTER TEN

Notes from Lili Castelli

"Inquire not what I am, nor wherefore I bide in the darkness," said he . . .
"Henceforth, I am nothing but a shadow behind her footsteps . . ."

Nathaniel Hawthorne, "The Marble Faun"

April 17, 2002

My Dearest Kendall,

A copy of your manuscript has come to me by way of Paolo Cavaluzzi, whom you evidently number among the "friends" with whom you chose to share this very intimate memoir. I truly hope you have not misplaced your trust in his confidentiality. He has already broken it by sending me this copy; you can judge his motives for yourself.

Well, I am prejudiced; perhaps he was honest with you. You tend to bring out the best in people, as does your dear Hannah, to whom I send my undying affection. Years have passed, but I remember always your kindness and the happy times we shared in Rome before the unfortunate incident which ultimately separated us.

Kendall, you have done a remarkable job of recreating the past, without having much more than your own observations and intuition to guide you. I never told you more than I believed necessary, and at times deliberately misled you (how annoyed you were with me!). But now, after the intervening years, I am able to reveal details which you may wish to include, should you choose to expand your narrative.

Also, in common with you, I wish to clarify my role. You have portrayed me much as I hoped, at the time, to be perceived, and there is some gratification in that. But the behavior which you considered out of character for Lili Castelli was that of the real woman behind the mask. You forgave me, but you never knew me. My fault.

Hannah has described the first encounter of our "charmed circle," as she liked to imagine us . . . and as we might have been, had not destiny at its most perverse deemed otherwise.

I was off guard at the exhibition opening. I had greatly admired the work of a young Finnish glass artist and had been following his career. When I learned that he was working on the *Inferno* pieces, I invited him to introduce the collection with a show at Galleria Castelli. It was quite a coup to get him and it required an incredible amount of time and money to mount the exhibition. You commented on the lighting, which alone cost a fortune. Yes, I had help with the initial expenses for the Galleria, but I prided myself on making the operation break even. I hoped to make it profitable. So I orchestrated a spectacular exhibition opening to which I could invite my clientele and cultivate new prospects for lucrative relationships.

It was a gamble, but as the party progressed, I began to relax. Pleased with the results of my efforts and throughly enjoying myself, I was completely unprepared for my other, darker endeavors to intrude. When my secretary told me that a Signor Destino was waiting in my office to speak with me, I merely shook my head and made some offhand remark to her about the unlikely surname, undoubtedly invented by one of the guests to intrigue me.

I walked into the office smiling, with my hand outstretched in welcome, and encountered the one man I had desperately hoped never to encounter again in my lifetime.

It had been almost twenty years, but I recognized him in one heart-stopping instant. Tall, lean, all in black—he had always worn black, and the color had become part of his mystique. He had the same flashing black eyes, black hair, and now a black beard.

We all must pay a price for our youthful foolishness, and I had been paying, through the years, with a shock of unreasoning fear each time he managed to get a message to me. I did not hear from him often, just frequently enough so that I could never really forget him, never really feel safe.

Now he was standing in front of me.

"Lili." His eyes burned with the wild light I remembered and once had found mesmerizing. "Even more beautiful than when you were a girl—and so much better dressed."

"What are you doing here?" I could not speak his name.

"Why, Lili, haven't you been receiving my little love notes? Didn't I say I would find you again? And here I am."

"'Signor Destino' is here, I was told." I struggled to regain my composure. "Not a very original pseudonym. Are you losing your flair, Khol?"

"It was a spur of the moment subterfuge, scarcely worthy of me, I agree. But I am your destiny, am I not? And you would do well not to taunt me, Lili, now that I have come to renew our . . ." he paused with a sardonic grin, "friendship."

"But why? What do you want?" My voice broke, control beginning to slip away again.

"Oh, my poor little Lili. Have I frightened you? Do you think I have come here to harm you? Perhaps you remember my bad temper."

I remembered. "Get out!"

He laughed. I remembered the laugh, too, most high-spirited when he was inflicting pain. "Yes, thank you for your courtesy, my dear, I will have a seat."

I sat too, behind my desk—there was a revolver in the gilt-trimmed drawer. He seemed to sense it.

"Relax, Lili. I am here only to do a little business."

"Blackmail? I'm not surprised."

He spread his arms, palms up, in mock dismay. "What do you take me for? No, I am not the villain here." Then he suddenly rose and leaned across the desk toward me, seething. "You are the traitor, you betrayed me. Do you deny it?"

I said nothing.

He resumed his seat. "But I am patient. I will have my revenge, Lili, count on it. But today, I have come to establish a mutually beneficial business arrangement with the esteemed Galleria Castelli."

"I don't want your business. Go away."

He reached across the desk, grabbed my wrist and pulled me toward him. "But you will. Does the name Carlino Dolata ring a little bell? He sent me—I think you will be wise to hear his proposal."

Dolata! The Mafia's *numero uno* in the south—it was the break we had been waiting for.

"I see that it does, yes. Signore Dolata had no idea he was bringing about a reunion with the woman I've been longing to see for so many years. He simply suggested I persuade the elegant and most discreet lady to effect the sale of a few dozen very old, very valuable . . . collectors' items, shall we say?"

My head reeled: first the shock of seeing Khol again; then learning that he was the long-hoped-for link with the Mafia. Now I remembered the coaching I had been given: Always appear reluctant, suspicious. Let them coerce you into cooperating. Then bargain.

I tried to forget it was Khol I was dealing with and simply play the game as I had been taught. I had done it before, successfully, albeit with less at stake. You remember what I told you, Kendall, about my rash behavior when Khol and I were students in Paris, and my later involvement with a secret police sting operation. I owed the authorities my cooperation for past favors, but I was not unwilling to be recruited. It gave me the opportunity to launch the Galleria, to be a player in the international art world, to travel, to promote my own work. Selfish goals, perhaps, but I also cared deeply about the preservation of antiquities. To allow priceless historic discoveries to be exploited for the enrichment of the mafiosi and the secret vaults of private collectors is unforgivable. If we could establish enough evidence to convict Dolata and his associates, we could go a long way toward stemming the illegal flow of art treasures out of Italy.

So, putting aside my forebodings, I did business with Khol. He would channel his "collectors' items" from archeological sites to the gallery or to go-betweens; I was to retrieve them, arrange suitable provenances, and see that the pieces made their way through customs to foreign buyers—at top price, of course. We haggled over my commission: I insisted on twenty percent.

"What a greedy capitalist you have become, Lili, you with your high ideals. You want to take my share of the profit," he upbraided me. Then, suddenly, he lashed out, "Wasn't it enough that you took my brother from me?"

"Your brother chose his path," I countered. "It has nothing to do with the subject at hand.

"Now—you are asking me to assume the greater risk in this project. And I will have expenses to cover. I will do it for twenty percent. Take it or leave it." I spoke firmly, but was dizzy with apprehension. What if he refused?

"Done, then." With one of his startling changes of mood, Khol became sweetly conciliatory. "Will you come and have a drink with me, Lili, to seal the bargain?"

"No. Can't you see I've giving a party?"

"Later, tonight?"

"Never. Now go, and don't come back here." His presence defiled the atmosphere, but I gave him a practical reason: "It would be wiser if we're not seen together."

I rose from the desk and gestured him out of my office.

He moved as if to leave, but stopped suddenly, blocking the doorway so that I stumbled into him. He looked down at me as though I were a cornered animal. "Oh, but we will see each other again, Lili. I promise you."

I shoved him then, and he stepped back, into the reception area.

Again I told him to go, and that is when you found us, Kendall.

I had seen you earlier, when you and the others were looking into the mirrors and laughing. You, Kendall, strong, earnest and intent; Hannah, with her shining hair and shining spirit. And Donatello, a bit of a playboy,

I thought then, but an uncommonly appealing one. I wanted to know who you were, but before I could introduce myself, I was called away to meet Signor Destino.

Then the three of you came to me—like a rescue party, I thought at the time—and Khol slithered away. Relief surged through me.

Like you, Kendall, I was wary of Donatello at first glance. I had had occasion to know a number of extraordinarily handsome men and had developed a protective skepticism. But I was amused by Donatello's quaint manners and surprised that so attractive a young man would approach me with gallant deference—I was accustomed to more sophisticated overtures. Gradually, as we toured the gallery, I became aware that his presence seemed to wrap me in a gentle, protective aura—there's no other way to describe it. The closer Donatello moved to me, the stronger this sensation became. I was almost afraid to look at him, for fear the feeling might evaporate. But when he began to tell me about the Monte Beni wine, I did look at him, deep into his eyes. I found myself imagining how incredibly safe it must feel to be enfolded in his arms.

It was the second time I had been caught off guard that evening.

After the exhibition, I went out to dinner with the Finnish artist and a few potential patrons I had lined up for him. Everyone was in a celebratory mood and I played the quintessential hostess, but my earlier euphoria had deserted me. Now I had other things on my mind. The artist took me home (my apartment was on the fourth floor of the gallery building) and tried to kiss me in the courtyard. He was quite full of himself and full of wine, and I had to have my security guard remove him.

Once rid of Lars, I took the private elevator to my apartment and immediately contacted my Carabinieri control, whom I knew only as Tozzi. I reported that Dolata had made contact through Khol.

Tozzi was ecstatic. "Great news, Lili! Now we can nail him!"

"But listen, Tozzi, this man Khol is dangerous. He knows me—from before—and he hates me."

Tozzi was unimpressed, so I had to tell him the whole miserable story.

"I don't believe you're in any immediate danger, Lili," Tozzi insisted. "After all, our so-called Signor Destino is playing with the big boys. He can't let old personal resentments interfere."

"But he's mad for revenge, crazy . . ." I was getting crazy, too.

"Just calm down. You've had a shock, but you can handle him, Lili. If you back out now, we'll lose Dolata, maybe for good. And you won't be any safer. Let's put both the bastards away."

I'm not a courageous person, Kendall, but I am a realist. Tozzi was right.

Chapter Eleven

Nathan Kendall's Narrative

Sipping, the guest longed to sip again . . . There was a deliciousness in it that eluded analysis and—like whatever else is superlatively good—was perhaps better appreciated in the memory than by present circumstances.

Nathaniel Hawthorne, "The Marble Faun"

After my encounter with Il Calabrone, I walked to Tre Scalini, arriving a few minutes early and opting to sit indoors where I could bask in the air conditioning. We would still have a good view of the famous fountain and the piazza.

Soon Hannah arrived. I felt the corners of my mouth turn up the moment I spotted her copper hair and bouncing walk. As she took my hand and settled into a chair beside me, I got a whiff of her perfume (warm, fruity) and wished that we were lunching alone.

Then Lili entered the restaurant. She was dressed very simply but she walked like a queen and heads turned. When Lili joined us, she took off her dark glasses and smiled. That smile was all the adornment she required.

"Mr. Kendall, Hannah, I'm delighted to see you again."

In the face of her graceful greeting, I felt somewhat chagrined for my skepticism.

We fell into easy conversation, first about the happenings in Rome—an Andrea Boccelli concert, the threat of another train strike, the disappearance of valuable artifacts from an archaeological site—and then about Hannah's frustration with the opera project.

Lili knew a great deal about the Cenci history and was able to suggest some new lines of approach to Hannah. "If you are free, say, Saturday—both of you—we could visit Castel Sant' Angelo. Beatrice was detained and interrogated there, as well as at the Corte Savelli.

"And there, Hannah," she added, "you can see where Puccini's Tosca leapt to her death,"

"I would love that," Hannah agreed.

"And we could visit the Tempietto at San Pietro in Montorio. Beatrice Cenci is buried there."

"Really!" Hannah turned to me. "Are you free, Kendall?"

"Unless something unexpected comes up, I'd be happy to join you," I said, and found an opening to get down to business with Lili. "You are obviously very knowledgeable about art and history. How did this interest develop?"

Lili told me that her father was Italian, from a prominent Milanese family. He was sent to Beirut as a diplomat and there met and married her mother, the daughter of a French-Lebanese hotelier. Her mother's parents were collectors of art and antiquities: "When I was very little, Mother and I had little tea parties for my dolls with dishes that should have been in a museum."

When she was six, her father was transferred to London where Lili received her early schooling. Then, when she was in her teens, her parents parted. Her father returned to Milan and his family business; her mother took Lili to Paris. She studied art there, encouraged by her mother. In short, Lili told me little that I didn't already know.

"Your father's name is Castelli?" Would she answer truthfully?

"No. Castelli is a name I assumed for business purposes."

I pressed on. "What is your father's name and business?"

She shook her head. "I think he would not want me to talk about him. We've not been on good terms ever since he separated from my mother, you understand."

I could not possibly be rude enough to insist that she give me a straight answer—not with Hannah, to whom she was being so generous with her time and interest, sitting between us. My suspicion that she had never intended to be very forthcoming was confirmed.

I tried another tack. "Your mother—what is she doing now?"

"She runs a little boutique in Paris. We do some business together, in antiques and estate jewelry."

"And your family in Beirut?"

She shrugged. "You know all about the political situation there, Kendall. I haven't been back in years."

"What made you decide to open the Galleria?" (I meant, where did you get the financing?)

"Well, I must make a living, and this is what I know how to do best. I understand and appreciate beautiful things and the people who make them; I like to be surrounded by mementos of the past." And then, as if hearing my unstated question, she added "It all became possible thanks to some friends. My . . . investors are very kind."

"And who are they?"

Hannah's foot nudged mine under the table.

For just a fraction of a second, Lili's eyes blazed. Then she replied mildly, but with finality, "I'm not at liberty to say."

I said nothing for a moment to let her know I wasn't satisfied. "Let's move on to more personal matters. Have you ever been married?"

Hannah kicked me again, harder. I ignored her.

"That is not something I care to discuss," Lili demurred.

I persisted. "You have a number of notable escorts, I understand. Anyone of particular interest?"

"None. They are all so kind, I would not like to single out one over another."

I was getting a bit testy by now. "There is a lot of gossip about you, Lili." (Another kick.) "I've been told that you were once a member of the Red Brigades, that you were married to an Arab prince, that you were involved through your father in Israeli espionage. Any comment?"

Lili was clearly not amused, but she tried to make light of the matter. "Fairy tales! If you must write something sensational, Kendall, say that I'm an assassin with a Palestinian terrorist group and a former mistress of Prince Charles—no, that's too ghastly, make it Tony Blair."

We laughed to break the tension, and the interview was over.

Hannah suggested dessert. We were discussing our choices when I caught sight of Donatello at the door. I waved him over, a superfluous gesture for he had obviously planned to join us, no doubt having overheard me setting up the time and place for the interview.

He looked as if he had just stepped out of the shower, fresh-scrubbed with his hair still damp where it curled over his ears. He wore a pale yellow silk sweater and slim white flannel trousers, making me, in my best khakis and a new striped shirt, feel unexpectedly conservative.

Donatello greeted us warmly and drew up a chair between Lili and me as if we had been expecting him.

Lili said to the count, "I want to thank you for the wine. It arrived at the Galleria this morning."

"Have you tasted it yet?" he asked.

"No, I seldom drink before noon."

"We will all have some now. I will speak with the wine steward." He jumped up headed for the kitchen.

"Lili, I hope he's not bothering you," Hannah voiced her concern.

"Dear Hannah, who could be annoyed by the attentions of such a beautiful young creature?" she laughed, and then said more seriously, "I don't mean that unkindly. Donatello is your friend, and he is very *simpatico*. I enjoy him." This time I kicked Hannah under the table.

"I'm sure you would rather be pursued by Donatello than by your other shadow," I fished.

"What are you talking about?"

"The ill-tempered buyer's agent. He was still waiting across the street from the gallery when we left the other evening."

She froze for an instant, then recovered her poise. "That one believes we have some unfinished business and he is not pleasant about it. But he need not concern us now." She brightened. "Here's Donatello with our 'liquid sunlight.'"

Donatello uncorked the bottle and poured with a flourish. We touched our glasses in a toast: "To Monte Beni!"

I was curious about this white wine from a region famous for its reds: Chianti, Montepulciano, Brunello. The only Tuscan white with which I was familiar was the Vernaccia, produced near San Gimignano for centuries and a favorite of our friend Dante.

The pale, greenish-gold Monte Beni is a softer wine than the slightly lean Vernaccia, somewhere between dry and semi-sweet with vanilla notes. The first glass was quite pleasant; the second even better. Donatello explained that he was experimenting with the addition of Chardonnay grapes to the traditional Trebbiano. We complimented him on the results.

The waiter bought a second bottle. We mellowed. Hannah had stopped kicking me, but allowed her sandaled foot to rest companionably on top of my loafer. Donatello was outrageous in his attempts to charm Lili, but when it came to flirt and dodge she was a master of the game. Hannah and I followed their repartee as if we were watching a tennis match. Finally conceding the last word to Lili, Donatello called for another bottle of Monte Beni. We all enjoyed ourselves immensely.

When we finished the second bottle of wine, Lili checked her watch and said that she was late for an appointment at the gallery.

"But we must get together again, we four," Donatello declared, and I thought it was good strategy on his part not to attempt a rendevous for two with his goddess and risk rejection.

"Please join us on Saturday then. We have already arranged to do some sightseeing," said Lili.

"I would be most happy. It is so kind of you to include me," he beamed.

It was then I remembered my photos, and I passed them around the table. Hannah and Lili put their heads together to scrutinize the shots from the Cinecittà set.

"He does look the very image of a faun in that costume," Hannah exclaimed.

"And you should see him leap out of the trees," I said. "Formidabile! I want to take his picture beside the Praxiteles statue to see if they might really be related."

Lili looked up from the photos. "We'll do it Saturday. I know exactly where to find the statue in the Capitoline. We can meet at the foot of the Cordonato and go from there—if Donatello is willing to hazard the comparison."

For once Donatello did not respond to her gentle jibe. He was intent on one of the photos I had taken at the gallery. He leaned toward me, to show me what had captured his attention.

"Ecco, il bruto!" he growled under his breath.

The photo was, I had thought, an excellent one of Lili standing beside one of the Inferno pieces. Behind her was a group of animated guests gesturing with champagne glasses.

Donatello indicated a corner in the background where, in the shadows, stood the lone figure of the bearded man. He was staring directly at Lili, in his face a fiendish malevolence which rivaled the glass depictions of Dante's hell.

CHAPTER TWELVE

Journal of Dr. Hannah Ingram

In Rome, there is something dreary and awful, which we can never quite escape.

Nathaniel Hawthorne, "The Marble Faun"

July 17

Lunch today at Tre Scalini—light on lunch, but incredible desserts (go back for chocolate tartufo).

When I arrived I saw Kendall right away—tall and so attractive with that great grin, he's not hard to spot. Then Lili arrived, looking meravigliosa in a pearl grey linen sheath dress and antique silver earrings. She was just as friendly and down-to-earth as she had been at the gallery. We were enjoying our conversation until Kendall began the interview and insisted on asking Lili questions that she obviously didn't want to answer. A journalist's prerogative, I suppose, but Kendall's inquisition, low-key as it was, made me really uncomfortable. Lili too, no doubt.

Finally he backed off, and I had just begun to relax again when who should come bounding in like a golden retriever puppy but the bellisimo Donatello. Of course he joined us. I was afraid Lili might be offended—he wasn't invited—but she seemed to enjoy sparring with him, and Donatello is such fun to be with. He made a fine ceremony of pouring his Monte Beni wine for us. It's an unusual celery color, dry but not too dry, with a whiff of herbs. *Very* good.

Kendall passed around the photos he'd taken of Donatello on the movie set—the costume and make-up are amazing! Donatello is quite striking as the faun, and I can well believe that women all around the world will be falling in love with him when the movie comes out. The shots of Lili and the glass art exhibit were exceptional, very dramatic. Lili photographs like a model, of course, and Kendall is a fine photographer. He even got some good shots of me on Via Veneto, and I'm not at all photogenic.

The four of us will go sightseeing together on Saturday—Lili's suggestion. I feel very fortunate that she's interested in helping me with the Cenci research. We're going to the Capitoline Museum to see the faun statue and then to Beatrice Cenci's burial place and Castel Sant'Angelo.

After lunch Kendall told me he'd hoped we could spend the afternoon together but an important assignment came up. He asked me to go to Tivoli with him on Thursday (guess I can work it into my schedule . . .).

July 20

I had a call last night from Evan, asking about my progress on the score. I was embarrassed that I had so little progress to report, and tried not to let him know how discouraged I'm getting. I've managed to produce some passages that I'm pleased with, but I'd expected to be much further along by now. I get up in the morning with a lot of energy and enthusiasm and by afternoon, lethargy sets in and all I can do is nap. Will I ever get acclimatized?

I told Evan that I'd be visiting Beatrice's burial place Saturday, and he reminded me that composing is more a matter of perspiration than inspiration. Thank you, Mr. Comstock. You know nothing about perspiring until you've spent July cooped up in a little tower room in Rome. But I can't blame my lack of productivity on the heat. Or even on being distracted by Rome, or my new friends. It's that blasted Beatrice. I just can't comprehend her.

Hoping to let Evan know I'm at least trying, I told him about discovering La Petrella on the map in the Vatican Museum. Evan was not impressed: "Most texts place La Petrella between Rome and Naples, dear girl. Perhaps I'll come over to Rome for a long weekend. We'll rent a car and look around. It will give you a break."

"That would be great, Evan."

Oh, sure. I was mortified that he felt he needed to check up on me.

Evan's call made me really uneasy about taking a day off but, as Kendall pointed out, a change is often the charm when you have writer's block.

And the day in Tivoli with Kendall was a tonic. No need to describe Villa d'Este and Hadrian's Villa here—I picked up brochures and Kendall took a lot of pictures.

I like him more and more. He's very self-sufficient and self-contained, but also open and communicative and interested in people (interested in me!). When we got back to Rome he took me to dinner again—a Bolognese restaurant, and the best food yet.

And this time he kissed me goodnight properly. I think he was disappointed that I didn't invite him up to my apartment.

Well, why didn't I? What's wrong with me?

July 21

Another day with no progress.

All morning I kept reliving the day with Kendall, strolling through the romantic ruins and gardens and fountains like a couple in a Victorian novel. I was so annoyed with myself that I went out for a long hike in the blazing sun. Along the river, across to Piazza del Popolo, up to the Pincio and the Villa Borghese park, where I could pick up the pace on the jogging trails. There were a few men running in the park, but no other women; I felt as if I were breaking some unwritten rule by exercising. Again there were comments and cluckings, from men lounging lizard-like on the park benches, and again it bothered me more than it should have.

It's hot, it's humid, but there's something more that makes this city oppressive—something dark. Kendall told me that Rome is a paradox. Like the Inferno pieces, it's both magnificent and squalid. Kendall has made peace with the inconsistencies, but I'm still trying to ignore the seamy side. Today it seems a losing battle.

I expected to love everything about Rome, to be inspired, to create, enjoy every minute I spent here. Unrealistic expectations, of course—a failing of mine.

I walked back by way of Via Veneto, over to the Spanish Steps on the route Donatello had taken us. Showered when I got home, ate some fruit and cheese, settled down at the desk. Nothing. When I'm in the apartment I'm always half-listening for the cell to ring—it's ridiculous. I can't allow myself to be distracted this way. Hopefully, after the visit to Beatrice's tomb and Castel Sant'Angelo tomorrow, I'll have a Beatrice breakthrough.

CHAPTER THIRTEEN

Notes from Lili Castelli

"I hardly know," said she, smiling, "whether you have sprouted out of the earth, or fallen from the clouds. In either case you are welcome."

Nathaniel Hawthorne, "The Marble Faun"

Publicity is publicity, Kendall, and I would have granted you an interview under any circumstances, although Hannah was quite correct in her comment that I found you attractive. I jotted down the date on my desk calendar in anticipation of one normal, non-threatening occasion I could enjoy.

You were not very complimentary, however, in thinking I planned to use Hannah as a shield. I felt quite able to deflect any verbal darts you might toss my way and, furthermore, by the time of our appointment, I had some information about you. As a matter of course, I had asked Tozzi to run a check. You may be amused, at this late date, to learn that the security agencies of several countries were keeping detailed dossiers on you. So I was prepared for inquiries which went beyond the name of my hairdresser and which fashion house I favored. Of course, I couldn't know that you would be prepped for the interview by Il Calabrone himself, who in his glory days had never missed an opportunity to embarrass and offend my father's family.

There was a time when a bright young person like Hannah, with legitimate business in Rome, might have been recruited by your CIA to gather some sort of peripherally useful intelligence, but I couldn't imagine it in her case. I did not even mention her to Tozzi. I included her in the lunch plans for no other reason than that I liked her and was sincerely interested in helping her with the Cenci opera.

I did ask Tozzi for information about the young count of Monte Beni. His villa and vineyard are quite close to some archaeological sites where poaching is prevalent; I could scarcely ignore the fact that he turned up at the gallery at the same time as Khol. There could be a connection and, yes, he intrigued me. I learned that he was orphaned early in life and was struggling to keep the family winery profitable. What he didn't tell you and Hannah was that he was managing to enjoy life in the meantime with numerous short-term flirtations and some high-risk adventuring—mountain climbing in the Alps, ski boarding in the Dolomites, deep sea diving in Sardinia. And now he was working as a bit player at Cinecittà—not bad for a country boy. Could he really be as ingenuous as he seemed?

On the morning of the interview one of my employees informed me that a delivery had arrived. I wasn't expecting anything for the gallery; I worried that it might be some of the clandestine artifacts that I would need to account for to the staff. I had warned Khol specifically not to send anything to the gallery without alerting me first. I was furious by the time I got to the loading dock, and then laughed with relief to find the case of Monte Beni wine.

So I was not completely surprised when Donatello joined us at Tre Scalini. I confess, Kendall, that I was a trifle distracted during our interview because, somewhere in my subconscious, I was expecting him.

Even so, I was startled when he appeared: more handsome—and younger—than I'd remembered. But the enveloping warmth when he sat down beside me was exactly the same sensation I had experienced at the gallery. Even as I welcomed it, I scolded myself for surrendering to what could only be an inappropriate and inconvenient physical attraction.

Ah, Kendall, you describe the wine, the conversation. I remember nothing of that, only the overwhelming presence of Donatello and a losing battle for control of my senses. I am amazed—and relieved—that you found our dialogue diverting. I was close to distraught. I invented an appointment at the gallery as a means of retreat.

And then you brought out the photographs from the film set. How can I explain the shock of recognition? When I was a little girl, my mother would read me to sleep with stories from Greek and Roman mythology, and I would dream of gods and heroes, nymphs and fauns and centaurs in the Arcadian forest. Donatello, to me, did not appear to be made-up and costumed to look like a faun. It was more that he had been stripped bare of contemporary trappings and the image in the photograph was his true self.

Was it just the wine or did you see it, too?

Chapter Fourteen

Nathan Kendall's Narrative

*The resemblance between the marble Faun and their living companion
had made a deep, half-serious, half-mirthful impression on these three
friends . . .*

Nathaniel Hawthorne, *"The Marble Faun"*

I had quickly pocketed the photo with Lili's stalker scowling in the
background. At any given moment, any one of us might make a ferocious
face for an innocuous reason. Maybe he had just gotten a bad shrimp. I
had already annoyed Hannah by asking embarrassing questions during
the interview; I wasn't eager to add fuel to her ire by confronting Lili with
the photo. Especially not when Hannah was being so uncharacteristically
cozy.

It was rotten luck that I had the bridge assignment to handle that
afternoon, but I did parlay lunch into a trip to Tivoli with Hannah.

Sharing some of my favorite places with her was remarkably gratifying.
Hadrian's melancholy estate, the fountains and grottos of Villa D'Este, an
open-air restaurant overhanging a deep ravine which reminded us of the
gorges along Lake Cayuga—Hannah explored each venue with intelligence
and enthusiasm. And she seemed happy—very happy—to be with me.

"Back in Lit class, would you ever have imagined we would be sitting
here, having lunch together in this incredibly beautiful place?" she mused.

"Not in a million years."

"As many as that?"

"Hannah, I'll be frank. You terrified me. The only time I fantasized
about you was when I heard you sing, and it wasn't about having lunch."

"Oh." She let that sink in a moment.

"And I'm waiting impatiently to hear you sing again."

She responded with that maddening, ambiguous smile that females have perfected over centuries.

I felt certain that by evening she would be comfortable enough to invite me up to her apartment, but it didn't happen. Could she still be pining for the professor?

I was determined that our Saturday outing would conclude differently.

We congregated as planned at the Cordonata, the great ramp designed by Michelangelo, and climbed to Piazza del Campodoglio. Here we followed Lili to the Palazzo Nuovo, the museum where we would find Praxiteles' faun.

As we entered, Lili told us that the faun, or Faunus, as he had been called in ancient times, was a rustic Roman deity: "He was revered as the protector of the forests and the animals that live in them, as well as shepherds and woodsmen." Although fauns are often depicted with horns, tails and goat legs, Lili explained, this Faun of Praxiteles has but one characteristic to distinguish him from a human being—the pointed, much elongated ears.

We found our faun in a small gallery on the second floor of the museum, just one among many great sculptures. Displayed in close company with mighty gods and goddesses, emperors and amazons, the faun did not immediately impress me. As I studied him, I began to appreciate his naturalness, his peaceful self-composure. He is not hunting or killing or making war, dallying, dancing or dying. He is simply himself, God's creature (or creature of the gods), the boy next door with strangely curved and tapered ears.

Donatello's reaction was characteristically playful as he gamboled around the figure, finding the appropriate pose for my photo. "I like him so much! Who knows, perhaps he is my ancestor."

"There is one way to find out," Lili observed. "The faun has pointed ears. We can't see your ears with all that hair, Donatello. Shall I look?"

As she reached toward him, Donatello grasped her outreached hand in midair and jumped back.

"No! I am sorry, Carissima, not even you may see my ears. It's an old family characteristic—my ears are very ugly."

Lili was astonished, then amused by his reaction. "Sciocchezza! You want us to believe you truly are a faun."

"Or maybe he doesn't want us to learn that he isn't." Hannah presented an alternative interpretation of Donatello's reluctance.

"More likely," I chimed in, "he has really ugly ears. I'd just as soon not see them."

The hallmark ears were immaterial in establishing the faun persona. Looking through the viewfinder at Donatello and the statue as I took photos for my story, I could see the resemblance was undeniable, even more in attitude and effect than in actual physical similarity.

We finished our tour of the museum in high good humor, trying to find a statue to resemble each of us. We settled on the Esquiline Venus for Hannah, which pleased her mightily, and lanky Alexander Severus, arm raised as if to serve a tennis ball, for me. Donatello could find no representation of a female, human or divine, to compare with Lili.

We circled the Capitoline Hill, enjoying the view over the old Roman forum, before descending the Cordonata. From there we walked past the Theater of Marcellus and across the the Fabricio bridge to the opposite side of the river, the picturesque Trastevere district.

Trastevere had been a rough section of the city in my mother's day; she told me she wouldn't venture there at night except with my father, usually to eat in one of the authentic old Roman restaurants. The restaurants are still an attraction, but now Trastevere has become gentrified and is the preferred venue of the entertainment types who used to frequent Via Veneto.

And here Donatello became our guide: "This is my part of the city." He led us along lively Via della Lunagaretta to Piazza di Santa Maria, where we stopped for a spremuta di limone and watched the activity around the fountain. It was nearly as mobbed as the Trevi, but with locals rather than tourists.

Donatello excused himself. He had ordered a lunch to take with us to Janiculum Hill, and went to pick it up from a restaurant around the corner. By the time we finished our drinks, he had returned with a large straw basket and a rolled-up quilt.

Donatello knew a shortcut to San Pietro In Montorio, he told us, and it was mostly uphill—a very long, very steep hill. Hannah and I were reminded of climbing to class on the Cornell campus, "high above Cayuga's waters:" the joke was that you could tell Cornell girls by their well-developed calf muscles. Donatello, of course, had no trouble forging up the incline and Lili surprised me by taking the hill apparently without effort.

But we were all panting by the time we reached our destination, the final resting place of Beatrice Cenci. And there was no reward for our efforts. The church, as well as its high-walled courtyard with the Tempietto, was locked and apparently deserted. No helpful signs informed us of the hour it might reopen.

"I'm so sorry. I should have checked before I suggested coming here," Lili apologized.

"It's not your fault," Hannah was quick to say. "I think Beatrice is simply determined to elude me." But I could see that she was frustrated. She had been counting on today's visits to Cenci sites to give her a jump start on her stalled opera score.

"I think we should have lunch now," was Donatello's pragmatic reaction to the setback.

Our climb had brought us more than halfway up Janiculum Hill, which is crowned by a beautifully wooded park. After ten minutes more hiking we had reached a grassy slope where we could sit in the shade and look out over the city. There was even a slight breeze.

Donatello spread the quilt; we plunged into the basket. He had brought a feast—ham, mortadella, bread, cheese, roasted peppers and ripe olives, a melon and two bottles of Monte Beni, still cool.

"I think I'm in heaven," Hannah sighed, her spirits restored, and I agreed. We ate and drank our fill and stretched out on the quilt—all but Lili, who sat in a cross-legged yoga pose beside the prone Donatello. He lay on his back, arms crossed behind his head, looking up at Lili and murmuring softly to her until his eyelids closed.

Hannah and I were on our stomachs, heads turned toward one another. The sun was warm on our shoulders; the breeze cooled the back of our necks. I looked at our clasped hands: mine large and tanned; hers smaller, with tapered fingers and a strong, square palm. I was uncommonly contented.

We dozed, until Lili gently touched my shoulder. "Rouse your sleeping beauty, Kendall. We should start for Castel Sant'Angelo now or we'll be locked out there, too."

Donatello bolted up. "Why did you let me sleep? I didn't want to leave you alone . . ." He was angry with himself for missing a moment of her company.

Our route now was mostly downhill, and within thirty minutes we had arrived at the imposing amber mass of Castel Sant'Angelo. It always reminded me of an overgrown sand castle.

We entered at the base and made our way up a long, dark spiral ramp in the core of the building. Lili explained that it was originally designed as a mausoleum for Hadrian, but by medieval times had taken on the functions of fortress and prison as well as a sort of safe house for the popes in times of peril. Beatrice Cenci may have been held in a cell on the lower level, Lili went on, and she underlined the hopelessness of one young woman pitted against the power of the papal court: "Imagine the weight of this massive fortress over your head."

Her commentary was most effective. I began to feel the claustrophobic panic of such imprisonment myself. Lili continued to speak effectively, almost passionately, of Beatrice's plight until we emerged from the dank interior to the welcome sunlight of the courtyard.

Next Lili led us through a labyrinth of frescoed halls and handsome salas and anterooms and passageways which comprised the papal apartments. Even with Lili as guide, we tended to lose track of one another—particularly Hannah, who was intent on exploring all the small dark recesses marked "*Vietato l'Ingresso,* entrance prohibited.

"You remind me of my nephews," I told her, thinking of Dani's sons Matt and Mark, nine and seven. "They would love this place. They could play here for hours."

"Me, too," Hannah agreed.

Lili corralled us to the terrace, which she designated as the scene of the last act of "Tosca." When her lover is killed, Tosca leaps from a parapet into the Tiber.

Hannah was entranced. She glanced around; we four were the only people on the terrace. "I've always wanted to play Tosca. Here goes . . ."

Hannah went part way up the steps to the castle's narrow encircling guard walk (vietato, or course), struck a pose, and began to sing the opening notes of "Vissi d'Arte," Tosca's signature aria.

Backlit by the late afternoon sun, she was a flame. Even in shorts and sneakers, she became Tosca, the passionate Puccini heroine. And her voice was even better than I remembered, richer, powerful, filled with emotion. I heard Lili catch her breath.

As Hannah sang, I felt myself identifying with Tosca's nemesis, the sexually obsessed Baron Scarpia. I wanted this woman, now. Or, at least, very soon. It was an incredible performance.

When she finished, Donatello shouted "Brava! Bravissima!" and we cheered wildly. Her singing had attracted some other late sightseers to the terrace and they joined in the applause.

Hannah was both elated and embarrassed: "I didn't intend to make a spectacle of myself."

I hugged her. "You were magnificent! I'll take you to Seville if you promise to sing 'Carmen' for me!"

It was then we realized that Lili was no longer with us. I wondered uncharitably if she had wandered off because she was piqued that another woman had become the center of attention. We waited a few minutes; then Donatello said he was going to look for her.

He returned about ten minutes later. "I can't find her anywhere. Help me look."

"She's probably in the ladies' room," Hannah said. "I'll check." But she came back quickly. "She's not there."

"Lili knows this place better than we do. Let's stay here and let her find us," I suggested sensibly.

Donatello was not content to wait. "Maybe she fell. She's wearing those silly little shoes," a reference to Lili's designer sandals. "I'm going to look again."

"Then let's go together so we don't lose you," said Hannah, and we started back down the winding ramp in the center of the fortress. I was beginning to worry, too. There were places where one could stumble and have a bad fall.

We began calling her name; our voices echoed eerily. Where was Lili?

"She wouldn't just leave us," Hannah reasoned. "Do you suppose she got locked in somewhere? In one of those 'vietato' places . . ."

"Ascolta!" Donatello hushed us. "I hear something."

There was a faint scuffling noise behind us on the ramp, and low voices.

"Lili!" Donatello shouted, and started running back up the ramp toward the sounds. I followed.

Then we heard Lili call "I'm here," and she appeared, walking toward us, apparently safe and serene.

But behind her, retreating quickly up the ramp and merging with the shadows, was a man. Perhaps I only imagined it was the bearded "buyer's agent;" I didn't get a good look at him. When Donatello moved as if to pursue the man, Lili held him back.

"I'm quite all right," she assured him. "I'm sorry if you were worried about me."

"*Come no?* You disappear, you tell me nothing . . ." Donatello began angrily, his face dark.

"Come on, let's just go," Hannah interrupted, hoping to forestall an argument.

"Yes, we will leave this place," Donatello agreed emphatically, glancing back in the direction of the fleeing figure.

Lili changed the subject. "Hannah, what a thrill you gave us. I've heard the 'Vissi d'arte' sung many times, but never in this setting."

"I couldn't resist the opportunity," Hannah confessed.

"I'm glad. You have a fine voice, and you're a real actress. You have my complete admiration."

"Mine, too." I squeezed Hannah's hand. I had misjudged the motive for Lili's disappearance and, as usual, she felt no necessity to explain herself.

Lili said it was time for her to leave us; she had to get ready for a dinner engagement. Donatello announced that he would accompany her back to Via Gregoriana. (I had guessed that she lived over the Galleria; Donatello had evidently made it his business to find out.) Lili thanked him and said she could manage quite well alone. He didn't argue with her, he simply took her arm—"Andiamo, Cara. Buona sera a tutti"—and marched her off.

"Donatello is certainly getting proprietary," I observed as I marched my lady home.

"He's worried about her, and so am I," Hannah said. "You must have seen that character behind Lili on the ramp—he's obviously stalking her. She tries to cover up, but I'm sure she's afraid of him."

"I'm not so sure. I think she's well able to cope."

"Do you? Suppose he's a vindictive ex-lover, or a blackmailer or even as she told us, just somebody she just doesn't want to do business with. She can't go to the police for protection until he does something to her. I would be terrified in her place."

More than Lili seems to be, I thought.

"You know, Hannah, it was Lili who suggested we go to Castel Sant'Angelo. Maybe she planned to meet the guy there."

"Oh, really!" Hannah was angry. "You just don't want to take this seriously. You don't trust Lili because she wouldn't answer all your impertinent questions."

"I didn't expect her to answer all my questions, Hannah—which were logical, not impertinent, by the way. The fact that we happen to like Lili doesn't mean she's above suspicion, however. The woman is hardly an open book."

"She's been nothing but kind to me, to all of us," Hannah argued. "Can't we allow her some privacy and still be concerned about her?

"So be it," I conceded, content to avert our first fight. "And if you're worried about her, remember that Donatello has appointed himself her protector."

"Yes, he has, bless him. Imagine how he must feel, leaving her at her apartment to get ready for a date with someone else."

I wanted to point out that Donatello wasn't the only one being left at the door lately, but thought better of it.

We arrived at Via dei Portoghesi. "I'm exhausted!" Hannah declared.

Here comes the dismissal, I thought.

She smiled up at me. "Would you like to have dinner at my place?"

We shopped for groceries and carried them up to her tower apartment which I dubbed, with suitable ceremony, "The Songbird's Nest."

We cooked together, laughing as we stumbled over each other in the cramped kitchen cubicle. Then we carried our meal—pasta with fresh tomatoes, olive oil, lots of garlic and basil—through her bedroom and up to the roof for our second picnic of the day.

Hannah put on a Resphigi tape, a soothing accompaniment to the sounds of the city. She showed me how she had 'trained" the doves to come to her roof for crumbs. By the time we finished dessert (chunks of cake and fruit stirred with whipped cream and Amaretto, my bachelor specialty) it was dark. Hannah lit a few candles.

It was very romantic there on the roof, but not as secluded as I might have wished.

"You're very quiet all of a sudden," Hannah said. "What are you thinking about?"

"I'm thinking that perhaps I should bring up a blanket. It's actually getting a bit chilly."

"I'll come with you," she said.

I went first, and helped her down the folding stairs. As she bent over the bed to gather up a blanket, Hannah's hair fell across her cheek. This time, I reached out and touched it, brushed it back over her ear.

"When you asked me what I was thinking about I lied," I said.

"Oh? What were you really thinking about?" Her voice was husky.

I told her. I held out my arms, and she came to me.

CHAPTER FIFTEEN

Journal of Dr. Hannah Ingram

She continually brought to . . . mind the image of a child, making a playing of every object, but sporting in good faith, and with a kind of seriousness.

Nathaniel Hawthorne, "The Marble Faun"

July 23

I don't like things to just happen. I prefer to explore, consider options, plot a course—to compose my life. Then Nathan Kendall called my name—a week ago?

And now we're lovers. Happenstance. Rome.

Or did I take a hand in the orchestration? If so, I did well.

When I awoke this morning Kendall was up and dressed, standing over the bed and smiling at me.

"Time for breakfast."

He had been out already and brought back a tray with cappuccino and pastries and that red orange juice I adore. And a bouquet of pink lilies—the room smells like a garden.

We ate and showered and went back to bed and then showered again. It was one o'clock before I began to feel guilty.

"I know it's Sunday, Kendall, but I really have to get some work done." I told him about the call from Evan, that he might pay a surprise visit to Rome, and that I was at a virtual standstill on the opera score.

"Obviously, you can get into Tosca's skin—I don't understand why you're having such trouble with Beatrice," Kendall said. "There are similarities, aren't there? They were both tormented, and both killed their tormentors."

"That's true, but the characters are quite different: Tosca was a famous actress, the toast of Rome; Beatrice was fresh out of a convent."

"I don't know the Cenci story well. How about letting me have a look at the libretto?"

I handed the pages to Kendall and he scanned them as I dressed.

"The lawyer has all the good lines," he commented.

"Of course." I told him about Evan.

"I thinks that's admirable," Kendall commented. "The man's made his reputation as an attorney, and now he's willing to gamble on his talent in a totally different field."

"He's gambling on me, too, Kendall. I can't let him down."

"I think I can see one problem," Kendall said. "When Beatrice tells her story to the lawyer and to the court, she's hiding the truth, or putting a spin on it. The only time she's the real Beatrice is in the flashbacks—the duet with Olimpio, the Cenci quartet. And in the scene with Lucrezia before the execution. That could be a heart-breaker, by the way."

As he spoke, I nodded agreement. Beatrice's arias could be technical showpieces for the soprano, but her true character had to come out in the ensemble numbers. The duet with Lucrezia takes place in prison while they are helping one another dress for the last time, trying to find the courage to make a proud appearance at the execution.

"You've got something there, Kendall. I think I'll get started on the prison duet. The visit to Castel Sant'Angelo gave me some ideas: I'll use tolling bells, maybe even some pipe organ, overpowering, ominous. And for Beatrice and Lucrezia . . . frail yet valiant . . . flute, clarinet . . ."

"I can see I've already been mentally dismissed," Kendall said. He kissed my shoulder. "I'll call you."

I spent a couple of hours at work; then needed to stretch and went out for a walk. I stopped in front of Palazzo Cenci and stared, wondering what it had been like for Beatrice there, first suffering her father's brutality and later, after his death, fearing discovery—regretting the act, perhaps. But no amount of conjecture could put me inside her head or her heart.

I came back and now all I can think about is Kendall. I don't want to eat dinner alone tonight. Or sleep alone.

Back to the keyboard.

July 30

Lili phoned and suggested we go to the flea market at Porta Portese today. It's a real Roman institution, she said, and she occasionally she ferrets out a few treasures for the Galleria there.

We met in Piazza Navona for a late breakfast, and afterward I showed her my tower. She told me there's a legend about it.

"For many years it was called La Torre della Scimmia—the Monkey's Tower. Supposedly a monkey or chimpanzee stole a baby and carried it up to the top."

"Good heavens! Like a miniature version of King Kong on the Empire State Building! Was the baby rescued?" I wanted to know.

"Oh, yes. The story ends happily."

"Good. I saw the King Kong movie when I was seven and I cried at the end, to my father's intense embarrassment." I've always preferred happy endings. Could that be why I'm having problems with the opera score? Suddenly I saw that I heartily dislike the whole sordid Cenci story and its pitiful protagonist. A revelation. Now, how will I overcome this revulsion? When?

'So I'm living in the Tower of the Monkey," I continued the conversation. "Kendall calls it the Songbird's Nest."

Lili smiled, and I saw that she sensed the change in my relationship with Kendall.

"He's a good man, your Kendall," she said.

My Kendall. I felt myself blushing and changed the subject. "Yes, he's even given me some good advice about the opera." I told her about my work on the prison duet. "The visit to Castel Sant'Angelo inspired some interesting ideas. Thank you so much for taking me there."

In truth, after that first flurry of creativity, I haven't made a lot of progress. The old afternoon malaise is still with me. And now there's Kendall, who monopolizes my thoughts more than I would like. We've had dinner together every night this week, at my place or his or out somewhere. I think we've surprised ourselves with the intensity of the attraction. It's disconcerting. Ever since coming to Rome, I've felt somehow out of control.

The flea market is held every Sunday morning at Porta Portese, just across the Sublicio bridge in Trastevere. Booths and stalls extend for what seems a mile along the old wall which parallels the river. As soon as Lili and I crossed the bridge, we were accosted by peddlers and hawkers. Except for one junior entrepreneur offering goldfish in plastic baggies, they were selling much the same tourist trash that's touted in piazzas and on street corners throughout the city. I was disappointed.

Once through the arched stone gate to the market itself, however, where bargain-hunters were already milling about elbow-to-elbow, I caught flea market fever. Here the booths and tables and stalls displayed that combination of things ancient and modern which is the hallmark of Rome.

And some of the display devices were ingenious—packets of pantyhose cradled in an upside-down beach umbrella, cigarette lighters lined up on an ironing board. And a man just sitting cross-legged on the ground with plastic handbags hanging from his shoulders and elbows and ears and a pile of wallets in his lap.

I tried to follow Lili's magenta jacket while weaving my way through kitchen cutlery, canaries, mini racing cars. Over the noise of the crowd, competing CD dealers blasted the latest hit songs at ear-splitting decibel levels, so I was always having to run up beside Lili to hear what she was saying.

"Don't be discouraged, Hannah, we'll get to the good part soon," Lili all but shouted.

"But wait a minute!" I wanted to linger and look at the little watercolor sketches, the fine marbled papers, the scandalous bras and panties which hung beside sturdy mamma-mia size corsets. After some bilingual bargaining, I purchased a silk scarf with a fake designer label which looks great with my black dress.

"You could have won a prettier scarf over there," Lili teased me, gesturing toward a carnival-type game booth which exhibited an amazingly garish orange-sequined scarf as one of the prizes.

"I think one of these furs would look elegant on you," I shot back, as we passed a table piled with mangy pelts reminiscent of the feral cats that plague parts of the city. Lili made a mean little cat face and meowed—how that bit of silliness disarmed me!

We pressed on. I clutched my shoulder bag tightly, under prior instructions from Lili, and kept alert to the people who brushed against me. And, after the unsettling experience at Castel Sant'Angelo, I also had an eye out for Lili's stalker. It was possible he would turn up here. I did see a tall, dark, furtive man with a beard who might be following us—I saw a half-dozen of them. I couldn't remember the stalker's features well enough to distinguish him from anyone else of the same general description. And Lili seemed quite oblivious to any threat—she was obviously in her element.

We came at last to the area of the market where antiques are interspersed with old junk and only an expert like Lili can tell them apart. I was attracted to a "silver" salt cellar and a "crystal" decanter, but Lili firmly steered me away.

Lili found an earthenware pot which interested her, and she told me it might be Etruscan. She had bought items from this vendor before, she said. They began negotiating in Italian, and the man brought out some other pieces, perhaps trying to persuade Lili with a package deal. It seemed that they had reached an agreement, but in the end Lili came away empty-handed.

"The things aren't authentic?" I asked her.

"I think some may be. You know there was a theft at an archaeological site recently . . . I must be very careful not to touch anything that might have been acquired illegally. By definition, antiquities belong to the state and there are strict laws protecting them."

So much for your suppositions, Kendall, I thought.

We looked at oil paintings, mirrors, lamps, figurines, jewelry. Lili purchased a few enameled pill boxes "just for fun." I bought one, too, and then spotted a tarnished silver music box inlaid with a cameo of a man and woman, their hands clasped. I wound the key and the box played an unfamiliar waltz tune in minor key.

"You have a good eye. It's charming," Lili said, and examined the music box closely. "It's mid-nineteenth century, very well made and in reasonably good condition."

She exchanged a few sentences with the vendor.

"She wants about $400 dollars for it," Lili told me. "It's a fair price."

I paled. "I'm sure it's fair, but way out of my price range."

"*Mi dispiace, Signora,*" I told the vendor. I was truly sorry.

Lili spoke to the woman again, trying to get the price down, but she was unsuccessful.

The heat and the crowd and the noise were starting to be oppressive, and I was glad when Lili reversed direction. As we made our way back to the gate, I noticed still another dark bearded man—I was getting paranoid. I was relieved when we were finally out of the stifling press of bodies and in sight of the bridge.

Then Lili said, "I forgot something, Hannah. Wait right here by the arch—I'll be back in a moment." She disappeared back into the market throng.

I was immediately apprehensive—Kendall's influence, no doubt. Was one of those bearded men waiting for her somewhere in the market? I checked my watch. If she wasn't back in ten minutes, I was going in after her.

The minutes were long, but she returned before my deadline.

"Good! That's taken care of." She took my arm as we walked back across the bridge.

I never walked arm-in-arm with a woman in the States—but I never had a really close woman friend. Here, with Lili, it feels comfortable, companionable. She's like a sister in some ways, in spite of her glossy magazine lifestyle.

I think she feels that way, too.

"You know, Hannah, I really appreciate the times we spend together. When I saw you and Kendall and Donatello that first day at the Galleria, having such fun together, I was envious."

"Of us?" I was surprised.

"Yes. I wished I could be part of a group of friends like you. The people I associate with are just . . . people who are useful, do you understand? There is no one but Hannah whom I would call to say 'Let's go to Porta Portese.'"

I was surprised again, and touched. "Lili, I feel honored to be your friend. I hope we'll spend a lot more time together."

We chatted casually about this and that, and Lili asked me to tell her more about Kendall. I told her that we had met when we were students at Cornell and that we debated a lot in Lit class. When I mentioned that Kendall had been on the tennis team, she said she would like to invite us to play doubles at her tennis club.

"The four of us? What fun!"

"No, no. Not Donatello. We'll play with one of the club pros." Then she softened her exclusion of the count. "I think he's busy at Cinecittà during the day, anyway. They have expanded his part."

"Lili, how do you feel about Donatello, really?" I asked.

"I believe that he is someone quite special" she replied, and led me to a stone bench where we sat for a moment before she continued.

"He's infatuated with me and that is very flattering, of course, but . . . he isn't like other young men."

"How do you mean?"

Lili told me about a morning she had taken her sketchbook to the Villa Borghese park.

"Once in awhile I like to just put on old clothes, let my hair down and go off and sketch somewhere quiet, away from the demands of the gallery."

She had settled into a secluded spot and was limning a landscape when Donatello came running up and sprawled at her feet. He said had been using one of the jogging paths and "just happened" to find her.

"While he was catching his breath, I did a sketch of him, incorporating the ears of the Faun of Praxiteles. When I showed it to him he seemed pleased, but he took my pencil and added curls over the ears to hide the points."

"What would it mean, Lili, if Donatello does have faun ears?" I wondered. "You don't believe that he could have some special powers, do you? That he's superhuman in some way? That seems pretty farfetched."

Lili shrugged. "Of course. It's not possible. And yet . . ." She paused, considering her words carefully before speaking. "Listen, Hannah. You've noticed that Donatello has trouble sitting still? All that nervous energy, like a wild thing."

I nodded agreement, and Lili continued.

"He asked me to walk with him, but soon we were running, skipping, hiding, chasing one another, even rolling in the grass. Like children. I don't know what came over me."

"But you enjoyed it?"

"Oh, yes. Who wouldn't like to be a child again, for a little while?" I remember how she had laughed and made a face at me at the flea market.

Then, Lili told me, they sat down beside the lake and Donatello began to make little chirping, chuckling noises, something like bird calls.

"And, Hannah, I swear the birds answered him! I saw a squirrel on a tree trunk stop and listen—it was uncanny. At that moment, I could almost believe that Donatello is a faun. He is so very close to nature, like man before sin came into the world."

I was amazed to hear Lili speak about him this way, and didn't know how to respond.

"Then what happened?"

"We walked through the Orangerie, just enjoying our surroundings, and came to a piece of statuary—not a particularly good one, but sweet. It includes a faun, with a tail as well as the pointed ears, and a nymph. They are holding an infant faun. Have you ever seen it?"

I nodded.

"Well, Donatello stopped and stared at the statue. He said 'Perhaps we will be happy together like this some time.'

"Hannah, I just froze!"

Even as she was telling the story, Lili's eyes widened with dismay.

"My mythological playmate had become a man like any other," she continued, "with desires far exceeding my own, and I realized I shouldn't see him any more."

She is probably right. I remember Donatello's statement that he is expected to fill the Monte Beni villa with bambini and I can't picture Lili as the *mamma*, wife of a grape farmer, stuck in some crumbling country castle far from the glamour and excitement of her present life.

I felt mounting sympathy for the infatuated Donatello. "Surely, you could be just friends?"

Lili shook her head. "Surely, we could not be just friends."

Again I could think of no response.

As we parted she said, "'A happy person is such an unaccustomed and holy creature in this sad world . . .' Donatello is one, and it would be a sin to change him"

I thought I recognized the quotation. "Hawthorne?"

"I think so." Lili leaned over to deliver the air kisses, one side then the other—another first for me. "Take care of yourself, Hannah."

All this time I've been thinking that Lili is simply humoring Donatello, toying with him, like a queen with a courtier. Now I see that he has touched her deeply and that she cares for him far more than I would ever have imagined.

Lili's paintings come to mind, with their intricate interplay of light and shadow, reality and illusion. How like the woman herself—except that Lili has no illusions, I think.

CHAPTER SIXTEEN

Notes from Lili Castelli

*"I tell you . . . there is a great evil hanging over me.
. . . It will crush you, too, if you stand at my side!"*

Nathaniel Hawthorne, "The Marble Faun"

When one falls in love, there is an incubation period. You hold the precious, fragile feeling close to your heart—and any information about it close to your chest. Eventually, though, your love swells and bursts into exuberant bloom and then you want to shout it to the world. Or at least confide in a friend.

Looking back, this may have been a motive in my inviting Hannah to go to Porta Portese with me. That and my pleasure in her company and desire to entertain her. If I also planned to make contact with one of Khol's go-betweens there, what did it matter? Hannah would not be in danger, would not even be aware of my activity.

I knew that Khol was still trailing me. It was completely unnecessary so far as the conduct of our "business" was concerned: it was personal, vindictive. Or it was possible that he suspected my true role. Neither explanation was reassuring, and Tozzi was no help. He said that assigning an operative to watch Khol watching me was a luxury he couldn't afford. If Khol got wise to it, the whole plan would be compromised.

"And he's not going after you until you've finished your work for his Mafia pals—unless you provoke him in some way. Be very careful."

Careful! Wasn't I always? But living carefully becomes tedious.

On that Saturday when we four went sightseeing together, I had resolved to dispense with my dark thoughts and savor the moment. I certainly savored the sight of Donatello, and his delight at encountering the marble faun. Kendall, I cannot completely agree with you about his resemblance to the statue. It is as though Praxiteles sculpted a pale copy of the original creature.

What made me try to uncover Donatello's ears? Did I think to reveal him to you the way the photographs had revealed him to me? It was the first time I had reached out to touch him, and he backed away. For an instant I was devastated, as though by invading his privacy, I had earned his rejection. I didn't consider until later, after our meeting in the park, the ramifications of Donatello's possible kinship with a mythological being.

It was in Piazza di Santa Maria, while we were waiting for Donatello to collect our lunch, that I first noticed Khol. He was half hidden in the shadows under a shop awning—black shirt, black pants, a black stare in my direction.

Of course, once I had seen Khol, I couldn't stop looking at him, or for him. It was impossible for me to nap after the picnic like the rest of you. Do you imagine I wasn't aching to lie down beside Donatello, to hold his hand as you held Hannah's? I was on guard, watching for Khol, hating him for spoiling our lovely day. But I also watched Donatello as he slept, invading his privacy again in my imagination, running my fingers through his hair, along his chin, over his eyelids, his lips.

Didn't we have a grand time at Castel Sant'Angelo? I could almost see the wheels of inspiration spinning in Hannah's head as I told her about Beatrice. And when she began to sing, I was so proud to know this extraordinary young woman, proud to believe that perhaps I had been of assistance to her.

Then, as Hannah was singing the final phases of the aria, I felt someone brush against me from behind. "Come. We must talk. Now."

I followed Khol quickly, stealthily, into one of the off-limits passageways before Donatello could take notice and intervene. We rounded a corner and descended a short stairway, took another turn, another stairway. I was lost, and I could barely see in the gloom. This was typical terrorist strategy: surprise, disorient, intimidate. I was not afraid of the dark, but I was afraid of Khol. I supposed we must be in one of the pope's escape tunnels, and I thought wildly that it could take weeks before my lifeless body would be discovered.

I found the courage to confront Khol and stopped short. "Far enough. What do you want? This is a foolish way to contact me."

"All business, eh, Lili? Yes, I have some information for you . . ." and he told me where I should retrieve several of the stolen Etruscan pieces—urns, jewelry, a mirror.

"I understand. I have a buyer in mind, and he should pay an excellent price for the items," I assured him, trying to sound pleased. "Now stop following me and let us communicate only by prearrangement."

"But I have been so careful not to impose myself on you and your fine friends. That journalist—are you sure he suspects nothing?"

"Do you think I am a fool?"

"And the pretty boy," he sneered. "How much are you paying for his attentions?"

I ignored the insult. "He's is just a casual friend, Khol. Why should you care?"

"There was another young man, remember? My brother, who is rotting in a prison cell. Do you ever think about him while you are playing with your pretty boy?" His fingers dug into my arms as he shook me. I remembered how his strength seemed to increase with his anger.

"Take your hands off me! You're hurting me, Khol."

"I have scarcely begun to hurt you, Lili. When I think of what you did to my brother, to me . . ." He was losing control, and I was losing the circulation in my arms.

"Don't be a fool, Khol. Forget the past. We have obligations . . ."

"Forget? Never!" He loosened his grip. "I'll let you go now, but I will be watching you, and the *contino*. Perhaps I will take my revenge on him. A boy for a boy, eh, Lili?" He laughed, and with another of his disconcerting mood swings, became almost courtly. "Come. I will escort you back to your party."

"Just to the ramp. We shouldn't be seen . . . they will ask questions."

"It shall be as you wish, ma fleur." My flower. So he had called me when we first met in Paris and he discovered how he could use me. In my naivete, I had gloried in being his flower. Now I shuddered.

Khol noticed. "Ah, Lili, you do remember the old days, after all."

"It was a long time ago, and better forgotten."

"Perhaps you remember how I dealt with those who betrayed me . . ."

"I'd rather not . . ."

In a single, swift movement he forced me back against the rough stone wall.

"I never could quite bring myself to damage you then. You were so lovely, and so . . . young. But now?"

"Don't touch me!" I was horrified to hear myself beg.

Khol was reveling in my humiliation. Tears came to my eyes; I was grateful that he couldn't see them.

"Lili! Dove sei? Rispondi!" Donatello's voice.

Khol released me. "Yes, it was a long time ago. And now we are partners again. Be very careful this time, Lili." I ruefully recalled Tozzi's similar admonition as I made my way toward your voices and the light.

And I was careful. I invented an evening appointment and bid Donatello a firm farewell at the Galleria gate. It was clear that Khol's quarrel with me was at least partially fueled by jealousy. I would, as Tozzi cautioned, "do nothing to provoke him."

But that night, I could picture Donatello sleeping in my bed as he had slept on Janiculum Hill.

The next morning, Donatello called with an invitation for dinner and a movie. A movie! You can imagine, Kendall, how many years it had been since anyone asked Lili Castelli to go to a movie. I was completely disarmed and sorely tempted, but I pleaded a previous engagement.

Donatello was disappointed. "I must work all week. I don't know when I will be free again. I will call you, Lili."

On Monday, Tuesday, Wednesday he sent flowers, with sad little notes saying he missed me. I tried to avoid his calls, but he quickly charmed Silvia, my secretary, into putting him through. I began our conversations by thanking him for the flowers and apologizing for being unavailable. I could not bring myself to simply cut him off. But each conversation was longer than the one before as we discussed my day at the gallery and his on the set. I felt I could indulge myself in those conversations as compensation for not actually being with him.

Then came the encounter in Villa Borghese. Was it really just coincidence, or had Silvia told him where I'd be? When he found me sketching there, I suspected that Donatello, as well as Khol, was following me, and that could be dangerous for him. But those few magical hours, for me, were worth a lifetime.

I told you, Kendall, how the old myths inspired my dreamworld fantasies when I was a child. I've recaptured some of those dream visions in my paintings. Now I was living in one, frolicking with a faun—a beautiful, loving faun—in the Arcadian forest! It was pure enchantment, until we came to that statue of the faun family and Donatello's suggestion, which awoke me to reality.

And what happened next was a nightmare that convinced me I must not be with him again.

No, I didn't tell Hannah the whole truth about what happened and why I was determined to avoid Donatello. There was sufficient reason without disclosing the exact nature of the peril into which he had innocently placed himself.

CHAPTER SEVENTEEN

Nathan Kendall's Narrative

The more her secret struggled and fought to be told, The more certain would it change all former relations that had subsisted between herself and the friend for whom she might reveal it.

Nathaniel Hawthorne, "The Marble Faun"

I was out of practice, but my game came back quickly and it felt great to be racing around a tennis court again.

The heat was oppressive that morning, and I hadn't been even slightly tempted to ride my bike to the tennis club. I opted for an air-conditioned cab ride, picking Hannah up on the way.

The posh club was air-conditioned, as well. Lili had left our names at the reception desk, and an attendant led us to handsomely appointed dressing rooms. I had my old Prince racket with me; Hannah was loaned a courtesy racket of the most advanced design. I pointed out that she had an unfair advantage right from the start, and she took a practice swing in the general direction of my nose.

When we reached our court, Lili was warming up with one of the pros. She was hitting long, low baseline balls with more force and accuracy than I had expected. She asked me to be her partner: "I need a champion on my team." Hannah was paired with Sergio, the pro.

There is something intimate about sweating and panting in partnership with a member of the opposite sex. Lili didn't look particularly athletic, but she proved to be an intelligent and intuitive player. We moved well together. She told me under her breath to watch out for Sergio's serve down the center line, applauded my smarter moves at the net, congratulated me on an occasional ace. She sometimes berated herself in *sotto voce* Italian, but never lost control.

On the other side of the net was a different sort of player. Hannah's strength was visible in her well-defined muscles. Her energy and determination were also obvious—red hair flying, she would dive for and occasionally make impossible returns. She shouted a lot. While her game lacked finesse, her enthusiasm was infectious. I'm sure Sergio was playing harder than a polite pro probably should. And when Hannah hit a smashing cross court volley past Lili to clinch a game, he patted her approvingly on the fanny with his racket.

Lili and I won the final set in a tie-breaker when Hannah double-faulted. The pro went off to a lesson, and the three of us gathered around a court-side table to cool off with iced tea.

"Thank you, Lili, for inviting us. That felt great!" I said.

"It was a real workout," Hannah agreed, breathing hard from the fray.

"I'm glad you could join me. It's much more fun to play with friends," Lili said, "even though Sergio is very nice."

"Yes, and very talented," Hannah seconded, baiting me. "And next time, we'll win!"

"In your dreams!" I made a swat at her with a towel. "Lili, you're an excellent player."

She shrugged. "Sergio says I play with no passion. He's right—it's mainly just exercise to me. But I admit, today I wanted to win!" We clinked glasses.

Hannah grinned. She was happy to see us getting along so well. She still believed that I didn't like Lili; in truth, I wasn't sure how I felt about her. To me, she was an enigma. Until I understood her, I couldn't really trust her.

Sergio came to our table. "My student didn't show up. Hannah, if you like, I can give you a few pointers on your serve."

Hannah was willing and eager. It seemed to me Sergio hadn't waited very long for his student.

Left alone with Lili, and feeling quite at ease with her now, I took the opportunity to dispel some of my doubts.

Lili had tossed a light sweater around her shoulders, but it didn't hide the bruises on her upper arms. I hadn't noticed them until we sat down and I put on my glasses. I was fairly certain that Donatello hadn't handled her that way.

"I'm glad your bearded buddy isn't a tennis buff, Lili. It's a relief not to have him skulking around, isn't it?"

"Oh Kendall, let's not talk about him." Her eyes left my face; she focused somewhere over my shoulder.

"I think we should. You know, Hannah is really worried about this character." Lili began to interrupt, but I refused to be cut off. "She's afraid

you're in some kind of danger from him." I glanced pointedly at her bruises.
"I'm beginning to agree with her."

Lili squeezed lemon into her tea. "I'm sorry that Hannah is so
concerned. The situation really needn't trouble either of you." It was a
nice way to tell me to mind my own business.

"I'm not interviewing you now, Lili, damn it. I'm asking as a friend."
How could I reach this woman?

Lili sighed, put her hand on my arm and finally looked me full in the face,
her eyes solemn. "Dear Kendall, it would be a great relief for me to confide
in you. But if I were to do that, perhaps we could not remain friends."

"Try me," I urged.

She shook her head. "It is a matter I must resolve by myself. I do not
want it touch you or Hannah in any way—or Donatello."

"Donatello? Hannah told me you had decided not to see him any
more."

Her lips curved up involuntarily, the way mine do whenever someone
mentions Hannah. "I've refused his invitations, but he seems to just show
up where I am. And when I see him . . . well, the heart is not so wise as
the head."

When Hannah told me Lili's story of the romp in the park I had found
it almost impossible to imagine the elegant Lili playing games in the grass.
I recalled how she had sat up, proper and composed, while the rest of us
sprawled sleepily on the quilt at our Janiculum Hill picnic. Looking at her
now—raven hair in a girlish ponytail, face still a trifle flushed from the
game, eyes bright with emotion—I could believe that she was at least part
dryad after all, and that Donatello had brought her out of the tree trunk
in which she had been imprisoned.

Hannah and Sergio returned; we set a date for a rematch. Lili left for
the gallery. Hannah needed to cash some traveler's checks at American
Express near the Spanish Steps, so we decided to have lunch nearby. We
chose Babington's Tea Rooms, opened by some enterprising Englishwomen
100 years ago. Tea and scones and shepherd's pie continue to appear on
the menu. Over berry tarts, we rehashed the tennis match and agreed that
it felt good to get some much-needed exercise.

"I never guessed you were an athlete as well as a scholar," I told her.

"I try—Dad was an All State linebacker."

"But you couldn't even make the team." I began to see some
disadvantages in having a father to live up to.

"No contact sports, and tennis isn't really my game, either. But I bet I
can beat you in swimming."

I wondered if the competitive streak was a legacy from her father. "I'm
not so bad," I countered. "You might be surprised."

"I'd really love to go to the beach."

"The beach is no place for a swim race. We'll need a pool."

"But the beach is much more romantic . . . the scent of the sea, the cry of the gulls, the sand between your toes . . ."

"Ouch! I'm not sure how I feel about sandy toes . . ."

"Oh, Kendall!"

I loved to make her blush. "Well, we could take the train to the beach at Ostia."

"And let's invite Lili and Donatello."

I'd been finessed. "Hold on a minute. I thought you didn't approve of that match. And Lili just told me she's turning down his invitations . . ."

"But she misses him, I can tell. Tennis was fun, but it just isn't the same as when the four of us get together," Hannah said wistfully.

I couldn't deny that Donatello's presence added an element of playful exuberance to our group. I missed him too. "Lili's had every opportunity to see him, if she wishes. She's obviously made up her mind."

"But by avoiding Donatello, Lili is denying her feelings for him," Hannah argued. "Perhaps she needs to just give in to the attraction, get it over with and let them both move on."

"Dr. Ingram, I'm shocked!" I was, a little. "Is that how you feel about us? Are we just getting it over with so we can move on.?"

"Well, no . . ." Hannah was flustered, deservedly so. She was not a woman to take romantic liaisons lightly, and I wondered how long ours could continue before she found herself more committed than she wanted to be. "I guess I haven't thought about what comes next. Have you?"

I hadn't. "No . . . perhaps we should."

She looked surprised. "But not yet, Kendall." Hannah still had her priorities. I'm not sure whether I felt relieved or deflated.

"So, how about a day at Ostia?" she pressed on. "Lili may not agree to be alone with Donatello, but this would be the four of us."

"I suppose you want me to set it up?"

"I'll invite Lili—you invite Donatello."

When I got back to my apartment the next morning there was a message from Raffaella Bianco on my machine. It occurred to me that perhaps Raffi and Bruno might be persuaded to join our beach party. I dialed her office and found her in.

"I have some news for you," she announced. "Perhaps you can add it to your piece on Donatello di Monte Beni." She told me that the director had been very impressed with Donatello in the daily rushes and had expanded his part. "Now he's also playing Praxiteles' son, who poses for the statue and becomes a sculptor himself."

"That's great!" I said. "Do you think this is a big career break for him?"

"Of course, but that's not all: the production company, Chiara Vista, is so enthusiastic that they have asked him to star in a series of Tarzan remakes!"

"Really? But he said he can't act . . ." I hoped my initial disbelief didn't deflate Raffaella's ballooning hopes.

"I know, but he doesn't have to act, not very much, anyway. You remember Johnny Weismuller as Tarzan? He just swung on vines and went swimming and played with the monkey. Donatello's a natural. People will love him!"

Raffaella was right, of course. The idea was intriguing. After a decade or two of violent science fiction adventure films the public might well be ready to applaud a hero without high-tech weaponry—a pure-of-heart natural man like Donatello.

"This could be huge," I thought out loud.

"And listen to this, Kendall. The company assigned me to handle Donatello's publicity exclusively. With a raise. He's wonderful to work with—a real gentleman. I couldn't ask for a better situation."

"Congratulations, Raffi. I'm really delighted for you." I was. I could tell by her voice that she was already a happier woman.

Then I issued the invitation for our Ostia excursion.

"I would love that, Kendall, thank you. Of course, I'll have to check with Bruno and let you know. He's not too pleased about the Donatello business. Perhaps if he sees 'Tello with someone else it will reassure him."

My apprehensions about the beach party were growing.

I called Donatello and suggested he meet me for lunch at the press club the next day. I owed him one, and I thought the exposure might lead to some useful contacts in furthering his film career.

We met at the club bar, where I introduced the count to some of my media contacts before we sat down to lunch. Then I congratulated him on the Tarzan deal.

"Raffaella told you? She is so excited, but I haven't signed anything yet, Kendall. You understand, it's a big decision."

Donatello had been pleased when he was given more to do in the Praxiteles film, he said, because it gave him an excuse—and the funds—to stay longer in Rome. "You know why I want to stay, Kendall." But the Tarzan films would mean a commitment for the future: "I'm not sure I want to change my whole life."

I saw Il Calabrone, Paolo Cavalucci, eyeing us intently from his corner table. I nodded a greeting and remembered what he had told me about the wine business. "Surely you could put the money to good use, Donatello. You could expand the winery."

"You're right, Kendall, I owe much to the people who work there. They have a hard life now. But I am a little afraid of the film business." I couldn't fault him for that.

He told me that he must return to Monte Beni soon to prepare for the harvesting of the grapes. "The vendemmia is a busy time, much work, but I always enjoy it. I love the land, the people, my home, it gives me . . . it fills me . . ."

"It nourishes you?" I finished for him, already writing my story in my head.

"Esattamente. But now I am not so happy to go. I will worry about Lili."

Then Donatello told me his version of the Villa Borghese encounter. According to Donatello, he often ran in the park. "One morning I am running and I catch something in the air . . . her perfume? I feel that she is near, and soon I find her.

"She was a different woman there, Kendall, so free, gioiosa, like a little girl. And I think how much I would like to take her home to Monte Beni, how happy we will be together there.

"We walk, we talk, we play. Then, would you believe it? That schifoso shows his face again! I'm so angry! And Lili, she leaves me to go with him—I can't believe it! Why, Kendall?"

The stalker again. I noted that Lili had deleted this incident when relating the story to Hannah. A significant omission, I thought. I remembered Lili's stated intention not to involve the rest of us in her trouble. Was that why she had left Donatello and gone off with a man who appeared to be persecuting her? Or was she involved in some scheme or scam that she must keep hidden from us?

"Why did she leave me and go with him?" Donatello asked again, with both anger and puzzlement easy to read in his expression.

"I can't imagine," I answered. "It's Lili's business, after all."

"It is bad business, I say." His fork rang against his plate. "I promise you, if that mascalzone tries to hurt her, I will kill him!"

I assumed this was just Italian hyperbole, but Donatello was visibly upset, and from the corner of my eye I saw Paolo taking it all in with a smirk. I tried to calm my friend.

"Lili is a very capable person. I think we must trust her to deal with the problem," I said.

Donatello shook his head, dismissing my assessment of the situation. "You have seen her paintings, Kendall. This man is the dark one in the paintings, you agree? He has been in her life a long time. If she can deal with him, as you say, why does he still make trouble for her?"

I had asked myself—and Lili—pretty much the same question, and had no answer. Instead I presented Donatello with the opportunity to be Lili's protector at the beach.

"I will go, but she will not go with me. I don't know why. I would do anything for her." Donatello looked miserable.

"Well, this time Hannah is inviting her, and I think she will come."

"You know I will come, also. Che será, será . . ."

I was not surprised to see Il Calabrone heading toward our table. I was glad he was no longer writing his column.

Donatello rose to shake his hand as I introduced them. They exchanged some cordialities, Paolo telling Donatello how much he enjoyed the Monte Beni wine. Then he said to me, "You might want to pick up some background on that Etruscan tomb robbery from your lovely friend, the art expert. I understand the authorities are closing in for the kill."

"Thanks for the tip, Paolo," I said to be polite. "but I'm out of the news business now, remember?"

One of the reasons I'd quit BNN was so I wouldn't have to jump, like an old fighter hearing the bell, whenever I got a news lead. In no way was I going to pursue that story with Lili.

"A mistake, ragazzo mio," Paolo said with his masculine version of the Mona Lisa smile, leaving me to guess if the mistake were his or mine.

"Auguri for a most successful cinematic career, Conte." He bowed slightly to Donatello and returned to his table. I wondered, as always, how much he knew that he wasn't letting on.

"Your friend?" Donatello asked.

"An old colleague."

"He said something about Lili, she knows about that robbery?"

"No, no. Just that she is an expert on the sort of items that were stolen."

Donatello said simply, "I don't like him."

"Not many people do," I concurred, explaining that Paolo had been an outspoken critic of the rich, famous and powerful in his column and knew too many of their secrets. "But he's a great source of information."

"I understand." Donatello was silent for a moment. "Kendall, I hope you will visit me at Monte Beni. You could see the country, relax. Perhaps you can write about the wine, or Toscana. I know you are busy, and I don't want to waste your time . . ."

"Visiting you wouldn't be a waste of time, Donatello," I assured him. "I would love to see Monte Beni."

Tuscany is probably my favorite part of Italy—of the world—and I could find much to write about while I was there, including what might turn out to be the first in-depth interview with the new movie Tarzan!

CHAPTER EIGHTEEN

Nathan Kendall's Narrative

*Now comes Donatello, with natural sunshine enough for himself and her,
and offers her the opportunity of making her heart and life all new . . .
It is the surest test of genuine love that it brings back our early simplicity
to the worldliest of us.*

Nathaniel Hawthorne, "The Marble Faun"

Our Ostia outing was a mixed success.

It began with a flurry of introductions as we boarded the train at Termini. Bruno, at least as rugged and intense as the myriad photos I'd seen of him, immediately established himself as the dominant male, regaling Donatello and me with highlights of his recent soccer exploits.

The three women kept up a lively conversation in English. As they grew more animated, Bruno directed some brusque comments in Italian to Raffaella, asking what the hens were cackling about. They switched to Italian then, trying to include him, but he showed little interest in non-soccer subjects.

When we arrived at Lido di Ostia, we could smell the sea and could hardly wait to be immersed in it. Bruno knew the territory; he led us to the most expensive—and gaudy—of the swim clubs. Despite its dated design and decor, the club boasted a freshwater pool, a bar, a dance floor, all the amenities of a luxury beach resort. As he arranged rental cabanas for our party, Bruno had the attendants bowing and scraping. I had forgotten that he was a national celebrity. We were no sooner settled in than two grinning teenage boys loped over to ask for his autograph.

"You see how it will be when you are a star, 'Tello—constant adulation," Raffaella told the count.

"I see, and I don't think I like it," Dontello replied. He and Lili were together but uncomfortable—too polite, too careful of one another. They made me nervous.

The day was hot and sultry; a sun-drenched haze hovered over the turquoise Tyrrhenian. We slathered on sunscreen and lay back on our lounge chairs, agreeing that the beach was the only civilized place to be on such a day. Hannah and I read paperbacks, Donatello fussed about arranging Lili's towels; Bruno signed a few more autographs and posed for a snapshot with a group of feminine fans. We were too hot to talk, which was probably just as well.

After about twenty sweltering minutes, our somewhat fractious aggregation reached a unanimous decision. We got up, sped across the hot sand, and plunged into the sea.

Now I got my wish to see Raffaella with her face washed. She was without make-up and her hair, worn loose, was a mass of damp ringlets. Thin and pale skinned, she looked about fifteen years old and very vulnerable beside her deeply-tanned, heavily-muscled husband. Bruno splashed her and laughed and picked her up and tossed her into the deeper water. I watched to make sure she surfaced safely.

Donatello was a beautiful swimmer, of course. He slowed his stroke to match Lili's, and the two swam far out into the sea before they stopped and floated on their backs, oblivious. The physical activity had broken the tension between them.

Hannah, who looked even more seductive in a sleek blue racing suit than the other women in their bikinis, swam like a dolphin. We dove and dumped each other and raced out to join Donatello and Lili.

Hannah and I had wondered earlier whether we might get a glimpse of Donatello's ears at the beach. Now we felt a bit like voyeurs and actually avoided peering at his ears—which, in any case, were still camouflaged by wet curls. If Donatello did indeed have the ears of a faun, we mused, would it mean that our friend was significantly different from us at the core of his being, a member of some heretofore unidentified species? We were more comfortable not knowing.

The afternoon passed in a bright blur of sun and sea spray. We snacked on slices of watermelon and fresh coconut and dozed in the shade of our cabana.

It was Raffaella who decided to organize a race in the pool. As the least expert swimmer, she appointed herself the official. Bruno said the race was a silly idea, but allowed himself to be coaxed into joining the lineup. We decided to do two lengths of the pool, choice of strokes.

Raffaella played sports announcer and introduced us with her usual flair for publicity: Hannah Ingram, former Cornell University women's team captain and holder of the regional intercollegiate record for backstroke (she hadn't told me that); Lili Castelli, internationally-acclaimed artist and gallery owner; Bruno Bianco, starring forward of the Lazio team and World Cup stand-out (some onlookers let up a cheer); Conte Donatello di Monte Beni, soon to appear in a new Chiara Vista film, "The Marble and the Muse," (a few feminine whistles); and Nathan Kendall, noted American writer and TV newsman (no applause). A couple of people with cameras took positions around the pool, a manifestation of Bruno's notoriety, no doubt.

Raffi had borrowed a lifeguard's whistle to signal the start, and we were off. I quickly passed Lili and Bruno, who hadn't thought he would have to take this race very seriously, but passing Donatello was tougher. Hannah was way out in front, with Raffi cheering her on: "You go, girl!"

I passed Donatello and was gaining on Hannah when we came to the end of the pool, and there she lost me. She did a slick flip turn and by the time I had turned she was a quarter of the way down the last lap, swimming backstroke. Bruno had caught on that this was a real race and pulled past me to come in second. Donatello and I tied for third; Lili was a game fourth.

There was a spatter of applause as Raffaella crowned Hannah with a watermelon rind, and we all congratulated her . . . even Bruno, although it was obvious he was not pleased to have come in second to a female.

I was not surprised when, a few minutes later, Raffi said that the Biancos had to leave. "Thank you for inviting us. I had a wonderful time."

"You added a lot to the party, Raffi. I'm glad you came," Hannah said and gave her a hug before Bruno dragged her away.

The four of us melted into our beach chairs and sipped vodka tonic with lime while the shadows lengthened. The sea was still now, smooth and pale as pearl. From somewhere music started—an Andrea Bocelli ballad, almost unbearably romantic. Hannah began humming along, and I told her to stop: "You know I can't keep my hands off you when you sing."

The tenor must have had a similar effect on Donatello. He drew Lili to her feet: "Dance with me?"

She paused to pull on a white caftan. Barefoot, with her long black hair still wet and glossy, she looked more exotic than ever.

At first Donatello held her somewhat stiffly, not quite cheek to cheek, as though afraid to embrace her. But the music was sensuous, compelling. Donatello pulled Lili close to him. They were soon lost together in the rhythm—a tango? Hannah and I were not the only ones watching. You could believe they had danced many times together and had learned to respond to one another's lightest touch or glance.

Hannah reached for my hand. "We've got to try that."

"You're too short."

"You're too tall, but let's try anyway."

When the dance was finished, Donatello did not release Lili. His arms were around her waist and he was smiling down at her.

His arm was around her on the train as we rode back to Rome.

Later, in my apartment, feeling intensely passionate but painfully sunburned, Hannah and I pondered their relationship.

"They are so in love, but I feel guilty now about bringing them together again. Their situation is sure to end unhappily," Hannah sighed.

She would have felt even worse if I had told her about my conversation with Lili at the tennis club, and Donatello's disclosure that she had dismissed him and gone off with the stalker in the park. If Lili really cared for Donatello, would she allow him to come close to her if it meant danger for him? Or was the danger, whatever it might have been, over?

"Just because their relationship might not last doesn't mean it's a tragedy," I pointed out. "It's been said that the nicest gift two people can give each other is happy memories."

We proceeded to make memories.

In *Il Messaggero* the next morning there was a fabulous photo of Hannah climbing out of the pool with Bruno flailing the water few strokes behind. The caption translated into something like "American woman beats soccer star swimming backwards."

CHAPTER NINETEEN

Journal of Dr. Hannah Ingram

The only way, in such cases, is to stare the ugly horrour right in the face; never a sidelong glance, nor a half-look, for those are what show a frightful thing in it frightfullest aspect.

Nathaniel Hawthorne, "The Marble Faun"

August 6

Spent the night at Kendall's apartment. Thank God for his air-conditioner—with the sunburn we picked up at the beach yesterday, we would have been miserable without it.

Kendall brought breakfast in, and with it some copies of the newspaper. One of the photographers at the beach club took my picture climbing out of the pool and there I am—right on page 3 of the sports section! I'm sending a copy to Dad—he should be tickled that I beat a soccer player.

Apart from the sunburn, the trip to Ostia was wonderful. Everyone seemed to enjoy it, except that Bruno. I'm very fond of Raffaella (Kendall confessed that he had been attracted to her when he first came to Rome). But Bruno? Soccer star or no, in college we would have labeled him a male chauvinist pig. I don't know how Raffi puts up with him.

Kendall's place has none of the charm of my tower, but it's more practical in many ways—I could kill for his desk—and I take my work over there sometimes. Not that it helps much.

Lili loaned me a copy of Corrado Ricci's book, published in 1923. He did an intense investigation of the Cenci story, using the records of the papal magistrates. Ricci wrote about the major players in great detail, but even he seemed baffled by Beatrice. Was she in love with Olimpio at all, or just using him to get rid of her father? Her attempts to escape her father, both legal and lethal, had only made her life more miserable—and exceedingly short. And was it her pretty face that won the hearts of her fellow Romans or did she, at the end of the day, possess some qualities of grace and courage?

Of course, other opera heroines have lived recklessly and died violently—Tosca, Carmen, Desdemona. It is not their deeds, but their glorious music that immortalizes them. For Beatrice, it must be my music.

Evan could not have encountered Ricci's text when he was researching the libretto, because it includes an entire chapter on La Petrella. I was right—it's "a village almost on the Slato river . . . on the road which leads from Rieti to Avezzano." Just where I found it on the map in the Vatican Museum. The fortress began to crumble in the 18th century and an earthquake in 1915 finished it off. But Ricci's verbal reconstruction of the castle is very evocative and I'm copying it for the set designer to use.

The book also has graphic descriptions of torture techniques. One time when Kendall and I were walking along the Corso, we saw a series of bright banners with gold fringe announcing a museum exhibition: Antique Torture Implements.

"Would you like to see it?" Kendall asked me. "Research for the opera?"

"I'm not even remotely interested," I told him. "Why in the world would anyone put such horrors on display, much less advertise the show like a gala event?".

Kendall just grinned. "I'll bet the place will be mobbed."

He's right, no doubt. I was reminded of the deadly games that took place in the Colosseum centuries before—and that the Romans seem not to have outgrown their taste for mayhem. Perhaps people need to feel pain and horror vicariously to steel themselves against the shock of actual experience. Or is it simply the thrill, an adrenaline rush—the kind I felt singing doomed Tosca's aria?

August 8

Kendall took me to lunch at the Stampa Estera today and I met some of his media pals—an interesting lot from all around the world, all happy to be working in Rome. I enjoyed chatting with them. Then he introduced me to Paolo Cavalucci, a famous columnist and a special friend. Paolo was absolutely charming—impeccable clothes and manners, a wonderful raconteur. When we said goodbye, he kissed my hand—just a light brush with dry lips. But he looked at me in way that suddenly made me feel defiled. An overreaction, perhaps—he didn't say or do anything out of line. But I was very thankful he didn't join us for lunch, and later I told Kendall I find the man repulsive.

Kendall laughed and said, "Yes, he is repulsive in a way, but I enjoy him."

Well, Kendall's considerably more worldly than I. I wish I could emulate his easy acceptance of human inconsistency. I'd understand Beatrice better.

August 9

Letter from Margaret today. She's vacationing on Prince Edward Island but says she'd rather be in Rome—must have forgotten the heat. She says Karl Hoffman, one of our old profs, is here working on a project with the American Academy. It would be nice to see him—I'll look him up. He might have some helpful suggestions for the opera score.

Kendall's off to Bologna on a story—an electronic five-fingered robot tortellini-making machine or some such marvel. Wish I were with him. For his company, of course, and because it might be a few degrees cooler there.

K. got a big check for an article on security systems at the Vatican, and said he'd take me to Hostaria dell'Orso for my birthday. Then he found out that Placido Domingo is singing at the Baths of Caracalla, so we're going to the opera instead—Lili and Donatello, too. After the performance, Donatello is treating us to dinner at La Pergola, the restaurant on the roof of the Cavalieri Hilton Hotel. Perhaps he thinks this is his last chance to impress Lili before he leaves Rome—the film is finished and he's got to get back to his vineyard.

Poor Donatello! He tries to be suave and sophisticated and all the while it's his natural simplicity that endears him to Lili. I'm thrilled that he's been chosen to play Tarzan—from faun to ape man isn't such a great leap, after all, and I have a feeling he'll be a huge success. I wonder how money and fame will affect him—was this what Lili was concerned about when she said it would be a sin to change him? He's already besieged by starlets and groupies, I'm sure, and he still has the good taste to prefer Lili. He might eventually become a Galleria Castelli client, and Lili could choose art and antiques to decorate his villa.

There I go with my happy endings . . .

Kendall will see Monte Beni soon—Donatello has invited him to visit and K. plans to do a story on the Tuscan vineyards. I wonder if Monte Beni is a place where Lili could conceivably be content.

August 12—My Birthday

Tonight—"Aida" at the Baths of Caracalla. I'll probably be too tired to write by the time I get home, so I'm doing my journal entry now. It's hard to know what to write in this journal, what will be important ten or twenty years from now and what's just trivia.

Trivia. I had my hair done at a parrucchiere on Via Margutta—curled and teased and piled on top of my head. I went shopping on Via Condotti and splurged on a luscious silk knit dress and matching jacket, deep apricot color. Topaz earrings. Terra Rossa cologne. All this is to make me look beautiful in Kendall's eyes, when I know perfectly well it's not my appearance that keeps him by my side.

Important. When I read this page twenty years from now I'll remember how it felt to be in Rome and in love.

CHAPTER TWENTY

Notes from Lili Castelli

She must have cause to dread some unspeakable evil from this strange persecutor, and to know that this was the very crisis of her calamity; for, as he drew near, such a cold, sick despair crept over her, that it impeded her breath, and benumbed her natural promptitude of thought.

Nathaniel Hawthorne, "The Marble Faun"

So Donatello told you about the ending of our idyll in the park. As much as he knew.

We were strolling aimlessly, arm in arm, to the Pincio gardens, carefree and reveling in one another's company, when suddenly Khol emerged from the shrubbery like the serpent in the Garden of Eden.

It took all my strength to send Donatello away. I wondered how long Khol had been following us, what he had seen. He immediately confirmed my fear.

"You always pretended to be such a lady, Lili," he spat at me. "And now you play the whore with your gigolo for everyone to see. Charming!

I had retrieved my sketch pad from Donatello when he left; now I held it in front of me like a shield. "Do you have something to discuss with me or not?"

Khol snatched the sketch pad and tore out the sketch I'd made of Donatello. Something flashed; the halves of Donatello's face fluttered to the ground.

"Too bad. He's ruined."

In another man, I would have interpreted the gesture as a childish tantrum, or perhaps a warning; in Khol, I knew it to be a demonstration of his intentions.

"Donatello has nothing to do with our business. Would Dolata approve of your threatening me or my friend?

"Do I care what Dolata thinks?" There was a manic light in his eyes and I was afraid of what he might do next, even in this public place.

"You should care. We need each other in this enterprise. We need to keep our heads."

"Yes, the enterprise. I'm not sure that I can completely trust you with it, Lili. You betrayed me once—why should I give you another chance? Perhaps I no longer need you."

"Then let's call if off. I don't need you, either. Most of the antiquities are in my possession now," I reminded him.

Khol was agitated; he wasn't totally irrational. "Touché, ma fleur. But do not imagine I will let you out of my sight for a moment until your task is completed."

"Waste your time then, if you must," I replied angrily, "but stop playing the fool."

His face contorted with fury. "You dare to call me fool?" I half expected him to bring out the knife and plunge it into me then and there. I looked around wildly, praying there was someone who would come to my assistance if he tried.

"Leave me alone," I cried. A couple strolling nearby discreetly turned their faces.

"We have a score to settle, Lili—you will not escape. And if you play me false this time, I swear, your young count will pay the price."

Then Khol strode away, leaving me weak and trembling.

"Just stay away from the count and try to string Khol along a while longer," Tozzi responded when I asked to be relieved of the assignment. "Take the goods to your usual contact in Geneva and have the provenances prepared. While you're there, we'll pick up Khol on some pretext or another. He's probably in the country illegally."

"Won't that be a signal to Dolata that we're on to him?" I worried.

"He's too greedy—and too arrogant—to call off the deal now. Just proceed as if you're expecting Khol to contact you when you get back from Switzerland. Dolata will eventually send someone else. From his point of view, Khol is expendable."

It had seemed like an elaborate game when we started the operation. Tozzi could always make it seem like a game, but he was sitting in an office somewhere, safe from a madman with a knife and a vendetta.

I couldn't protect myself, but I could try to protect Donatello. If Khol didn't see him with me again, he might forget about him. I filled my appointment book so that no waking hour would be available for Donatello. I arranged the gallery exhibition schedule for the next year. I prepared brochures and catalogues and advertisements. I contacted collectors of antiquities who might be interested in the Etruscan finds and not ask too many questions. I went to parties. I played tennis.

But Donatello was not to be denied. I attended a cocktail party one night in Parioli. I don't know whether Donatello was invited or not; he just appeared beside me at the buffet table. He whisked me off to the balcony where he sang a little lullaby about the moon. (I can still hum the tune, Kendall.) Then, mysteriously, he managed to secure the seat behind me at a chamber music concert: I imagined I could hear his breathing in the violins. Another time, he followed me to the greengrocer's and juggled oranges until even the proprietor was helpless with laughter.

Then came the afternoon at Ostia, and I could no longer keep him at arm's length. Hannah had not warned me Donatello would be in the group. When Silvia called my apartment to tell me, "That gorgeous count is here to accompany you to the beach," I was thoroughly disconcerted, and annoyed that Hannah had inveigled me this way when I was trying valiantly to avoid Donatello. Of course, I could not be angry with her for long, and concentrated on conversing with her and Raffaella Bianco (a lovely person and quite capable—I do admire your taste in women, Kendall). Engaged in the group, I was able to fend off Donatello's overtures.

Then we plunged into the sea, and I was lost.

Dontatello, gleaming bronze, cut through the water like a Triton, more than ever a creature from mythology. We swam until we were breathless and then surrendered ourselves to the gentle rhythm of the sea. I felt released into a magical, watery world where nothing could harm us. Pleasure is too bland a word: it was bliss.

When we returned to shore, Donatello rose from the water, shook the sparkling droplets from his hair, threw his arms wide and laughed for joy. I wanted to forget everything and go with him—somewhere, anywhere, merge with him and become a part of his time and place. I had felt this way before, in the park, when Donatello had alluded to the delight of the faun family and said we could be similarly happy at Monte Beni. I knew it was not possible, and yet I wanted it with all my being.

I'm sure my emotions were obvious to you at Ostia, especially when we danced. But even after that enchanted afternoon, I was mindful of Tozzi's warning and Kohl's threats. When we got back to the Rome station, I ducked into a cab and locked the door before Dontello could join me. I could not even look at him to wave goodbye because I was close to weeping with frustration and longing.

The physical attraction I felt for Donatello was so overpowering I was almost sick with the strain of resisting it. But Donatello's feeling for me was something else, something sweeter and somehow innocent. To become his lover without reciprocating his devotion, I felt, would not only exacerbate the danger from Khol but also be a terrible betrayal.

You were kind, Kendall, in your narrative not to question Donatello's unshakable, almost fierce attachment to me. I did. After all, there were many more beautiful, younger, less complicated women who would readily have reciprocated his attentions. I believe now that when Donatello saw my paintings, he recognized in them a kindred spirit. We met, and he felt an innate empathy which I soon shared. Then he saw Khol. With his exceptional intuitiveness, Donatello sensed the danger long before the rest of you became seriously concerned. Like Faunus, whom he so resembles, Donatello is first of all a protector.

Hannah has recorded, with vivid detail, her excitement in preparing for our evening at the opera. I, too, had great expectations.

In the intervening days, I had received the remainder of the stolen artifacts and concealed the lot within shipments appropriately documented for delivery to my mother's shop in Paris. But I would not be going to Paris. I would cross the border into Switzerland and intercept the shipment at Lucerne, separate the contraband from the legitimate merchandise and arrange for the provenances. From there, the items would be forwarded, not to my mother, but to buyers in London, Beirut, Philadelphia, Seattle, Shanghai. Before this last phase of the plan would take place, however, Tozzi's team would apprehend Khol, Dolata, and certain of the receivers, as well. My mission would be complete, and my life would resume without the poisonous presence of Khol.

So the end of the nightmare was in sight. I felt confident enough of our safety to invite Donatello to call for me at my apartment before the opera. It would be the first time I had invited anyone to share my sanctuary. You and Hannah have described the Galleria Castelli as "the epitome of elegance" and "a wonderland." My apartment was in distinct contrast, with nothing to overload the senses: oversize sofas, low tables stacked with books and magazines, thick Chinese carpets, a few favorite art objects and paintings from my grandparents in Beirut. Simple shapes, soft textures, soothing colors.

You will chuckle, Kendall, because I prepared for Donatello's arrival as if I were intending to seduce him. I chilled wine, arranged flowers, plumped pillows, put fresh, herb-scented sheets on the bed. Our farewell celebration would not end at La Pergola; Donatello and I would have our long-delayed time together. (Didn't Hannah, with her artless insight, suggest a similar solution to our dilemma?) Then I would go to Switzerland and Donatello would return to Monte Beni to tend to his vineyards. He would have a motion picture career; I would paint. The intensity of our feelings for one another would fade, and eventually beautiful memories would replace regrets.

CHAPTER TWENTY-ONE

Nathan Kendall's Narrative

. . a deeper wisdom, that stoops to be gay as often as occasion serves, and oftenest avails itself of shallow and trifling grounds, because, if we wait for more substantial ones, we seldom can be gay at all.

Nathaniel Hawthorne, "The Marble Faun"

Each year in recent memory there has been controversy about staging opera at the Baths of Caracalla. The magnificent open-air setting is immensely popular with music-lovers, but archaeologists worry about damaging the ancient site. Usually a compromise is reached and come summer, the show goes on.

As we passed through the imposing ruins to the theater, Lili related the history of the Baths, a pleasure palace for Rome's elite: "More than a thousand Romans could bathe here at one time. And there were steam rooms, pools and gymnasiums, even art galleries and gardens."

The elaborate marble decorations have disappeared, but the bare remains are grand enough to impress. Hannah, alight with excitement and particularly appetizing in a new outfit, squeezed my arm. "It's overwhelming, Kendall. I wonder if Beatrice ever saw this."

Donatello escorted Lili to our seats with great dignity, a *conte* with his *contessa*. He wore a beautifully-tailored light suit for the occasion; Lili was exquisite as always in what Hannah described as black chiffon evening pajamas with a long, luxurious shawl of richly embroidered cashmere.

This night, Donatello and Lili looked as though they belonged together, but according to Hannah, they had seen each other only casually since the day at Ostia. Indeed none of us had seen much of Donatello, who told us he had been putting in long hours at Cinecittà. Lili had lunched once with Hannah, and we had played tennis again, but she, too, had been preoccupied with other activities. Now we happily updated one another until the conductor entered and raised his baton.

The first familiar notes of the overture were heart-stopping; the scenery, costumes and choreography even more spectacular than we had anticipated, particularly the triumphal procession complete with live camels and an elephant. But I think Donatello found the opera hard going, mainly because the seats were only semi-comfortable and he was too skittish to stay still for so long. Between acts, we considered skipping a *recitativo* or two in favor of a jog around the ruins. But we persevered and were rewarded—it was a thrilling performance.

In the last act the lovers, Aida and Radames, are sealed in a vault under the Egyptian temple and left to die in each other's arms. That night, the great walls of the Baths were an integral and extremely effective element of the set. Hannah whispered that the somber scene reminded her of our visit to the bowels of Castel Sant'Angelo.

A chilling mist swirled into the amphitheater and around the stage, adding to the ominous atmosphere. Hannah began to shiver; Lili moved to the seat beside her and wrapped them both in her shawl.

Even after the final bows, Hannah continued to shiver.

"That last scene had a strange effect on me," she confided. "I kept thinking about the time we lost Lili in Castel Sant'Angelo and for a moment I even thought I saw the stalker lurking in the ruins." Then, with a shaky giggle, "He was wearing a tux."

I'd stopped thinking about Lili's shadow in the past few weeks and I thought Hannah had, too. I put my arm around her and pulled her close. "Before long, we'll be at the restaurant and we'll have some supper to warm you up." I was ready for some sustenance myself.

The Rome Cavalieri Hilton is situated high above the city atop Monte Mario. As our cab wound its way upward, the hotel came into view like a dream castle rising from the mist. The Hilton is as impressive a playground for Rome's well-to-do today as were the Baths in Caracalla's time.

The elevator took us up seven flights to the roof and La Pergola. The view was awe-inspiring that night, with phantom swirls of mist and fog alternately revealing and obscuring the city lights spread far below.

By now Hannah had recovered her good spirits, noting with pleasure La Pergola's frescoed ceiling, fine paintings and rich furnishings. Lili commented on the linens and tableware: "These are Austrian glasses, very fine, hand-blown. The china is a special design from Luxembourg." The strategically-positioned mirrors intrigued me: they reflected lights and shadows, angles and aspects, in an intricate pattern which made the room seem at once larger and more intimate.

"You chose a magnificent setting for a celebration, *Conte*" I said.

Donatello basked in our appreciation and made the most of his role as host. He conferred at length with the waiter in animated Italian, devising a menu which began with paper-thin cannelloni stuffed with creamy chunks of lobster and truffles. The dish was so incredible that I can't even remember what came next.

"This wonderful restaurant does not have Monte Beni on the wine list—yet—so I have ordered Moet et Chandon in honor of La Parisienne," Donatello nodded to Lili. We drank toasts to Donatello's film success, Lili's gallery, Hannah's opera, and the Great American Novel I would some day write. We drank to Rome, to Tuscany, to Cornell, to Praxiteles, to Verdi, and we probably drank too much.

Hannah announced over her favorite *zabaglione* with orange, "This the best night of my life."

"You've drunk the most champagne of your life," I amended.

"Probably. But it's not just that. It's the four of us—we're almost like a charmed circle, together in Rome."

We drank to our charmed circle, and the waiter brought espresso to finish the feast.

"I guess I'll be the only one of us in town for Ferragosto," Hannah lamented. She was referring to the annual August holiday when most businesses close for two weeks and vacationing Romans desert the city, leaving it to the tourists. "I'll miss you all."

"You're not supposed to miss them—only me," I complained. I had scheduled my visit to Monte Beni during this down time in the city.

"And I'll only be away for a week or so," Lili added.

"What part of Switzerland are you going to visit?" Hannah asked.

"First Lucerne," Lili replied and went on to give us her itinerary. "I have a contact in Neuchatel who has offered me some interesting wooden sculptures. Neuchatel is a fairy-tale town—you would adore it, Hannah. It's on the loveliest lake . . ." she began, and then suddenly stopped mid-sentence. "Oh!" She put a hand to her throat.

"Excuse me, I guess I shouldn't have had that last glass of champagne." She gave us a wan smile. "I feel a little dizzy. Perhaps I should get some fresh air."

Lili rose to her feet. Donatello was beside her immediately, wrapping the cashmere shawl around her as they hurried out to the rooftop terrace.

Left to ourselves, Hannah and I fell into a mellow silence. We finished our espresso; ordered a liqueur. I started to yawn. "I'm really ready to leave."

"Me, too," Hannah's eyelids were heavy.

"I'll go down and ask the doorman to rustle up a taxi while you find Lili and Donatello, all right?"

"Fine. If they're not ready to leave yet, I'll just thank Donatello for us and join you." Hannah headed for the terrace.

I had been waiting with the taxi in front of the hotel scarcely five minutes when Hannah appeared, out of breath and pale as the statue of Venus she resembled.

"What's wrong?" I asked, hustling her into the cab.

"I just want to go home." She sounded awful.

"What about the others?"

She closed her eyes and shook her head.

I gave her address to the driver.

"What on earth is the matter, Hannah?"

She swallowed hard before answering. "I feel really sick."

"Too much champagne? Or the zabaglione? Just put your head on my shoulder—we'll be home before long."

But she sat rigid, her arms crossed over her ribs, head bent forward. "No! I . . . maybe it was the seafood. I feel terrible."

I tried to hold her but she resisted. I thought she was afraid she might throw up on me. I couldn't get another word out of her until we arrived at her building.

"Don't come up tonight, Kendall, please. I really need to be alone."

"But I'm worried about you, Hannah."

She unlocked the heavy outer door and as I began to follow, she actually shoved me back. She managed a weak smile. "Goodnight, Kendall. I'm sorry."

I was floored. What had happened to change "the best night" of her life? I called her as soon as I got home to ask how she was feeling, but there was no answer. I left a message saying I would phone around noon so we could have late breakfast together. I hoped she was already sleeping it off, whatever it was.

CHAPTER TWENTY-TWO

Nathan Kendall's Narrative

"They are aware of some misfortune that concerns me deeply. How soon am I too know it too?"

Nathaniel Hawthorne, "The Marble Faun"

I awoke late the next morning after a fitful sleep and immediately phoned Hannah. There was no answer. She might have gone out for some groceries or something, but I was uneasy that she hadn't called me. I tried again after fifteen minutes; showered, dressed and called again. No answer.

At this point, I was less worried than annoyed. I certainly didn't want to spend Sunday by myself and in suspense, so I got on my bike and pedaled to Via dei Portoghesi. Hannah had given me copies of her keys; I unlocked the outer door of the building, ran up the stairs to the apartment and knocked. There was no response. I didn't feel I should invade her privacy; it was possible she had called me while I was riding over, and had gone to our usual cappuccino place in Piazza Navona. I went to the Piazza but I couldn't find her.

Now I was more concerned than angry. I ran back to her apartment and used the key, privacy be damned.

"Hannah!"

She was not in the living room. I checked the bedroom, the bath, even the roof. Hannah was not in her tower.

Perhaps she had left a note for me somewhere. I went to her desk, but found nothing; in fact, the desk looked unusually bare. Her laptop computer and keyboard were gone, and some files. Frantic now, I looked in the closet, in the dresser drawers. Items of her clothing were missing, as well. The bathroom had been cleared of toiletries.

Feelings of anger and relief fought for control. She was not ill in a hospital; she had not been murdered or kidnapped, thank God. She had merely gone away, taking her work with her. But not permanently, because she'd left most of her belongings in the apartment.

But she had departed very suddenly, without telling me. It was irresponsible and unlike her. Then I remembered her mentioning that Evan Comstock, the librettist, might be coming to Rome, and that they might go together to look for La Petrella, the site of the Cenci killing. That could be the answer: Comstock had arrived unexpectedly; they had left in a hurry. Hannah would probably call me when they got to L'Aquila or wherever.

I had breakfast alone in Piazza Navona and returned home to tackle some writing assignments. All afternoon I was expecting her to call; I even tried her apartment a time or two, an exercise in futility. By evening I had worked up to a real sulk. It was obvious that Hannah simply didn't want to be in touch with me for some reason.

What had happened last night at the hotel? Hannah had been affected by more than indigestion or superfluous champagne to behave this way.

I considered calling Donatello, then remembered that he was leaving that day for Monte Beni. The close-mouthed Lili would simply have to tell me what had happened. I dialed Galleria Castelli and got a recorded message—of course, it was Sunday and the gallery was closed. I would have to go in person tomorrow morning and find a way to get the story from her.

The night was endless. Intermittently I dozed and had mad dreams of being buried under an Egyptian temple, which morphed into Castel Sant'Angelo . . . climbing to the roof of Hannah's tower where she knocked me over the side with a tennis racket . . . Paolo Cavaluzzi waving a ringed finger at me and gloating "Your mistake, *ragazzo*."

Morning came as a blessing. I extricated myself from the tangled sheets, showered, dressed, walked to Piazza Repubblica where I picked up a paper to read with my morning coffee. I sat under the arcade and savored the brew, somewhat reassured by the customary bustle all about me—traffic roaring, people rushing to work, tourists consulting their maps. Just another hot summer day in Rome.

I scanned the headlines in *Il Messaggero*: the usual political shenanigans, yet another strike, a dead body discovered . . . my heart skipped a beat.

A body had been discovered on the grounds of the Rome Cavalieri Hilton, a probable suicide. The corpse was found where it would have landed had the man jumped from the hotel's heliport, located on the opposite end of the roof from La Pergola restaurant. The article made a point of that, speculating that "While late diners enjoyed elegant food and drink in one of Rome's classic restaurants, just meters away a man met violent death in the thick early morning fog . . ."

We had been among the "late diners." It was possible that Hannah had seen something, something shocking that had left her sick with fright.

And what about Donatello and Lili, who had been out on the roof getting some air? God forbid it was Donatello who had fallen . . .

I read further. The body was as yet unidentified: dressed in evening clothes, probably in his mid-forties, dark-complected, over six feet tall, bearded. Not Donatello, then. But Hannah thought she had seen someone of that description skulking in the ruins of the Baths of Caracalla . . .

It was imperative that I find Lili. I ran to the Galleria Castelli, oblivious to traffic, endangering myself and those I jostled on the way, but I was desperate. When I reached Via Gregoriana, the gallery was closed. Closed for Ferragosto, according to a notice on the gate, and I remembered that Lili was going to Switzerland this week. Gone.

That left Donatello. He had invited me to visit him; I would leave immediately. I'd be arriving a few days earlier than planned and he would just have to cope.

I felt abandoned. I had introduced these three people to each other; they had made me a sort of father confessor (even Lili, to some extent). Now they had some knowledge they had chosen not to share with me and had simply disappeared. What did they think I would do? Twiddle my thumbs and wait for them to write or call or come back to Rome as though nothing had happened?

On the way back to my apartment I stopped briefly at Stampa Estera to pick up messages. Paolo Cavaluzzi was there. As I sped down the stairs he called after me, "Did you see *Il Messagero* today, Kendall? That man who took a tumble—I know who he is."

I stopped and turned. "Do you care to share that information or are you just bragging?"

"Touchy today, aren't you?" he observed blandly. "He's Egyptian, from a prominent family and expensively educated in France, but a bad apple. He did a turn with the Red Brigades, got into arms smuggling, drugs, the usual."

Paolo paused for effect. "Now he's a tombarolo. Or, was."

A tomb robber. In some regions of Italy, the tombaroli were protected by the Mafia, who shared the profits from the illegally acquired antiquities.

"I trust you've given this information to the police?" I challenged Paolo.

"Oh, they already know, of course," he replied with a lazy wave of his hand. "They're keeping it quiet for their own good reasons."

I turned to go.

Paolo called after me. "Get to work, giovanotto. You're missing out on a great story."

That wasn't all I was missing. I packed, arranged to rent a car, and within two hours was on my way to Monte Beni.

CHAPTER TWENTY-THREE

Notes from Lili Castelli

"I see a spectre now!"

Nathaniel Hawthorne, "The Marble Faun"

The cashmere shawl was a gift from Donatello.

He brought it when he came to my apartment before the opera.

"Here is something to hold you safe while I'm away," he said, almost shyly presenting the beautifully wrapped package.

I made quite a show of opening the box and admiring the gift, although I was dismayed that he had spent that kind of money on me when I had more than enough finery. But the shawl was exceptional, feathery light and soft, and embroidered with a delicate design of grapevines and lilies. The tears in my eyes when I thanked him were genuine.

Then I poured us each a glass of Monte Beni, which delighted him. Oh, how happy he was, Kendall! It was to be a night of joyous celebration with good friends, a night of love.

And how proud I was—Lili Castelli, whose escorts included princes and famous actors and tycoons—to take the arm of this young count from the country. For this one night, I would be his *contessa*, his nymph, whatever he wanted me to be.

Hannah told you, not quite believing it herself, I think, that she saw "the stalker" at the Baths of Caracalla. I did not see him until later, at La Pergola. When I caught Khol's reflection in a mirror it was like a sudden descent into hell. I knew at once disaster was imminent; my flight out to the roof was as much a physical reaction as a tactical move. Perhaps, I hoped desperately, Khol merely wanted to be sure that our plans were on schedule: he would follow me to the roof and I would reassure him and he would be gone.

But Donatello saw him, too. Donatello came with me, out into that choking fog.

When we reached the end of the roof, Donatello spun me around to face him. "Basta, Lili. Enough! Now you will tell me about this schifoso and I will finish with him."

"It is not that simple. I have business with him . . ."

"Business? Do you think I have no brain? He does not follow you, make you afraid, because of business! Tell me the truth, Lili."

While intending to protect him with my silence, I had underestimated Donatello's accuity. Now, as succinctly as I could, I explained my connection with the Carabinieri, our plan to trap the smugglers, and Khol's part in it.

"Ah no, Lili, this is foolishness. You put yourself in so much danger for what? To save these old things?"

"These old things are archaeological treasures, . . ."

"No, you are the treasure, Lili, tesoro mio. I will not let you risk your life . . . ."

"It will be over soon. Leave me alone now and let me deal with Khol. If you think I am in danger, you can stay out here on the roof. Just go where he can't see you."

"You want me to hide?" Donatello was indignant. "No, Lili. This is crazy. Come with me now, I beg you. I will take you home. You will call this Tozzi and tell him you are through."

I wanted to do what he asked. I couldn't. "I am going to finish what I started, Donatello. If you don't understand that, I'm sorry. Just go away!"

He disappeared into the fog.

I waited for Khol.

PART TWO

Tuscany

If the ancient Faun were other than a mere creation of old poetry, and could have appeared anywhere, it must have been in such a scene as this.

—*Nathaniel Hawthorne, "The Marble Faun"*

Chapter Twenty-Four

Nathan Kendall's Narrative

The world has grown either too evil, or else too wise and sad, for such men as the old Counts of Monte Beni used to be.

Nathaniel Hawthorne, *"the Marble Faun"*

I had to concentrate on my driving. I didn't find myself behind the wheel very often in those days, and I was never truly comfortable with a stick shift. But by the time I left the outskirts of Rome and headed north, I felt more at ease with it and my mind turned back to the disturbing and possibly dangerous situation in which Hannah—and I—found ourselves.

I could assume that there had been an incident on the roof of the Cavalieri Hilton involving Lili and Donatello and resulting in the death of a man who may have been stalker. Hannah had probably been a witness. She had suffered a terrible shock, which explained her strange behavior, to a point. Why she hadn't told me what she'd seen, and why she had fled Rome without contacting me, remained a mystery.

Setting aside my bruised ego, I acknowledged that Hannah, like myself, was essentially a loner and accustomed to steering her own course. Her much-loved and admired companions had, before her eyes, changed into strangers capable of . . . whatever dark deed had occurred. Sorely shaken, she might well be wondering whether I, too, was not all she had believed me to be. She would need time alone before she could trust me again; that was the least ominous explanation I could conceive.

Paolo's taunt came back to sting me. I was on the inside of what could well turn out to be a major story involving the theft of antiquities from an archaeological site, not to mention the violent death of a *tombarolo*, most likely at the hands of a glamorous gallery owner and a young count on the brink of a movie career. With a lovely but maddening young American composer as an eyewitness. Great stuff! But it was too late now, because I cared about these people. I wanted to help them, not expose them.

Paolo had given me several cues which I'd ignored because I was too busy grinding out little 500-word tidbits on automated tortellini twisters and such. Trivia had become my livelihood. In disassociating from my BNN career had I also disengaged my journalistic instincts, my aptitude for investigation? I'd certainly lost my objectivity: I was emotionally involved, totally. It was a sobering realization.

After I passed Terni, little hill towns appeared with increasing frequency until it seemed that every major mound was crowned with an ancient walled village. The red earth of Tuscany was baked dry in the August sun, but the vineyards were green, the grapes heavy on the vines.

I bypassed Siena and took the Chianti wine route towards Florence, finding myself entranced with the scenery in spite of my preoccupations. Green-black cypress trees, silvery olive groves—how Hannah would love it, I thought, and I felt a gnawing emptiness in my chest. Where in God's name was she, anyway?

The nearest town to Monte Beni, Donatello had told me, was San Gimignano. I could recognize it at a distance because of its unique skyline, punctuated by more than a dozen medieval stone towers. I decided to stop there and call him. I should give him that courtesy, no matter how disturbed I might be. In my haste to leave Rome, I had forgotten my cell, so I wound my way up to the center of the town and found a public telephone in the piazza.

My call to Monte Beni was answered by a Signor Belgioso who spoke a little English and explained that il Conte would not return until dinner time. After I explained that I was a writer friend whom Donatello had invited to visit, he was most cordial, even offering to meet me in the piazza and lead me to Monte Beni.

"We are on the next hill to the south, Signore."

I settled for directions, and said I would time my arrival for early evening. Donatello would have returned by then, and we could dine together.

This gave me an hour or so to kill, and meandering through the streets of San Gimignano was as good a way as any to do it. I got my camera out of the car and took some photos. I needed to do a story or two in Tuscany if I were to pay the rent back in Rome.

After stopping for a cold drink I climbed to the Rocca, a 14th-century fortress with a tower and incredible views of the countryside. The hills were like stained-glass windows—rectangles of green, gold and rich red-brown outlined by the black cypress trees. I wondered which of the hillside vineyards and villas might be Monte Beni, and how I would approach

Donatello when I arrived. With Lili out of reach, he was the only one who might be able to tell me what had happened at the Hilton, but confronting him directly could be counter-productive. If he had wanted my counsel, he could have contacted me in Rome. I would try, at least in the beginning, to stifle my impatience and hope that he would eventually confide in me.

Following Signor Belgioso's instructions, I easily found the sign for the Monte Beni vineyards and turned onto a narrow paved road which curved up the hillside. Even at this time of year, the hill was lush and green, dense forest curved around small circles of meadow.

The paving came to an end at a great iron gate. I parked the car and proceeded up a dirt road on foot. Coming into view above the treetops was an ancient stone tower not unlike those of San Gimignano, rectangular and battlemented. As I rounded a corner, the path widened into a dusty courtyard and I saw, at last, the Villa Monte Beni.

Donatello's ancestral home was larger in scale than a typical Tuscan country house and very, very old. Of no particular architectural style, it had been painted a pale ochre color, but not recently—heavy vines clung to the crumbing walls. While the villa was impressive overall in its quintessential Tuscan setting, it was obviously in decline, a forlorn relic of better times.

Now I could see Donatello himself on battlements of the tower, silhouetted against the early evening sky. He might be watching for me, or merely surveying his vineyards. Rose-gold light painted the tower and trees with rich, romantic color; I took a photo before calling to him.

My friend waved and within a few moments came out the main entrance of the villa to welcome me. He looked the part of a working vineyard owner in a dark sweater, work pants and boots. Perhaps it was the bulky clothing and the muted light, but Donatello appeared both heavier of muscle and gaunter of face than when I had last seen him, and his customary glow of good spirits was considerably dimmed. He could, of course, be affected by the demands of overseeing the harvest, but if my suspicions were correct, he had darker matters to contend with. Then, too, his parting from Lili may have been a wrenching one, under the circumstances.

After he had greeted me, Donatello asked about Hannah.

"I haven't seen Hannah since the opera and I don't know where she is. It appears she packed up her computer and went somewhere to work uninterrupted by me," I told him, not hiding my ruffled feelings.

Donatello's mouth hardened. "*Eh, le donne. Sempre misteriose.*" He shook his head. "But this is not like Hannah. I'm sure she will return to you soon."

I wanted to shout at him, "What happened? What frightened her?" but I was somehow subdued by this new, somber Donatello, so different from the green-and-gold young man who had danced like a faun. The demand for an immediate explanation died in my throat.

Donatello took my bags; I followed with my desktop computer and camera equipment. The villa was dark within, unlighted except for the afterglow of the sunset. We passed through several sparsely furnished rooms, refreshingly cool but with a faint aura of decay. In the shadows I could discern faded frescoes on the walls and ceiling, mythological scenes, perhaps, and a scattering of formal portraits.

"The former counts," Donatello said. They looked more like rugged men of the land in period costume than titled aristocrats, and seemed ill at ease in their ornate frames.

The present count led me up the stairs to the second of three floors and down a long hallway with a multitude of closed doors. The villa could once have accommodated several Monte Beni generations along with their family retainers. Donatello should consider converting this venerable albatross into a hotel or a bed and breakfast, I thought.

The room prepared for me was freshly-scrubbed and spacious, its windows looking out over the wooded hills. With more furnishings, it might have been quite inviting. But with only a bed, a small table and lamp beside it, a single chair and much-scuffed armadio by way of a closet, the room seemed barren and cheerless.

Perhaps Donatello sensed my reaction to the lack of amenities. He said, "There is only one desk in the villa and I use it for the business, but I will have a table brought up for you to work on."

"That will be perfect, thank you," I assured him. "Your ancestral home is huge, Donatello. It must be a major burden to maintain it."

"Yes, I have only Sofia to help. She is the housekeeper and cook; some of the vineyard workers take care of the grounds. Tommaso—Signor Belgioso who spoke with you on the phone—is an old friend of my father and my vineyard manager. He lives in a little house near the winery. Sometimes he joins us for meals."

Donatello was apologetic. "We are few people in a very large house, and not . . . spiritoso. I hope you won't be bored."

"How could I be? Monte Beni seems to be the center of the most beautiful part of the world."

That comment managed to coax a smile from the count. "I always thought so."

"And where in this palazzo grande will I find you?" I asked.

"My room is in the tower. If you like, I will show you."

Now I recalled Donatello's telling Hannah he lived in a tower. But how different a tower! The room he claimed for himself was far less hospitable than the one he had allotted me. It would be no exaggeration to call it dismal, with only a small arched window in each wall. A stone stairway, without a railing, led to the roof.

Donatello lit a gas lamp (electricity had evidently not been extended to this section of the villa). "You can see my life is very simple," he explained. "When I was a boy, I loved to play here and pretend I was a knight defending my castle. I had many sword fights on the stairs." He took the classic *en garde* stance to demonstrate, and I grinned, seeing him again as the playful companion he had been in Rome.

"And I shot arrows from these windows, like Robin Hood in the old Errol Flynn movies," he continued. "I always won the fight and married the beautiful princess."

"Of course!" Poor Donatello was destined do battle for his lady; he had practiced overpowering the enemy . . .

At this instant a huge hairy animal unfolded itself from the twisted blankets on Donatello's bed, stretched and yawned mightily. Some sort of mastiff? A small horse?

"It's my old friend Romeo. I call him that because he is a great lover. I hope you like dogs, Kendall. I have several and they go all over the house."

I held out my hand; Romeo approached and sniffed. Evidently I passed muster because he did not eat my hand and allowed me to scratch behind his ears. I wondered if I would be sharing my bed with an equally massive canine companion.

Although the accommodations were more rustic than I had anticipated, and the atmosphere decidedly melancholy, I was calmer now that I was here and quite comfortable as I settled into my room. Something about the age and simplicity and quiet of the place soothed me and cleared my mind. I felt strongly the connection with the past that I treasure so greatly in Italy. These feelings would grow over the next days as Donatello, Tommaso and others told me about the Monte Beni history and legend. It began that first evening at dinner.

The dining room was by far the most hospitable place in the villa. A great trestle table, dark with age, was set in front of a stone fireplace. A fire was lit against the chill of the evening. The only other illumination was from candles in a multi-branched wrought iron candelabrum on the table. "I prefer the candles to electricity—I grew up with them," Donatello explained.

The candlelight revealed details of the frescoes on the walls and vaulted ceiling.

"What a coincidence!" I exclaimed. "There are fauns on your walls." The frescos pictured a paradise of trees and vines and flowers, birds and animals, nymphs and shepherds, not unlike the Cinecittà set I had visited when I first saw Donatello. "They're wonderful."

"Yes, I've always loved these frescoes," Donatello said. "Our family is a very old one, going back to the Etruscans. I'm not a student of the past, you understand, but there is a story that our first ancestor was a faun."

"And you never told me? It would have added a lot to my story," I couldn't resist pointing out.

"I know," admitted the count, "but it is such a private thing.

"You see the faun in the center," he went on, "with the very pointed ears, like the statue we saw. He is the first, the original. There, above you, is another, from much later. The painter, they told me, copied the face of my great-great-grandfather. His ears are long, but with no points. I did tell you, Kendall, about the family ears."

"Yes, I remember," I replied, although I had almost forgotten. I had become accustomed to Donatello's long locks hiding his ears. His hair now, I noted, was almost as shaggy as Romeo's, and he hadn't shaved for a day or two.

Sofia came in, a very small, bent woman with a big, toothy smile and a white apron wrapped around her skinny middle. Donatello introduced her as "one of the family" and me as "mio amico molto caro." Sofia brought us bowls of sausage-stuffed tortellini *in brodo* and passed a dish of pungent grated cheese to sprinkle on top. With this we ate sunflower bread, tearing chunks from a still warm-from-the-oven round.

"I'm glad you are here, my friend. Once there were many family and friends around this table and Monte Beni was a very happy place," Donatello sighed.

"It's a wonderful place," I said encouragingly, thinking that it could be. Then I blurted, unthinking, "All it needs is a woman's touch."

There was a slight pause. "*Davvero*," Donatello agreed, without further comment. He finished his soup, mopping the bowl with a crust of bread. "Before, we had feasts and parties here, and played games together, young, old, everyone. Now all the young people go to the city, to the cinema or the disco."

"In America, they go to the malls or the sports bars," I said, wondering why we were bemoaning the good old days like a couple of octogenarians. The absence of our women was to blame, no doubt.

"It's time for some sunlight," declared Donatello, and poured Monte Beni wine from a large carafe. He raised his glass: "Cin cin!"

"Happy days!" I responded.

Sofia brought in a chicken roasted with herbs for our main course. By the time she offered fresh figs with goat's cheese for dessert, we had imbibed sufficient sunlight to be mellow, if not actually cheerful.

"Kendall, tell me what I can do for you here, anything you want to see, anywhere you want to go."

I explained my ideas for a travel piece on small Tuscan wineries, and told him that I would appreciate some introductions to his counterparts at other vineyards.

"*Niente problema,*" he replied. "Although there are not so many of us any more."

"Of course, I will concentrate on Monte Beni. And I'll need to take some more photos of you, if I may." I didn't want to bring up the Tarzan business just yet.

"As you wish," he agreed. "Just don't show my ears."

"I won't even try," I laughed, "since even Lili wasn't permitted a peek at your ears."

This time Donatello did not recover so smoothly from my gaffe. He glared at me with anger or sorrow, I couldn't determine which. Although I was alarmed, I managed to keep my own expression benign, and gradually Donatello regained his composure.

"*Allora,* you have said her name," he all but groaned. "What can you tell me about her?"

"Nothing, really. I went to find her at the Galleria this morning and it was already closed for Ferragosto. She's probably in Switzerland." For the first time, I realized both women were missing and that they might be together. I was about to mention this possibility to Donatello when he suddenly rose from the table.

"If you will excuse me, I am very tired. I rise very early these days. You remember how to reach your room?"

I assured him I could find my way, and we said goodnight.

Once bedded down, I found the utter silence strangely unsettling: I had learned to lull myself to sleep with street noise in Rome. My former calm deserted me. I tried to read myself to sleep by the meager light of the little lamp with a Dick Francis mystery I'd borrowed from Hannah—Hannah!—but my thoughts kept wandering back to the sadly-changed Donatello, the likely demise of the stalker, and Hannah's unexplained absence.

The Monte Beni ancestors, nymphs and fauns and satyrs, all cavorted in my confused consciousness. My eyes closed and I drifted into a dream vision like Praxiteles'. In this scenario, Donatello was again the Faun, but he was fierce and threatening rather than playful. Lili was a nymph with flowing onyx hair, but instead of gracefully eluding the faun, she clung to him, entwining her body with his in a vulgar parody of the tango they had danced at the beach.

Hannah appeared, at first her shining self, smiling and reaching out to me. But when I approached she became frightened and started to run. I pursued her all around the fresco but Donatello and Lili kept coming between us. I awoke with a start as my book thudded to the floor.

I vowed to limit my intake of liquid sunlight in the future, turned out the light, rolled over and finally slept.

CHAPTER TWENTY-FIVE

Nathan Kendall's Narrative

They were strong, active, genial, cheerful as the sunshine, passionate as the tornado. Their lives were rendered blissful by an unsought harmony with nature.

Nathaniel Hawthorne, "The Marble Faun"

Despite a troubled night, I awoke refreshed, although the morning was already hot. I put on shorts, loafers and a polo shirt, my usual work-at-home garb, and went downstairs to find Donatello and a cup of coffee.

Donatello had already left for the winery, Sofia told me. She bustled me into a big old-fashioned kitchen, redolent of fresh-cut herbs and coffee, and provided me with café latte, bread and cheese and apricot jam. She explained in Italian that Tommaso would be along soon to show me around the estate.

Tommaso appeared to be a hardy seventy-or-so, grey-haired, sunburned, energetic. He started our tour at the back of the villa, where extensive landscaping had been done in times long past. A circular pool and three-tiered fountain were dry and stained; wild vines vied with spice-scented roses on the arched trellises. Shrubs were overgrown; trees were in desperate need of pruning. Tommaso explained that maintaining the gardens had become a great expense: "*Molto costoso, troppo.*"

From the gardens we could view the entire estate which, he informed me with pride, included three large hills in addition to the one on which we stood: two planted with grapes and olive trees; one remaining thickly forested.

We walked about a quarter-mile down the road I had come up the day before and took a sharp turn to arrive at the winery; a great rectangular box of a building dating from the 14th century, Tommaso informed me.

Within was a secret passageway to the villa, originally an escape route during the wars between the Guelphs and Ghibellines and a favorite place for youngsters in recent generations to play hide-and-seek. Tommaso led me on through the cellars where last year's wine was aging in massive barrels of Syrian oak: "Fifteen months, Signore, and then it is ready for bottling, although we drink some sooner," he explained.

"Here we grow only the old grapes, Trebbiano. The larger vineyards have imported vines—Chardonnay, Pinot Noir, Pinot Grigio. These grapes grow faster, lower to the ground than the old native varieties . . . it is the modern way. Even the count is experimenting with blending juice from other grapes."

I could see that Tommaso had mixed emotions. "You disapprove?"

He shrugged. "I am getting old, *Signore*. Nowadays, the count says—and he knows, he talks to the hotels, restaurants, wholesalers—now people want their wine to taste the same every year, and the big companies adjust the taste by mixing juice from different grapes, adding sugar. Bah!" Adding sugar, evidently was the ultimate degradation. Tommaso continued, "Our Monte Beni wine is a little different each year, depending on the sun, the rain, the temperature. Lovers of fine wine anticipate that difference and appreciate it. That's why Monte Beni wine is so special."

And not very well known, widely distributed or profitable, I might have added, but I said "I suppose Donatello feels he must change with the times."

"He does—but one must also preserve the best of the past," Tommaso replied.

As we toured, I could see that Monte Beni was employing current technology in some aspects of operation and timeworn methods and equipment in others. Just as Paolo Cavaluzzi had implied, unless the winery could invest in modernization and expansion, it probably would not survive.

We found Donatello in a small anteroom outfitted as an office where he was busy on the telephone. He looked up to acknowledge us and continued his conversation; we backed out to give him privacy. Tommaso took me to his own little cubbyhole, produced a pair of glasses and poured a taste of his riserva speciale. Lovely, but it would never replace my mid-morning espresso.

I used Tommaso's phone for the first of many futile calls to Hannah's cell. If she were to try to reach me, she would get no answer at my Rome apartment or on the cell. Perhaps coming to Monte Beni had been a mistake, but here I was, and I would have to make the best of it.

I thanked Tommaso for the tour, and he assured me it had been his pleasure. Then he said, in a hushed voice, "Perhaps it is not my place to suggest, Signor Kendall, but I hope you will urge the count to enjoy himself a little, go to the village or to Florence. He used to be the liveliest of all the young people, but since he has returned from Rome, he is changed. He is all business, very serious, too quiet."

Tommaso leaned forward and put a hand on my forearm. "Signor Kendall, you are his friend. Tell me, did something bad happen in Rome?"

So Tommaso had seen the change. He was an old family friend; he was concerned. What could I say? "Well, there was a woman . . ."

Tommaso grinned, evidently relieved. "A woman! But never have I seen the count so troubled because of a woman."

"An older woman, very fascinating, perhaps . . . dangerous."

"Aha! Well, when she is finished with him perhaps he will be ready to settle down with a nice local girl and do his duty." He winked.

Tommaso told me that Donatello was not only the last of the Monte Beni dynasty but, according to legend, a so-called Golden One. Once or twice in a century, he said, the family produced a male child who closely resembled the progenitor—il Fauno. In their youth, these special sons were exceptionally beautiful, strong, brave and kind. They were endowed with an affinity for all living creatures and aspects of nature. Sadly, these gifts and graces often faded with maturity and were not replaced by other, more sober attributes of character and intellect. I recalled the portraits of the former counts, most of whom looked substantial enough but scarcely noble.

"The family, of course, is not fond of this legend, and the count will not permit himself to be referred to as The Golden One," Tommaso added. I promised not to repeat his words to Donatello, and also agreed to lure the count away from the estate for some recreation.

An opportunity presented itself at dinner when Sofia reminded him about the upcoming annual wine festival in the nearby town of San Barnaba.

Donatello began to explain to Sofia that he didn't have time for such foolishness any more. I quickly interjected that I would like to go and take some photographs for my story. He reluctantly agreed to take an afternoon off and accompany me. In the meantime, he said, I should learn to ride one of the various scooters or motor bikes he kept at the winery.

"You are in the campagna now, Kendall. Motorini are best on these roads. And it must be expensive to rent the car."

I agreed to drop off the Fiat in Siena, the closest rental office, and Donatello had one of his workers follow in a beat-up truck to drive me back to Monte Beni. I regretted not having arranged to spend the day in Siena; I had always found it soothing to the soul just to wander through the medieval city's myriad narrow streets and twisting passageways. I'd been planning to take Hannah there to see the Palio with me. Would she return from wherever she was in time for that? I was angry with myself for missing her so much and angry with her for not being with me.

That evening, Donatello gave me a moped lesson. I was apprehensive, and rightly so. I proved my lack of aptitude early on by skidding off the road and into the woods. Donatello was all patience and concern, but before the instruction was over I had been able to give him a good laugh or two.

In succeeding days, I learned to appreciate this mode of transportation. I was able to negotiate the winding back roads efficiently (and with an awe-inspiring wake of red dust) while visiting neighboring vintners.

Those I interviewed, like Donatello, were struggling. Some had decided to produce only specialty wines, such as the potent Vin Santo; others were resigned to eventually selling their grapes to the big producers and making wine only for their own family use.

When I asked Donatello about his plans for Monte Beni, he confessed to frustration. "The winery is in trouble . . . you can see how much we need to do. The bank will not lend me more money. But how can I give it up? It is all I know, and so many people depend on me."

I had seen how the employees at the winery deferred to Donatello, which could be expected—he was the *padrone*. But it was more than that: they sincerely respected him and trusted his judgment. Their faces would light up when he stopped to exchange a few words, or give a pat on the shoulder. Indeed, for them, he was The Golden One.

Frankly, I was surprised at both his competence and his diligence. In Rome, as a minor movie actor, he had seemed somewhat of a lightweight, if a likeable one. Here, he had a real life role which he took seriously.

"But surely the film contract would bring in enough money to keep you going," I said.

"For next year, perhaps. But things have changed, Kendall. Nothing is certain anymore," the count replied cryptically, and changed the subject.

We went to San Barnaba via Vespa. In contrast to San Gimignano with its many towers, this town is completely encircled by a high wall which conceals the roofs of buildings within. We parked outside the wall, and walked through an arched gate into an earlier time. I had visited several similar Tuscan hill towns, but familiarity does not diminish their enchantment.

The festival would follow a traditional format, Donatello told me: There would be a parade, participants in medieval costume marching along beside the school band with baton twirlers and acrobats and anyone else who wanted to join in. There would be flags and floats, balloons and banners and bicycles. The parade would terminate at the piazza centrale, where various pompous dignitaries would hold forth until the long-awaited moment when the town fountain would be turned on and—miracles of miracles!—flow with new wine in place of water. There would be a mad rush as the crowd converged on the fountain with mugs, cups, glasses and bottles. Then the real fun would begin.

Events proceeded accordingly, and I forgot myself in a flurry of photography, finding unusual angles and capturing unexpected action. I snapped a tiny girl with red ribbons in her hair riding on a flower-bedecked donkey; an unapologetic hound relieving himself on the trouser leg of a uniformed dignitary

Donatello, following my erratic path, was frequently hailed by the townspeople. He always responded genially, with hugs and jests. They chided him for staying so long in Rome—*"Perchè sei stato tanti mesi là?"*—as though Rome were some sort of purgatory. He simply shrugged, too modest to mention his stint in the movies.

"Ai forse trovato una bella Romana, Conte?" one bright-eyed teenager teased as she wrapped her arms around his neck: Have you found a beautiful Roman girl?

Donatello paled, but quickly recovered himself. *"Perchè cercare a Roma le belle donne? Francesca sta qui!"* (Why look in Rome? Francesca is here.) He kissed her cheek and she squealed with delight.

A fine effort on his part, I acknowledged, considering his current despondency. And if Donatello could draw this sort of response as a minor local celebrity, imagine what admiration he would engender as an international film star! Would it ever happen?

Donatello had brought mugs for us to fill at the fountain, and I took a break from the camera to sample the wine. It was, surprisingly, cold and quite pleasant.

All around the piazza and streets leading from it, the balconies and window sills were exhuberantly festooned with flowers and streamers and bunches of grapes.

"Watch now," Donatello said.

The people at the windows began to dismantle their decorations, lowering the grape bunches on strings to the revelers below.

"Try to get some grapes," Donatello urged me, and I willingly joined the fun. When I reached for a particularly tempting bunch, the laughing woman on the other end of the string yanked it up and out of my reach.

Now I understood the game, and I'm tall, and I used to play basketball . . . The next time she lowered the grapes, I leaped up and snagged them, earning a roar of approval from Donatello and some onlookers.

Then Donatello joined in, albeit with less than his usual whole-hearted abandon. He raised his empty mug and shook it. A giggling youngster leaned over a balcony rail and, with admirable aim, tossed a bunch of grapes into it. Soon the air was full of flying fruit; both Donatello and I got thoroughly pelted. Of course, those of us in the street threw grapes back at the folks in the windows and on the balconies. It was a fabulous food fight and continued until all the grapes had been squashed.

Now we were sticky as well as hot, and we sat down in the shade at one of the rude wooden tables in front of an osteria.

A group of raucous young people, former schoolmates of Donatello, joined us. They drank a lot of wine and joked and insulted each other with good humor. The friends wanted to get together with Donatello later and he agreed, but pointedly didn't set a definite time. When they left us, he became quiet and preoccupied again. I could see that, with all his recent troubles, he had outgrown his childhood friends and their light-hearted horseplay, and that it saddened him.

Of course, we all face this sobering process as we mature. I thought of my father, who had not managed the transition successfully. He doubtless had fancied himself in love forever with the fair-haired Americanina, never suspecting that she might one day request him to change a diaper or run the vacuum cleaner. He had never imagined that his life on the gold-paved streets of the Stati Uniti would require him to take two jobs just to pay the rent. He had started out like one of legendary Golden Ones in Tommaso's tale—charming, happy and brave as my mother described him—but had lacked the inner resources to carry his "gifts and graces" into later life. I hoped Donatello would find the fortitude to deal with his disillusionments more creditably and emerge with his essential character intact

CHAPTER TWENTY-SIX

Nathan Kendall's Narrative

In Donatello's case, it was pitiful, and almost ludicrous, to observe the confused struggle that he made, how completely he was taken by surprise; how ill-prepared he stood, on this old battlefield of the world, to fight with such an inevitable foe as mortal calamity, and sin for its stronger ally.

Nathaniel Hawthorne, "The Marble Faun"

Mindful of Tommaso's request, and with concerns of my own, I lured Donatello away from his work long enough to hike the Monte Beni hill that remained uncultivated. He began the trek happily enough, but soon grew pensive.

"I used to spend so much time in these woods, I knew every tree and bush. It all looks different now, *più selvaggio,* wilder."

He led me to what he recalled as his favorite childhood hideaway on the hillside. We had to fight through thick clusters of shrubbery and brambles to find it, a secluded hollow where there was a crumbling, time-worn statue of a nymph holding an urn from which water must once have flowed. A trace of ground water still trickled through the cracked basin at the foot of the statue.

This evidence of someone's yearning, centuries ago, to create a thing of beauty here aroused a sweet sort of sadness.

"I can see why you love this place," I mused. Green light filtered through the foliage overhead and dappled the aged nymph, the ferns around the basin, our faces. "It's magical. It inspires me to try some poetry." I hadn't written any since high school.

"Yes, there is magic, a story, if you want to believe it," Donatello said. "My oldest ancestor, the faun, loved a human girl and brought her to live in this place. The fountain is where they had their well."

"Of course, the faun must have had a human mate." I was pleased that returning to his childhood sanctuary had put Donatello in a communicative mood. "It's a lovely legend."

"There's more. The man who made the statue, many hundreds of years ago, said that one who knew how to call the nymph could bring her to life."

"And did you ever try to summon the nymph from the fountain?"

"Oh yes, when I was very young. Of course, she did not come," he said, with a self-deprecatory smile. "But sometimes when I called, birds answered me. And I could make noises so that little animals would come, too."

I was amazed at this disclosure and wanted to pursue the subject with him. "I've heard that some people have that gift. Try it now. See if you can summon up a chipmunk or something."

"It's been a long time. I don't know . . ." Donatello sat beside the fountain and began to make a chucking sound deep in his throat. Then he brought the sound forward, clicking his tongue, and finally produced a sort of whistle, rhythmic and repetitive. The sounds were soothing, beguiling, a murmuring which gradually grew and seemed to arouse a rustling in the foliage and a stirring in the underbrush.

Perhaps my imagination got the better of me in that sylvan setting: I was ready to believe that Donatello was, indeed, a faun.

But no creatures appeared.

Donatello stopped his calling with a heavy sigh, almost a groan. "Impossibile!" Everything has changed with me. Even the animals know it, what I have done."

Much as I was moved by his distress, I had to grasp the opportunity. "What have you done?"

There, at last, was the question I had come here to ask, but Donatello gave me no answer other than to hide his head in his arms.

I should have persisted, but instead I tried to reassure him. "It's probably just because I'm here that your animal friends won't come out."

"They are not my friends now," he said softly, not raising his head, like a schoolboy shunned at the playground. But this was a grown man.

"Well, unfortunately, when we grow older, we sometimes lose our closeness with nature," I offered in banal explanation.

"I prefer to be what I was before."

Platitudes poured into mind, but I rejected them in the face of Donatello's misery. Eventually he rose to his feet and busied himself with pulling some burrs off his pants. "All this talk about nymphs and fountains and calling animals seems foolish now. What you say is true, Kendall—with more experience of life, we change, not always for the good." He straightened; squared his shoulders. "If you are ready?"

I followed him down the hill without further attempts at conversation.

I had successfully interviewed dozens of celebrities and world leaders, and wrested information from hundreds of sources, but now, when it was so crucial to me personally, I seemed to have lost the skill.

We had been making it a habit to take our after-dinner coffee on the battlements and watch the sun set. That night the sky was almost cloudless, a vast ink-blue bowl with just a narrow band of vermilion defining the horizon. Fireflies flashed in the garden below and we could see the faint glow of San Gimignano's towers in the distance.

"It's so clear tonight, I can almost imagine I see Rome to the south," I ventured as an opening, then immediately felt a tightening in my stomach—Hannah. Was she somewhere in Rome?

Donatello didn't respond.

"Are you looking forward to going back to Rome?" I asked him.

"No. I hate Rome now!" he replied.

"But we had good times together there, didn't we? And the Tarzan film should be fun to do."

Dontello gave a bitter laugh. "I am no longer a man who can talk to rabbits; how can I pretend to talk to a chimpanzee or an elephant? No, Kendall, I don't think I will ever be Tarzan."

I couldn't offer a glib response. Our uneasy silence was broken only by bells announcing Compline at the monastery in the neighboring valley.

Donatello said ruefully, "The bells are calling to me. Perhaps I will become a monk instead of a movie actor, and trade my tower for a cell. It would be . . . *appropriato.*"

"What? That's a drastic prospect." I had never heard my friend say anything so despondent before. It must be guilt that was preying on him—I had to know, to come out of the infernal labyrinth of half-truths and evasions into which Lili had led us all. With a sudden inspiration, I declared, "I'd rather throw myself off this tower than be shut up in a monastery for the rest of my life."

"No!" Donatello looked at me with an expression of horror. "What a terrible death!"

"Don't worry," I hastily reassured him. "I'm not planning to leap from your battlements. But they say that if you jump from a great height, you die in the air and never know when you hit the ground."

"*Non e vero!* Not true! Imagine someone alive one moment, looking at you, and then he's falling down, down, screaming, and there is no way you can bring him back. He screams until he strikes the earth and lies there broken, *tutto contorto . . .*"

"Enough, you've convinced me!" I interrupted, stunned at this graphic confirmation of my suspicions. It was only too obvious that Donatello was describing the death of the stalker.

"Donatello, I know something terrible happened in Rome, with you and Lili and the bearded man. Tell me about it. Perhaps I can help."

He shook his head. "My friend, how I can I burden you with such knowledge? I have done a very bad thing and I cannot escape it. That is all."

His face, in the light of the rising moon, was colorless, chiaroscuro, like that of Praxiteles' marble statue. But, etched with remorse, his features were less those of a faun and more a mortal man's.

CHAPTER TWENTY-SEVEN

Journal of Dr. Hannah Ingram

"I must keep your secret, and die of it . . ."

Nathaniel Hawthorne, "The Marble Faun"

Siena, August 13

Away from Rome, thank God.

I'm at the Sanctuary of St. Catherine, in a claustrophobic little room, but I feel safe here. I was very lucky to find a room at all this time of year.

As compensation for the cramped quarters, I have a small balcony with a view of the cathedral. I can make out a long, steep street that climbs along the wall to the old section of the city. I'll walk there tomorrow.

Now I need to get things under control—myself, mainly.

Last night, after I got back to my room and locked the door, I just collapsed. I felt dizzy and nauseous and I couldn't seem to stop shaking. I wrapped myself in a blanket and rocked and moaned and replayed the scene in my mind, hoping that somehow it might end differently.

It might help to write about it.

At La Pergola, when Kendall left to get a taxi, I went out to the roof to find Lili and Donatello. The fog had thickened so that I couldn't even see the stars or the city lights. It was damp and bone-chilling, the atmosphere so heavy that it was hard to breath. I remember thinking that Donatello and Lili must really be wrapped up in themselves to stay out there so long on such a miserable night.

It took me a few moments to make them out. I spotted Lili first because of her light shawl. She was standing by the railing on the far corner of the terrace, looking down toward the city—although there was nothing to see. She seemed to be waiting for something.

Donatello, just a blur, was at the other corner, head bowed and shoulders hunched as though they had been quarreling and he had walked away from her or—more likely—been sent away.

What's gone wrong now?, I wondered. It was like a scene from an old horror movie—everything in murky shades of black and gray, no dialogue.

I was about to call out to them when I sensed another presence.

Dimly, in the gloom, I discerned a third figure, dashing across the terrace toward Lili.

"*Finito*, Lili. *Vengo!*"

A sickening wave of terror engulfed me. I tried to call out, to warn her, but no sound came. I had no doubt at all who it was that lunged at Lili, seized her and twisted her down to the pavement of the terrace. Run, help her!, my inner voice commanded but, again, it was like a *film noir* and I was relegated to the audience.

The man raised an arm to strike her, and in that moment Donatello was on him, grasping him from behind, almost lifting him off his feet.

The stalker cursed and writhed; Donatello struggled to restrain him and called something to Lili in Italian.

She lifted her head to answer him, but I couldn't hear her response. Whatever she said, Donatello instantly hefted the man over the railing and into the blackness. The man was clutching Lili's shawl and it trailed after him like an unopened parachute. The fog swallowed his scream.

Still I couldn't speak; I couldn't move.

Donatello and Lili, too, were silent and motionless.

Then, uttering no more than a gasp, I turned and ran.

Kendall was waiting with a taxi. I wanted to rush to his arms for consolation and reassurance. But what was I to say—I've just seen a murder, our friends are killers? Once I'd said that, I knew, Kendall would go to the police. He has his journalist's objectivity, and no matter how much he cares for me and the others, he would do the right thing. The repercussions for the three of us would be disastrous—and for Kendall, too, if I put him in the position having to choose between his integrity and his friends. Was I wrong to spare him this?

And I wasn't completely convinced that what I had seen on the roof was real—God knows, I didn't want it to be real. It was dark, foggy, I had drunk a lot of champagne. Could it all have been a hallucination?

I know I heard the stalker threaten Lili. Or did he? His voice was threatening but the words—"It's finished, I'm coming"—could have meant almost anything.

Clearly, he attacked her. Did he have a gun, or a knife? If he had, Donatello saved Lili's life; he's a hero. But he didn't just save Lili—he destroyed the man. Tossed him off the roof like so much garbage.

The kind, charming, lovable Faun. I still can't comprehend it. And Lili, my beautiful friend, whom I trusted, even defended when Kendall doubted her? Maybe she told him to do it, maybe not. Either way, he did it because of her, because of something that was between her and the wretched stalker.

Just as I had settled down enough to make myself a cup of tea, the phone rang and startled me. It was Kendall: "Hannah, are you there? Please, talk to me. I'm worried about you." How I wanted to beg him to come to me, to tell him everything I was feeling. But I let the machine take the message. And I switched off my cell.

It may have been the wrong decision. My judgement hasn't been very reliable lately.

I believed in these people. Yes, I was aware that Lili had a past and that she might still be involved in some shady activity. I realized that the stalker might try to hurt Lili, and that Donatello was determined to protect her. But I didn't expect to see my friends do murder. I felt as battered and betrayed as if they had thrown me off the roof. I actually started to cry, as much from anger and disappointment as from shock.

Then I heard footsteps on the stairs—a woman's heels. There was a tentative knock at my door.

"Hannah, are you there? It's Lili." Her voice was soft, intimate, cajoling.

I stiffened. How had she gotten into the building? I had locked the heavy outside door when I said goodnight to Kendall. Was picking locks another of Lili's esoteric talents?

And why had she come here? Perhaps, after all, she had an explanation . . .

Hope—and curiosity—conquered my fear. I took a deep breath, went to the door and let her in.

"Hannah, you look dreadful. I'm so sorry." Lili, all concern, reached out to me, and I backed away. She looked dreadful herself, haggard and disheveled, her mascara smudged, the diamonds dangling at her ears a macabre touch. "You saw what happened, didn't you? No wonder you ran away."

Even after what I'd seen, I was stung by her implication. She thought me a coward; I probably was. "What are you doing here?"

"I came because I wanted to make sure you're all right."

"All right? How can I be all right? Or you either? It was all your fault, wasn't it?" My accusation sounded hysterical, even to myself.

"I will have to live with it as best I can. There are reasons. I'm just sorry that you had to see it."

"And poor Donatello," I continued my diatribe. "You made him do it for you, didn't you?"

"Did I?" Lili looked even more distraught. "I blame myself that I ever let Donatello into my life . . ." She shook her head, as if in disbelief or remorse, before going on. "Hannah, I'm leaving Rome. I wanted to say goodbye and tell you, in the event we don't meet again, that your friendship has been very precious to me."

The irony of that remark! "I'm your friend? You've merely used me . . ."

Lili gestured helplessly. "I've been trying to protect you . . ."

"Protect yourself, I think." I was angry and indignant now. "And of course you must get away now. Switzerland . . . South America . . . wherever."

"Yes, I'm going."

"And I suppose you would prefer that I—your very good friend—not tell anyone what I saw?" She had earned the sarcasm.

"Then you didn't tell Kendall?" she asked.

I caught my breath. Unthinking, I had revealed to Lili not only that I was a witness to the killing but also that I had told no one about it. Was her purpose in coming here to make certain I never told?

I stared at Lili, no longer seeing her as glamorous and intriguing, but as a desperate, dangerous woman with few scruples.

"I didn't actually tell him, but he certainly knows something's wrong . . ." I stammered. What a naive fool I had been!

Lili looked at me appraisingly. Was she considering how best to dispose of me? I mentally searched for a weapon, some means of defending myself. But she took me by surprise.

"Tell him. Or someone else you can trust. You must not try to bear this alone, Hannah—it will consume you. Perhaps, one day, you'll understand and want to see me again. I hope so."

And she was gone.

I sat up through the early morning hours, playing Bach on the Yahama to sooth my nerves—unsuccessfully. I was jumping out of my skin, the fight or flight reaction. Flight was the obvious course—I was in over my head in Rome. A too-fast love affair, an unfinished opera score, delightful new friends who turned out to be not at all what they had seemed. If I had felt out of control before, now I was panicked.

For one fleeting moment I considered going home to Buffalo—how blissfully cool a Buffalo summer would seem, and how welcome the strong, protective figure of my father. But ultimately, he would expect me to handle my own problems. And how could I go back without completing my work?

Then I remembered Margaret mentioning a place she and Kim had stayed in Siena—not a hotel but a guest house run by a religious order. St. Catherine's. I waited impatiently until it was a decent hour to call; they had a room. My sanctuary.

I've been unkind to Kendall. I'm sure he's worried and probably furious as well by now. I should at least have left him a message, made up some excuse. But I can never lie to him. And I need to be on my own now for awhile. I need time to sort things out.

CHAPTER TWENTY-EIGHT

Notes from Lili Castelli

Was it horror?—or ecstasy? Or both in one?

Nathaniel Hawthorne, "The Marble Faun"

"Lascialo andare." Let him go.

That is what I intended to tell Donatello on the roof when he asked what he should do with Khol, and then he dropped him over the edge.

Did he misunderstand me, hearing *"Lascialo cadere,"* let him fall? Perhaps that is what I said, or wanted to say. Or perhaps Donatello saved me from making the fatal decision as he had saved me from Khol.

Khol had attacked me believing that he could end my life, clean his knife with my shawl, replace it under his coat and be gone before anyone knew what had happened. But that would not have been possible for him after a violent struggle with Donatello, even if he had prevailed. Khol must have believed, as I did, that Donatello had left me alone on the roof. Even in a homicidal rage, Khol was a physical coward, but Donatello could not know that about him.

He watched Khol fall to his death as I struggled to my feet. We were both stunned. We clung to each other, unable to comprehend what we had done, much less deal with the consequences. When at last we started back toward the restaurant, I saw Hannah rushing away and realized that she must have witnessed the scene. Whatever initial release or sense of satisfaction I'd felt at the death of my long-time enemy evaporated.

We were relieved to find that you, Kendall, as well as Hannah, had left. Donatello quickly paid the bill and we fled.

When we reached my apartment, where I had expected to play the paramour, I shamefully disclosed the whole story to Donatello: my past history with Khol, the reason for his hatred, the motive for his revenge.

Donatello, already traumatized by what he had done, was aghast.

"You should have told me everything in the beginning, Lili. If I had known before . . . He covered his face with his hands. "Now see what I have done. It is a sin. I am ruined." He began to sob, his shoulders heaving.

It was anguish, seeing him like that. I tried to take him in my arms, but he held me away.

"For you I did this terrible thing," he said. "And I will never be the man I was before."

He went to the door and I started to follow. "Please, *amore*, stay with me. Let me help . . ."

"No, Lili. It is not your fault, and there is nothing you can do, you understand?" He lowered his eyes, unwilling now to even look at me. "I must answer for what I did. And I won't see you again." He closed the door.

I might have gone after him, caught him before he got on the elevator, pleaded with him. But I knew it was useless. I poured myself a brandy, collected my thoughts, and called Tozzi.

He was angry. "You've given me a fine mess to clean up, Lili. Didn't I tell you to lay off the count?"

"Khol might have attacked me anyway," I pointed out. "And I told you from the beginning he was dangerous. You waited too long to take him seriously."

"And so you decided to take matters into your own hands, eh? Using yourself as bait, you set up the young fool to get rid of Khol for you."

I could barely reply. "That's an outrageous accusation, Tozzi! If you don't know me better than that, if you don't trust me, let me go."

"Well, it's water over the dam now or, rather, body over the roof," Tozzi said, backing off. "Think, Lili. Could anyone have seen what happened?"

I thought of Hannah. "No, no one."

"Thank the Lord for that. I'm going to contact the Rome police right away and get their cooperation in handling the investigation. Let's hope the media doesn't get on to it for awhile."

Then I thought of you, Kendall. When Hannah told you what she saw, would you feel you had to disclose the information? I believed you would not want to hurt us that way,

"You'll go to Switzerland today as planned," Tozzi said. "This needn't affect us—Khol's part in the scenario was over, anyway. Dolata won't care what happened to him. Just one less person on the payroll.

"And, Lili, Khol's no longer a threat to you," Tozzi concluded, sounding almost avuncular. "You must be relieved."

Relief was not what I was feeling. After I went to see Hannah, I returned to the apartment, showered, set the alarm so I could catch the early flight to Geneva. Then I went to bed. I covered my head with the herb-scented sheets and tried to imagine myself with Donatello again, blissfully floating far from shore on the Tyrrhenian Sea, sinking into deep blue oblivion.

CHAPTER TWENTY-NINE

Nathan Kendall's Narrative

". . . I seek to remedy the evil you have incurred for my sake."

Nathaniel Hawthorne, "The Marble Faun"

I was ready to leave Monte Beni.

I didn't like deserting Donatello in his morbid frame of mind, but he was unlikely to tell me more than I had already guessed. There was nothing I could do to help him, in any case. And I simply had to find Hannah.

After breakfast the next morning, Donatello left to run an errand in Siena and I went to my room to begin packing. I heaved Otello off the bed (the big black Lab had adopted me, and I had come to appreciate his patient, lumbering presence in my room). By now, I had made the sparsely furnished room my own and I wondered if I would ever return to it.

"Signore Kendall, come down, please! There is a lady here to speak with you," Sofia shouted from below. "Una bella donna!"

My heart leaped and I bolted down the stairs, expecting that by some miracle Hannah had come. But the woman who awaited me was Lili. She was beautiful, as Sophia had observed, but not the beauty I had hoped to see.

Lili stood in the parlor, studying the portraits of the early Monte Beni counts. Dressed in yellow, she seemed to have brought the morning sunlight into the villa with her, illuminating the joyless space with her presence.

"Lili! It's wonderful to see you," I said, hoping the greeting masked my disappointment. Then I added, all innocence, "How was Switzerland?"

Lili didn't deign to answer. There was an uncharacteristic urgency in her voice when she came forward and grasped my hand.

"I'm so glad to find you here, Kendall."

"You've come to visit Donatello, I assume?"

She shook her head. "Ah, no. I parked out of sight and waited until I saw him leave before I . . . The situation is very strange now, Kendall. I'm prepared to stay with Donatello under any conditions he might wish. I owe him my complete devotion, but I think he will reject it."

She had succeeded in surprising me. "Why would you think that?"

"When we parted in Rome, he almost ran from me. It's as if by abandoning me he can atone . . ."

"For God's sake, atone for what, Lili?" Again the question, and again, I was not to have the answer.

"You know he is an innocent soul, Kendall. He takes too much blame upon himself."

"He does, indeed. Last night he said that he might join a monastery." I had thought this unlikely prospect might ease the tension, but Lili turned pale.

"No, no. He mustn't feel like that. Lost, hopeless."

Lili looked so desolate that I took hold of her shoulders and gave her a little shake. I wanted to comfort her; I also wanted to shake her really hard.

"Look, Lili. Something terrible happened in Rome and no one wants to tell me about it. But I read the papers. I know your stalker took a dive from the Cavalieri Hilton roof the night we were there. I want the whole story—now!"

She gazed at me thoughtfully. "Then Hannah hasn't confided in you?"

"She's told me nothing. In fact, she's left Rome and I don't even know where she is. Tell me, is she in any danger because of what happened?"

"Surely not, but she saw what happened and she's understandably distraught." Lili began to pace; I waited, determined that she must speak.

"All right, Kendall, I will trust your discretion and your good heart."

We sat down on one of the threadbare brocade sofas, with only the ancestors' portraits to overhear the conversation.

Lili's first disclosure was that she had for some months been engaged by an arm of the Carabinieri, the Italian national police. Her gallery and related business dealings, financed largely by the police agency, gave her entree to the wealthy and influential of many countries, and to some of the less desirable elements—those involved in the theft of art and antiquities and spiriting them out of Italy. The rumors about her origins and activities, she said, had been circulated intentionally as part of her cover.

"You can understand now, Kendall, why I use an assumed name."

Most recently, she had been involved in a sting operation to trap the organization behind a series of thefts from sites at Cerveteri, Crustumerium and I Fucoli.

"Ironically, the man sent by the Mafia to contact me was someone I had known in the past," Lili continued, "the man you call the stalker. I didn't want to deal with him, but I couldn't refuse without endangering the operation. I had to convince him to trust me, no matter how terrified I was."

"Why did he terrify you?" I interrupted her narrative.

"This man hated me for something that happened a long time ago . . ." She stopped short, and gave me a rueful smile. "Forgive me, Kendall. I am so accustomed to prevaricating . . . the truth is, he was my lover. A long time ago, the first."

I was astonished. "Unbelievable!"

"You think it an unlikely match. But when we were at the Sorbonne together, he was a very charismatic figure—brilliant, witty, wildly romantic, a hero among the left-wing intellectuals. Who could tell that he was also mad? And I was going through a rebellious phase . . .

"Eventually we got involved with the Red Brigades."

This was the "naughtiness" to which Paolo had referred? The Red Brigades were terrorists, ruthless killers.

"Khol and I weren't together long until I realized he was cruel, violent. He enjoyed hurting people, and needed only the slightest provocation to do so," Lili continued. "He asked me to go to Italy with him on a secret mission. I begged off on some pretext or other—thank God. Later I learned that he had been instrumental in a high-profile political kidnaping and murder. You surely remember it, Kendall." I did indeed.

"I broke with him then, even gave information to Interpol and to the Carabinieri," Lili continued. "This led to the arrest of some of his comrades. One, his younger brother, was imprisoned for life. Khol managed to escape; he virtually disappeared. But occasionally he would get a message to me, wherever I happened to be, vowing to take his revenge.

"That he should become my contact—it was diabolical!"

Then Lili told me what happened on the roof of the Cavalieri Hilton.

"Khol had been following us all evening, I'm sure, but I only became aware of him at the restaurant—a reflection in a mirror. I had thought I was safe from Khol until the operation was completed, but his rage overcame his reason—perhaps because I was with Donatello." Lili's voice quavered. "Khol had seen me with Donatello before, and threatened to hurt him, too.

"He intended to kill me that night. Donatello stopped him the only way he could. My first reaction was relief at having escaped. It wasn't until later, with the realization of what we had done . . .

"I told Donatello what I've told you, that Khol had been my lover. Donatello didn't blame me for what happened, but he didn't want to touch me or even to look at me. He said he had sinned, and he would never be the same."

Lili's voice became husky; she paused to clear her throat. "Then he left me." She paused a moment, reliving the pain of that rejection, before she was able to go on.

"I realized Hannah had seen us and I went to her that night, to make sure she was all right. She was so horrified, Kendall, and repelled by me—even afraid of me. I hoped she would confide in you."

"If only she had!"

Lili continued. "Well, I pulled myself together and went to Switzerland as planned. I had to salvage the operation . . ." she shrugged.

"Of course," I nodded, understanding if not condoning Lili's pragmatism. "And now what?"

"Now, all I can think about is Donatello. I must help him, if he'll let me."

She could help by keeping him out of prison, I thought, considering her quasi-official status. "I assume your Carabinieri connections will see that the investigation does not become embarrassing and that there will be no legal punishment forthcoming?"

"You may assume that, but I must anticipate repercussions of some sort. There will be inquiries, accommodations . . ."

"Good Lord!" We sat quietly for a moment.

"How do you plan to approach Donatello?" I asked.

"I don't know." Lili was close to tears. "There's a risk . . . If he should turn away from me now, we will both be lost."

How their roles had reversed, with Lili now seeking Donatello's acceptance. In spite of the blame which surely lay at her feet, I was moved by her contrition.

"Lili, I have to believe Donatello still cares for you, perhaps more than ever after what you've been through together."

"Then I have hope. Kendall, can you help me find a way to reach him?"

"I'll try. I haven't much success with him." I thought of how drastically the happy Faun had changed, how deeply he mourned his loss of faith with the natural world. Did Lili imagine she could mend him as though he were one of the precious works of art in her gallery? Still, it was possible that Donatello could emerge a stronger person as a result of his experience (I tried to avoid thinking of it as a crime). I hoped with all my heart that he would, and perhaps Lili could be the catalyst.

"Donatello has been brooding here at Monte Beni too long," I said. "I'll suggest we go to Florence tomorrow. And we can find you there as if by chance."

She brightened. "That might be the way. Then, if he turns his back, at least I will not have come begging." She saw my puzzlement. "It's not just my pride, Kendall. If I'm to be of use to Donatello, he must want me, not merely permit me to be with him."

We arrranged our rendezvous for the loggia in Piazza della Signoria at four o'clock. There are cafés surrounding the piazza where one can settle with a drink and newspaper, or stroll to admire the sculpture, without appearing to watch or wait.

"Thank you, Kendall," Lili said. "I hope I can repay you somehow."

I didn't hesitate. "Find Hannah for me."

"I promise to have news when we meet in Florence." She pressed my hand. "Addio, and buona fortuna to us both."

CHAPTER THIRTY

Journal of Dr. Hannah Ingram

After long torpor, receiving back her intellectual activity, she derived an exquisite pleasure from the use of her faculties.

Nathaniel Hawthorne, *"The Marble Faun"*

August 20

I've been watching the newspapers, waiting to see some mention of the stalker's death before contacting Kendall. Once the story's out, he might not feel the need to relay anything additional I might tell him to the authorities. Strangely, I haven't seen any coverage yet—surely the stalker's body has been discovered by now.

And he was clutching Lili's shawl—very unusual and very expensive, no doubt—which the police might trace to her. Can they follow Lili into Switzerland? They'll be looking for Donatello, too—even Kendall and me, since we were with them at the Hilton. We're sure to be involved, sooner or later, so perhaps all I've accomplished by my silence is to delay the inevitable.

Suppose I should have to testify as a witness. Would I lie to save Donatello? Or Lili? What a sorry tangle our "charmed circle" has become! I'm reminded of our fractured reflections in the mirror at the Galleria—were the flaws in the mirror or in ourselves?

So today, more confused than ever and much in need of his support, I called Kendall, only to get a message that he's at Monte Beni. A surprise—I would have thought, after what happened at the Hilton, Donatello would forget about his invitation and perhaps even leave the country with Lili.

Next I tried to reach Kendall on his cell—not in operation.

I wonder if K. has learned anything at Monte Beni about what happened that night. Probably not. Donatello can't tell him without incriminating himself and Lili. But it makes me nervous that K. isn't using his cell phone—he's never without it. I suppose he's in no real danger—I can't imagine Donatello hurting anyone except to protect Lili. And Kendall can take care of himself, in any event. I probably should have let him take care of me.

I also called Evan Comstock today.

"What the hell are you doing in Siena?" he wanted to know.

I told him I simply needed a change, and that after immersing myself in Rome and the Cenci, it was helpful to just step back and get a new perspective. That mollified him; it also happens to be true.

Since coming to Siena, I've found my Beatrice. I was looking for her in the past, in Rome, but she's here, now—in Lili's haunted paintings, her subterfuges, her desperation. And in my own dreams, frustrations and fears. All the conflicting emotions I've felt and the inconsistencies I've observed, I can see in Beatrice, who struggles against a cruel, domineering father and is finally overcome by events—some of her own making. I'm enthralled with her now.

In the love duet with Olimpio, Beatrice manages to mesmerize the older, more experienced man while appearing to be seduced. Olimpio's line has the melody ("I can show you love"), a very straightforward approach, while Beatrice and a flute do some fluttering harmony—"How can I resist?" and so on. Gradually, Beatrice's notes coalesce into a counter harmony which becomes stronger and stronger ("Can you prove your love?") and it's a duel of wills until Olimpio acquiesces with "I cannot refuse." G minor, lots of diminished sevenths, modulation to the major at the end as both lovers achieve their goals—it works.

I had a start on the orchestration for the duet with Lucrezia back in Rome, and now I've completed it. By the time the women face execution, they have made peace and are helping each other dress, trying to keep up appearances to the end. Lucrezia is not courageous and loses heart, with lots of descending phrases; Beatrice, now resigned to her fate and determined to tough it out, supports her stepmother with the same melody, but it's inverted to sound almost triumphant. The final moments of the duet are in close harmony, thirds, and very tender. The women put their arms around each other (will I ever have such a reconciliation with Lili?) and exit the stage, heads held high. I was almost in tears when I finished it.

How I'd love to discuss all this with Kendall. Should I try to call him at Monte Beni? Or continue to wait it out?

Siena, August 22

Still nothing in the papers, and I still haven't called Monte Beni. Part of me wants to pour out the whole horrible story to Kendall and beg him to come for me in Siena; the other part still wants to avoid a confrontation and just finish my work. I settled the matter by writing Kendall a letter. I explained everything—what I saw, what Lili said afterward, why I couldn't bring myself to talk about it, even with him. Why I left Rome.

I also told him how much I miss him. They ran the famous horse race in the square last week—the Palio—that Kendall used to rave about. He said people come to Siena from all over the world to experience a few fabulous minutes of time warp—medieval pageantry, fierce competition, delirious celebration. From my balcony, I've watched the flag throwers and drummers practicing in the street below, and I got excited right along with them. But when the day of the Palio arrived, I just couldn't bring myself to go. I wanted to see it with Kendall or not at all.

And the other evening I was looking around for a place to have dinner and discovered a little gem of a restaurant near the Sanctuary—The Grillo (cricket). Tables and chairs were set out on the steep cobbled street and, incredibly, they were level—how could it be? I looked closely, and the legs on one side had been sawed off at the knees! I wanted so much for Kendall to see those tables and chairs. It's just the sort of offbeat ingenuity that delights him—he would be sure to take photos.

I wanted us to have ribollito together at The Grillo and share a bottle of Montepulciano. To come back to my little cell afterward and make love with the breeze from the balcony wafting over us.

When K. returns from Monte Beni, he'll find my letter. I know he'll understand.

And I'll go back to Rome this weekend.

CHAPTER THIRTY-ONE

Nathan Kendall's Narrative

*In circumstances of profound feeling and passion, there is often a sense
that too great a seclusion cannot be endured;
There is an indefinite dread of being quite alone with the object of our
deepest interest.*

Nathaniel Hawthorne, "The Marble Faun"

Perhaps Donatello was as weary as I of the gloom which seemed to
pervade Villa Monte Beni, for he agreed readily to the Florence excursion.

"We've both been working hard, Kendall. You're right—a weekend in
Florence will be good for us. There's always a lot to see and do there. And
then you'll leave with a better impression of my hospitality."

"Donatello, you've been a great host. I've loved seeing your home
and getting to know you better. And I have material for a couple of good
articles," I assured him. "But I need to get back to Rome . . ."

"I understand why you want to go," Donatello said, "but I'm not ready
for Rome." At least he didn't vow never to return. I took that as a favorable
omen for Lili's mission.

The next morning, while Donatello briefed Tommaso on some business
details, I said goodbye to Sofia, making a mental note to send her a thank-
you gift. Perhaps I would find something appropriate in Florence.

Otello, Romeo and the other dogs seemed to sense I was leaving and
congregated in the courtyard. I said goodbye to each of them, surprised to
find my emotions so at odds. My days spent in this ancient place, however
clouded with suspicion and anxiety, had been a retreat from present-day

realities, a reunion with the earth and its inhabitants of an earlier time. I cherished it.

We loaded our bags into one of the winery's aging pickup trucks, and Tommaso added a case of Monte Beni for me to take back to Rome. My parting words to him were mostly unspoken because Donatello was standing close by. I thanked him for all his assistance, and in our handshake was a pledge and a prayer for the future of *il Conte*.

As he drove, Donatello warned me that he had been unable to make reservations at a fine hotel, which I had scarcely expected anyway on short notice in the height of tourist season. "A cousin of Sofia's has a place on a little street behind the Uffizi and he has cleared a room for us."

We parked the truck and carried our bags down Via dei Guanti, which is in one of the city's many no-traffic zones. The cramped alley made Via dei Portoghesi look like a thoroughfare. And while we were greeted with cordiality, Sofia's cousin's place, Albergo Poco Bello, barely qualified for its three-star rating. Neither of us cared.

"*Ebbene*, Kendall, I know many wonderful restaurants in Florence, and museums, of course. Just let me know what you want to do."

I was pleased that Donatello had been able to tap some inner resources and to lift himself from his depression, even temporarily, and that he seemed eager to assume the role of guide. He did not disguise his relief, however, when I assured him that I had visited the Uffizi Gallery several times and was not about to stand in line for hours today, no matter how enticing the treasures within.

We settled for a stroll to Santa Croce. The Gothic style church boasts frescoes by Giotto and Gaddi, a chapel by Brunelleschi and the usual array of religious paintings and sculptures, but it's a favorite of mine because of the stunning assemblage of great human beings buried there—all Florentines! As Donatello and I circled the massive nave, we paused at the tombs of Galileo . . . Machiavelli . . . the composer Rossini.

"I hope you can bring Hannah here sometime," said Donatello, giving voice to my thoughts.

There is a memorial to Dante here (could we never escape him?), and the final resting place of Michelangelo, attended by three grieving figures representing painting, architecture and sculpture. We saw that a white rose had been placed on the great man's tomb, perhaps a tribute from a tourist.

On one of the streets leading from the piazza was a shop with a window display of colorful theatrical paraphernalia. I couldn't resist buying a commedia dell'arte mask for Hannah, partly as a talisman to insure that I would find her.

In another shop I selected a cameo pendant that Donatello agreed would delight Sofia. He purchased nothing, but I saw him examining some antique jewelry and wondered if, even subconsciously, he might have Lili on his mind.

At noon, Donatello steered us to a shaded courtyard restaurant where we shared antipasto and pizza. "We'll have the famous bistecca alla Fiorentina tonight," he promised, unaware that I had other plans for him.

We chose the Bargello for after-lunch sightseeing, intending to cross the Ponte Vecchio and see the Pitti Palace and Boboli Gardens later in the afternoon. The Bargello houses a superb selection of Renaissance sculpture, and Donatello did his best to provide ongoing commentary. But as time ticked by I found it harder and harder to concentrate on Della Robbia's cherubs.

I had suggested the surreptitious rendezvous on the spur of the moment, assuming that Donatello, in spite of his earlier flight from Lili, would be ready now to resume their relationship, in whatever form it might take. I could be wrong, of course, and merely be setting them up for further shock and distress. Distinctly unpleasant scenarios began to form in my mind, culminating in a double murder. By three-thirty I could bear no more of the Bargello.

"I'm ready for a drink," I told Donatello. "Let's get out of here and walk over to the Signoria."

"D'accordo!" He was relieved. I remembered that Donatello never liked to remain indoors for long periods.

The Piazza della Signoria is a unique outdoor sculpture gallery and one of the most elegant places in the world to sit and survey one's surroundings. In spite of my personal preoccupations, I felt a familiar stir of excitement we emerged from a small side street into that bright, broad, beloved space. I nudged Donatello to a café table where we had an unobstructed view of the Loggia dei Lanzi, the arcade where Lili was to appear.

We sat companionably with our drinks (Campari for me, acqua minerale for Donatello), making desultory conversation and watching the swirls and eddies of people passing by. It seemed a long time ago that Donatello, Hannah and I had sat together at a table like this on Via Veneto, never imagining the turns our lives would take. Suppose I hadn't remembered the opening at Galleria Castelli? Or suppose Donatello hadn't joined us for that event? What if we had been unable to find Lili at the gallery?

I checked my watch. Five to four.

Donatello noted my gesture and asked, "Shall we go?"

"No, not yet. I like just relaxing here," I replied, not relaxing at all.

Four o'clock . . . five after four. We were sitting in the shade but I was sweating.

The waiter, no doubt hoping to turn the table, brought our check and slapped it down with a brisk "Grazie, Signori, buona sera."

Taking the hint, Donatello picked up the check. "I suppose we should leave."

Damn it! Where was Lili? I peered at the shadowed loggia.

"No hurry—and let me take that." Perhaps I could delay a few minutes with a polite argument over who would pay.

Then I glimpsed a slender woman in a pink dress in the loggia. Her long black hair was loose around her shoulders; I had never seen Lili like that except at the beach. Was it she?

Then the woman removed her dark glasses and there was no doubt.

I tried, not too successfully, to sound casual. "Look, I believe that's Lili standing in the loggia."

I was too overwrought by this time to wait for Donatello's reaction. I sprang to my feet and dashed across the piazza.

"Lili! What news?"

She smiled, forgiving my abrupt greeting. "Hannah was at the Sanctuary of St. Catherine in Siena, but she's back in Rome now, safe in the Songbird's Tower. And no doubt eagerly awaiting your return."

With a rush of joy and relief, I took her hands and kissed them. "Bless you!"

"And Donatello? Isn't he going to speak to me?" Lili looked toward the table where Donatello sat watching us. "Won't he even acknowledge me?"

They faced one another for a long moment. Then Donatello rose and came slowly toward us.

"Lili?" I heard the old affection in his voice, the same warm delight with which he used to greet her.

When he spoke her name, Lili's face bloomed with hope, but she remained silent until he stood in front of her. "Donatello."

"*Cara*, I should not have left you like that in Rome."

"I understand why you could not bear to be with me . . ."

"But I was so confused. I was wrong; we need to be together."

"Yes. And now we are."

Gently but deliberately, the count gathered Lili into his arms, and she buried her face in the hollow of his shoulder. They clung to each other, oblivious to the passers-by who gaped and grinned as if at two carefree lovers. I knew the deeper significance of the embrace and felt myself an intruder.

I put a hand on the shoulder of each of my friends. "I think I'm not needed here. I must go to Rome."

They separated and began to speak at the same time: "No, Kendall, stay with us awhile; "Don't hurry off."

It appeared that my presence was still required. These first moments together were so emotional for Donatello and Lili that they needed a third party to steady them, to give them time to reconnect. Knowing where to find Hannah (perhaps even to be with her that night!) made me want to bolt to the train station, but at least now I was sure she was safe. A few more hours wouldn't matter . . . much.

I acquiesced. "Well, it would be nice to stroll around the Boboli Gardens and just talk . . ." But I remember little of the conversation as we walked past the Uffizi to the river, across the Ponte Vecchio and up Via de' Gucciardini to Palazzo Pitti. I recall that Lili asked Donatello about the harvest; I told her about the wine festival at San Barnaba. No one mentioned what was most on our minds.

We walked on, through the paved courtyard of the great sprawling palace and up a series of stairways to the gardens. I had previously visited the formal gardens which climb the hillside, the fountains, the grotto. Donatello told us there is a whole different world of deeply wooded paths encircling the landscaped area which most visitors miss—less tamed, with groves of holly and cypress. He led us past a statue of Pegasus and onto a secluded path. Here were thick, gnarled trees and dense shrubbery, feathered ferns and wild flowers.

On the foot path, walking a few steps behind Donatello and Lili, I could both see and sense their growing ease with one another. Donatello took Lili's hand to help her up a steep twist in the path, then put his arm around her waist. They began to speak softly to each other, carefully turning back to include me in the conversation from time to time.

Then, as we approached a particularly large and many-limbed tree, Donatello broke away, grasped a branch and swung himself up into the greenery. He let out a happy bellow and swung down to land almost on top of Lili.

"Buffone!" She jumped back and swung playfully at him with her handbag. "You're not Tarzan yet, you know."

He threw back his head and laughed.

As we walked on, my heart was full. Perhaps, just perhaps, everything would turn out all right.

Soon we came to the Boboli's fanciful, multi-colored Rococo restaurant and we stopped for cappuccino on the terrace. Below us, the grand panorama of Florence glowed in the golden afternoon light, but Lili and Donatello looked only at each other. Her hand moved slowly across the table to clasp his, a seemingly casual gesture that signaled their intimate attachment. Conversation ceased.

Enough, I thought. "I'm leaving now."

This time there was no objection. Donatello rose, reached into his pocket and brought out a set of keys. "Take the truck. I'll send someone to Rome to pick it up."

The truck had a stick shift.

"Thank you, that's very generous but I expect the train may be faster in the end."

Evidently Donatello remembered my learning curve with the moped and repocketed the keys. We hugged. I was getting used to this Italian custom, and it allowed me to express the affection I felt for him without straining to put it into words.

"Thank you and good luck, with everything, Donatello. Best of luck, Lili."

"We'll be in touch with you, Kendall," Lili said, her warm brown eyes making it a promise. "Please give my love to Hannah."

Hannah!

PART THREE

ROME

*When we have once known Rome, and left her where she lies . . .
hating her with all our might . . . we are astonished by the discovery,
by and by, that our heartstrings have mysteriously attached themselves to the
Eternal City, and are drawing us thitherward again, as if it were more familiar,
more intimately our home, than even the spot where we were born.*

Nathaniel Hawthorne, "The Marble Faun"

CHAPTER THIRTY-TWO

Journal of Dr. Hannah Ingram

It was not that the deed looked less wicked and terrible in retrospect, but she asked herself whether there were not other questions to be answered, aside from that single one of guilt or innocence . . .

Nathaniel Hawthorne, "The Marble Faun"

Rome, August 28

I've finished the Beatrice arias! I'm working on the remaining recitativi now, immersed in the music, doing what I came to Rome to do and trying to put the rooftop incident out of my mind.

But now that I'm back, there are so many reminders—the scarf I bought at Porta Portese, the newspaper clipping with the swim race photo, the program from "Aida." Every time I walk through Piazza Navona I see Tre Scalini and remember the lunch we had together there, and our first sip of "liquid sunlight." I can't forget that terrible night and yet I find myself remembering mostly the good times.

Still, I'm glad that Lili isn't in Rome. If I suddenly met her on the street, what would I do? What could I possibly say to her? In retrospect, I'm not proud of how I responded to her that night. Yes, I was sick with fright, but now I think of how terrified she must have been—and for how long. Lili was a good friend, regardless of what she did, and she deserved better from me.

I'm surprised that I've still seen nothing about the incident in the newspapers, and that no one from the police has tried to contact me—Signora Neri would certainly have told me if they had. I came back

171

to Rome prepared to face an inquisition. Could the storm I was expecting have blown over so quickly?

There are so many questions. I wonder if Kendall has learned any of the answers from Donatello. K.'s been at Monte Beni a long time now, it seems. Should I call? I really want him to read my letter before we talk. But if I don't hear from him soon, I'll contact Raffi and see if she knows what's going on there.

All this uncertainty is unnerving. Even the doves have deserted me, it seems—I must remember to put out some crumbs for them. Their cooing would be a comfort.

Rome, August 29

I'd just finished writing in my journal last night and was playing the Beatrice overture when I heard someone running up the stairs. Kendall!

I was so glad to see him I nearly knocked him over, but I don't think he minded a bit. He looks wonderful, all tanned from walking in the hills. We were up most of the night, too excited at being together again to sleep.

We talked a lot about Lili and Donatello. K. didn't stop at his apartment before coming here; he hadn't seen my carefully composed epistle. So I just poured out everything, unedited. How could I ever have hesitated to confide in him—he had no awkward questions, no reproof for my actions and decisions, even though I hurt him. Just gentleness and trust. Did I say I love him?

And Lili told him the rest of the story at Monte Beni: the stalker was her long-ago lover (as I guessed!), but also a terrorist, a thief, and probably deranged. Small wonder he haunted all her paintings! I can sympathize with her now.

Kendall is ready to accept that what happened on the roof was purely defensive. His only concern now is that Lili help Donatello work through his guilt and depression, and in so doing, assuage her own culpability. They are very fortunate—and I'm relieved—that Lili can use her connections to avoid legal prosecution. But it still makes me uneasy that a man has been killed and no one is called to account for it—some soul-searching is the least they can do.

Kendall and I had a sort of fight about it. He called me a narrow-minded moralist; I said he's a moral relativist, and so on.

"I don't understand you, Hannah. You consider Tosca a great heroine, and she stabbed Baron Scarpia to death. Now you've written wonderful music for Beatrice, and she had her daddy done in with a hammer.

"Furthermore, my dear Doctor," he continued, "You've done a complete about-face since we had that argument about *The Scarlet Letter* in Lit class.

You were such a feminist firebrand, you thought Hester Prynne should have squealed on the preacher and let him be hanged so that she could save her own skin."

"I can't believe you're bringing that up after all these years! I don't even remember saying anything like that!" I remembered very well, and it amused me that the incident still rankled.

"Be that as it may, my point is that Tosca was defending her honor and the life of her lover. Beatrice was trying to escape abuse and degradation. Did Lili and Donatello have a lesser reason to toss the stalker?"

"Of course they had a reason—that's not the same thing as moral justification. And those other cases are academic. It's different when actual living people are involved," I protested.

"Exactly. People we know and care about. You were there, Hannah. What would have happened if Donatello hadn't acted swiftly and decisively? If he had left Lili and gone for help?"

"Donatello could have stopped the man in some less drastic fashion."

"Could he? Donatello wasn't armed. How long could he hold off a crazed criminal? What would we have done in his place?"

"I guess I know what you would have done, Kendall." But what had I done?

I had watched, helplessly. And then I ran

I sighed. "You're right. Donatello did what he needed to do."

Kendall rolled his eyes in exaggerated disbelief. "I'm right? I've won an argument with Hannah Ingram? A first!"

"You can't be wrong all the time," I replied tartly. I was still assimilating my about-face on the issue, and a little afraid of the implications. "Gloat if you must, but if we dig deep enough we can probably find some rationale for Khol, as well."

"A reason, perhaps, not justification. He was clearly the aggressor."

"So it's motive that separates the hero from the villain? And our motives are seldom pure and simple."

"As you've discovered in your study of Beatrice. But we agree that Donatello's motive in this case was honorable." Kendall put his arms around me. I rubbed my cheek against his chest, contented, at peace.

"Yes, we agree." I like debating with Kendall; I love agreeing with him.

Later Kendall showed me the photos he'd taken of Donatello at Monte Beni. We compared them with the ones he took for the faun story, and there is a definite difference. Donatello looks older, sadder, wiser, and much less like a faun.

I asked if Kendall ever got a good look at Donatello's ears at Monte Beni: "Is he a real faun, with pointed ears?"

"Maybe yes, maybe no," he answered, teasing me. Then, "His hair is even longer now. I didn't see his ears," and he told me about the old Monte Beni family legends.

How wonderful—Donatello, The Golden One! "So it was destiny, not just coincidence, that he was chosen to be the Faun in the film," I concluded.

K. shrugged. "Don't get too exited, Hannah. Donatello put himself to the test and failed. You remember Lili telling you about their encounter in Villa Borghese Park, and how Donatello called the birds and animals? He tried it again in the woods at Monte Beni."

"What happened? What was it like?"

"Something happened; I'm not sure what. It was almost like entering another dimension, melding with nature. But no animals appeared, and Donatello was bitterly disappointed. He said the animals knew what he had done."

Poor Faun! I wonder if Donatello has lost his faunlike nature forever.

K. tries to view the change in a positive light: Donatello's traumatic experience has brought him to his knees and forced him to wrestle with his values and convictions. He has matured; he will be stronger, wiser. Good coming from evil . . .

But are we condemned to sin in order to have something to repent so that we can find our souls? Nonsense! We argued about that for awhile, too.

With Lili, I suspect, it's more a matter of trying to set things right than of finding her soul. She is a remarkable individual, granted, and I give her credit for trying to help Donatello instead of just going undercover or hiding out in Switzerland. Kendall told me how much she has changed toward Donatello, actually courting him now, in a way—but then, the Faun is not hard to love. K. thinks they have probably gone to Monte Beni and will get in touch with us when they've made peace with the past and reached some decisions about the future.

Kendall brought a present from Florence for me—it's delicious! A commedia dell'arte mask—the rascally Scapino character, with a long hooked nose and feathers, in green and gold and magenta.

"You were angry with me, and brought me a present anyway?"

"I was hurt and worried and extremely annoyed," he admitted. "But I saw the mask and it reminded me of you."

I tried it on. Kendall said it looks quite distinctive and I should wear it all the time—"It's you!" I slugged him with a pillow.

September 3

Evan called to tell me he's arriving Thursday. I'm actually eager to see him now and to have him hear what I've done. I think he's going to love it. There will be some fine-tuning to do, I'm sure, but that will be a pleasure.

Kendall says he's jealous—I'm much too excited about Evan's arrival. Ha! I told him Evan's old enough to be my father—in fact, he reminds me of my father quite a lot. They both respect me and are proud of my accomplishments. Neither would accept failure from me. Evan would probably cut me into very small pieces if I let him down; Dad would still love me, but he'd be disappointed. Kendall supports me totally, he will be happy for me if I succeed but it won't affect how he feels about me one way or the other, bless him. Perhaps that's because he's had such a different family life. He and his mom and sisters are like one big mutual admiration society. But while he seems so self-assured and resourceful, I wonder if Kendall knows what he really wants in life. He says he's writing a book, but I don't believe he's even started it yet.

Well, the creative process can be a painful one, as I've discovered . . .

CHAPTER THIRTY-THREE

Nathan Kendall's Narrative

Is it sin then—which we deem such a dreadful blackness in the universe—is it, like sorrow, merely an element of human education, through which we struggle to a higher and purer state than we could otherwise have attained?

Nathaniel Hawthorne, "The Marble Faun"

The train from Florence to Rome took about one hundred years that night.

When I finally arrived at Termini, I considered stopping at my apartment to freshen up and make myself presentable, but my patience was exhausted. I hopped into a cab, gave Hannah's address, and for the first time in Rome I told a driver to step on it.

Number 18, Via Portoghesi looked like Emerald City at the end of the yellow brick road. Hannah opened the door and threw herself into my arms—I was indescribably happy. We had a lot to talk about and spent half the night arguing, but the other half was ecstatic.

By noon the next day not even my beloved espresso could keep me from nodding off. I collected the luggage I'd left with Hannah's custodian the night before, called a cab and dragged myself home. I napped for a few hours and awoke refreshed and ready to resume my real life.

There was a series of semi-decipherable messages on my answering machine and a gratifying abundance of mail and e-mail; I had not been forgotten in my absence. But I would have a lot of catching up to do. One thing every good freelancer should be is available, and I'd missed two lucrative assignments while I'd been at Monte Beni.

I was about to head out to the Stampa Estera to pick up messages there when the phone rang. It was Lili, making sure I had arrived safely and informing me that she and Donatello were at the count's villa.

"How is Hannah?" she asked.

"Very well, all things considered. She's almost completed the opera."

"Really? That's wonderful!"

"I didn't say this to Hannah, but I think the whole traumatic situation released some creative energy that she's been able to channel into the Beatrice project."

"And perhaps she understands Beatrice better now, emotionally," Lili added. "I'm happy for her."

"Is everything all right at Monte Beni?" I asked.

"Fine. Although getting here in that truck was an experience I'd not care to repeat."

I grinned, picturing the elegant Lili jouncing along beside Donatello in the dusty old pickup.

"And did you survive the Poco Bello?" I asked, thinking a night in that no-frills establishment might have presented another sort of ordeal for her.

"Excuse me?"

"Poco Bello, the little back-street hotel."

"Oh. We didn't go there." She paused, and then I could hear the laughter in her voice. "We stayed all night in the gardens."

I had a flashback to the faun scene at Cinecittà and couldn't contain a chuckle. "Unconventional, but appropriate."

"Astonishing." She let me draw my own conclusions.

"Tell me about Donatello."

"He's struggling, Kendall. He seems to be his cheerful self again for an hour or two, and then gets very quiet and uncommunicative." She sighed. "It's going to take some time."

"Do you have time, Lili?" I remembered that she had hinted at eventual repercussions.

"I must," she said emphatically. "I will stay as long as Donatello needs me. I'm having some of my painting things sent here; I feel an overwhelming urge to paint. Monte Beni is so beautiful, and so strange. It's like living in a myth."

I wondered how different Lili's work might become, now, without her signature dark figure. What would take his place in her paintings?

At the press club, I had a before-dinner drink with some visiting BNN buddies, relieved that The Hornet was absent. I knew he was disappointed in me—he had expected me to pick up his clues and run with the story.

Perhaps I could have found a way to do it without compromising my friends, but I hadn't even considered it. I was disappointed in my performance, too. It was a new and disquieting sentiment.

My doubts about my suitability for my profession increased—or, rather, became focused—when Evan Comstock arrived in Rome.

Hannah had prepared me for a high-powered, high-strung egoist, and he was that—I could fully appreciate her earlier apprehension about not meeting his expectations. But he also had boundless curiosity, subtle wit, and a certain generosity of spirit.

Evan treated us to dinner at the Hostaria dell 'Orso. Knowing that the inn had existed in the time of the Cenci added particular enjoyment and significance to our being there; the food, the wine, and the conversation were splendid.

When Hannah and Evan got into heavy discussion of the opera, I began to take notes, belatedly remembering that I had intended to do a story about the project. The writing and producing of an opera is an immense undertaking, with a minefield of technical details to be navigated as well as the monumental creative aspects. My admiration of Hannah, already pretty high, towered.

In spite of all the summer's distractions and traumas, Hannah had reached deep into her talent, her intelligence, and her humanity and to create a major musical work.

Evan Comstock, with all the success in the world as an attorney, was contributing his extraordinary abilities, his (very expensive) time, and a portion of his fortune to that work.

Donatello, despite his shock and depression, was fulfilling his responsibilities at the winery with laudable dedication,

And Lili, impelled or compelled to play a dangerous game, had abandoned her glamorous life and beloved gallery for Monte Beni, where she was effecting Donatello's recovery—and where she continued to paint her intricate illusions.

Meantime, Nathan Kendall had dashed off some magazine articles and shot a few photos, "signifying nothing," in the words of the Bard.

I had talked about writing a book, but every journalist talks about a book. I saw now that freelancing, for me, had turned out to be little more than a way to pay for a time-out in Italy. I had stood by while Hannah struggled with her magnum opus and had not even started my own. Can a turning point in one's life take place over Lacrime Cristi in a famous restaurant? I vowed to begin.

Evan invited Hannah to return with him to New York and help with the staging of the opera. Hannah was flattered, but asked for another month to polish the score; she wasn't ready to leave Rome yet (nor I to have her go). However, the owner of the tower apartment would be back to reclaim it in a few weeks. I suggested to Hannah that we take a trip to the north of Italy and cool off in the Dolomite Alps for a week or so. She could bunk in my apartment when we got back, and then we could leave for the States together. (I hadn't been home for more than a year and I had promised my mother I would be there for a real family Thanksgiving.) Meantime, I could finish my pending assignments and get a good start on the outline for the book.

Hannah was happy with the plan. There were "a few" places she wanted to visit on our way north: Lucca, to see Puccini's birthplace; Florence, of course; Bologna, the old university city; the Palladian villas of the Veneto; Venice . . . our one week became three, and I began to worry about financing the tour. It was then Hannah told me that she received "a little allowance" from her mother's estate on a quarterly basis, and we could use that. I didn't object.

We would not be including Monte Beni on our itinerary. I hadn't heard from Lili again; I would wait and let her contact me when she and Donatello were ready to see us. And, I thought, Hannah needed to be free of troubling associations for awhile.

Before we left, I put in a call to Raffaella Bianco. If Donatello had signed the contract with the film company, it would be an indication that healing was underway.

The news was not promising. "I can't get him to make a commitment," Raffaella told me. "I'm afraid that Donatello has chickened out—he has the cold feet. Or is it chicken feet?" Raffi was testing her American idioms. "But he will be just fine as soon as that *vampira* Lili takes her teeth out of his neck."

"Ouch! You've got it all wrong, Raffi. Lili's at Monte Beni to help him get his confidence back."

"If you say so," she conceded. "Then I suppose I should be grateful to her. But it would be better if 'Tello were unattached . . . for publicity, you understand."

I understood, more than she realized.

"By the way, Kendall," Raffaella said, "you haven't asked me to go to dinner."

"I know. You've turned me down so often I've given up."

"This time I would have said yes."

Surprise. "Really? Would you explain your change of heart, dear lady?"

"Bruno and I have split up. So I'm available."

"*Che peccato*—too late for me. Should I say I'm sorry or congratulate you?"

"Both, thank you, Kendall."

"You're much too good for him, you know."

"I know." She sighed. "Bruno is convinced Donatello is to blame for my leaving because, well, you can imagine what he thinks. It isn't true. Or maybe it is, in a way. Now I know there are men who don't have to cheat and smack you around to prove how manly they are. Men who are warm and strong and kind . . ."

"You're referring to me, of course?" I teased.

"No! Yes . . . oh, you and 'Tello are both sweet, of course, Kendall. Now, tell me, how is Hannah? I like her so much."

"She's copacetic." There was a new word for Raffi to add to her English vocabulary. "We're about to leave on a trip north."

"Cool! Enjoy yourselves, and call me when you get back."

I was delighted that Raffaella was finally free of Bruno the Brute, but it was obvious she had transferred her affections to the count. They would be working closely together. I hoped she wouldn't get her heart broken.

CHAPTER THIRTY-FOUR

Nathan Kendall's Narrative

He has travelled in a circle, as all things heavenly and earthly do, and now comes back to the original self, with an inestimable treasure of improvement won from an experience of pain.

—Nathaniel Hawthorne, "The Marble Faun."

As we journeyed northward, Hannah and I were able to put our preoccupation with the plight of Donatello and Lili behind us along with the oppressive heat of Rome.

Hannah kept a journal of our travels; I took hundreds of photographs. But it is unlikely that either of us will forget that trip, even without such reminders.

When we returned to my apartment in Rome, there was an invitation awaiting me from Chiara Vista (silver raised lettering on marbled paper) requesting our presence at the opening of "The Marble and the Muse." On the back was a handwritten note: "Please come and bring Hannah. I am hoping to see you, D."

We were eager to see Donatello, certainly, and the film. It had been shown at the International Film Festival in Venice the week before Hannah and I passed through on our way to the Dolomites. "The Marble and the Muse" had been more or less snubbed by the judges, but audiences loved it, especially the "muse"—Fabrizia Milo, the so-called new Sophia Loren.

Also garnering more than his share of media mention was the Faun, Conte Donatello di Monte Beni. I recognized Raffaella's fine hand.

About Lili, we knew nothing. Hannah and I called the gallery several times and got no response. We even went to Via Gregoriana to see if she might have returned to Rome. The once-elegant Galleria Castelli was still closed. There were dead flowers in the courtyard and brown fronds on the palms. A notice on the gate announced that the building was available for sale.

"You don't suppose Lili is going to stay with Donatello at Monte Beni for good, do you?" Hannah wondered. I had told her about the deterioration of the villa and the poor prospects for the winery.

"Who knows? If you had seen her in that moldy old palazzo, Hannah—she brought it alive. And she's bringing Donatello to life, too. I can imagine her there, painting . . ." A pretty picture, but I didn't really believe it. Even if Lili wanted to stay (which, in spite of her affection for Donatello, was unlikely) I suspected that the Italian authorities were not through with her yet.

Hannah took out her opera outfit in preparation for the premiere; then sighed and hung it back in the closet.

"I don't think I can ever wear this dress again, Kendall. It brings the whole episode crashing back. I'll never get over it completely."

I took her in my arms, and after awhile we went shopping. Hannah chose a midnight blue cocktail suit with a deep V neckline, and I bought her "sapphire" earrings on the condition that she wear her hair up so they would show.

The days of the fabulous premieres, with the stars arriving in limousines to be greeted by thousands of adoring fans and *papparazzi*, were long past in Rome, I explained to Hannah. We would be attending the first night of a regular run in a downtown theater, and the stars would not even be there. They would be presented at the reception which was to follow in Rome's most prestigious hotel, the grand old Hassler. The reception would be staged primarily as a photo opportunity for the media, but we could expect it to be a glittering event,. And there we would see Donatello.

"I'm almost sick with excitement," Hannah confessed as we left for the theatre. I knew it was not just the premiere affecting her; it was the prospect of encountering Donatello for the first time since the night at the Hilton.

I'd seen "The Agony and the Ecstasy," the film in which Charlton Heston played Michelangelo, and "Lust for Life," with Kirk Douglas as Van Gogh. I expected "The Marble and the Muse" to be a similarly over-earnest endeavor, but I was happily surprised. It was more sophisticated than those earlier films, and directed with a lighter touch. The Englishman was serious enough about the authenticity of the art, but willing to be a bit tongue-and-cheek with the story. He allowed the script writers—and perhaps the actors—a lot of leeway.

The lead actor played Praxiteles, society sculptor of ancient Athens, with his usual charm and impeccable timing. It wasn't his fault that he was outshown by Fabrizia Milo, delectable as Phryne—she had most of the good lines, as well as incredible curves.

Hannah and I, from the moment the title appeared on the screen, were anticipating the appearance of the Faun. I nudged her at the part where Praxiteles drifts off to dreamland: "Here it comes!"

The scene dissolved to the Arcadian forest. Shot in soft focus, the overdressed set actually looked good. The shepherds wandered in, filmed through branches overhead. We heard only the rustling of the leaves; Hannah tightened her grip on my arm. Then came a harp glissando and a swoosh of foliage as a greenish-gold figure leaped from the tree and landed gracefully in front of the shepherds. The camera cut to a full-length view of the rising figure and gradually moved in for a close-up . . .

The Faun! The golden-eyed Golden One. Hannah's hand gripped my arm.

The rest of the montage was magical, reminding me of the Pastorale segment of Disney's "Fantasia," with the amorous centaurs at play. It had the same innocent appeal, with just a bit of bawdiness.

"The music is marvelous," Hannah whispered, and I agreed that the musical score had much to do with making the scene a fantasy instead of a farce.

Donatello's next appearance was as the son, modeling in Praxiteles' studio, with Phryne working him over while he blushingly tried to hold his pose and keep his composure.

"Hot!" was Hannah's succinct review of that scene.

He appeared only once more, as a foil for Praxiteles who was demonstrating a sculpting technique to him. Donatello spoke his few fragments of dialogue intelligently; his voice was distinctive, soft yet resonant.

The film won warm applause from the admittedly partisan audience. Hannah and I agreed that it was clever, fun, beautiful, and for us (for many reasons), memorable.

"Donatello was absolutely smashing," Hannah declared. "I can't wait to see him."

The Hotel Hassler is a Roman institution, the embodiment of tasteful elegance and discreet hospitality. Whenever I enter the lobby, I feel an urge to genuflect under its huge chandelier of overlapping crystal acanthus leaves.

Hannah and I were directed to the Medici Salon, a burgundy and gold magnificence, where the production company officials awaited. They looked relaxed and smiling, a confirmation that the film had been well received. A small orchestra played music from the film; TV cameras and lights were set up around a stage where the principals would be introduced. We chatted with some of my Stampa Estera colleagues, sipping champagne and sampling the Hassler's opulent assortment of hors d'oeuvres, until the Chiara Vista public relations chief came to the podium and suggested we take seats.

The dynamic president of Chiara Vista stepped forward and begged to say a few words. He delivered considerably more than a few before introducing the director, who modestly thanked the president of Chiara Vista, the assistant directors, the choreographer, the composer, the cameramen, the film editors, the costume and make-up people, the governments of Italy and Greece, and his favorite aunt.

The introduction of the stars was carefully choreographed for maximum drama and media coverage. With a musical fanfare, they entered from behind a screen at the opposite corner of the room where a spotlight found them and followed them along a strip of patterned carpet to the podium.

First came the popular American lead, pausing frequently to wave and shake hands and give the photographers plenty of time to get their shots. (It occurred to me then that I had forgotten to bring my camera—exit journalist; enter author!) The actor spoke with great sincerity and much-appreciated brevity, and then introduced his co-star.

Fabrizia Milo was greeted with a roar. She wore a short, skin-tight turquoise sheath with a feathery flounce and enough borrowed diamonds to finance her next film. The outfit was outrageous, but she looked spectacular as she sidled up to the stage. Her few comments were intelligent and witty, and I had the feeling she was getting a kick out of impersonating herself.

Next came the second leads, and Hannah was getting edgy. "When will we see Donatello?"

"Soon," I assured her. "Raffi's here." I had spotted her hovering at the screen in the back of the room, probably preparing her charge for his entrance. The new Raffaella was aglow with pride and particularly appealing with a few added pounds, her hair a mass of loose golden ringlets. And no tinted glasses.

The PR man spoke. "Now, a young actor who has made an amazing impact with his first brief appearance on the screen. I'm happy to say you will be seeing much more of him." He went on to announce that the company would be making a series of Tarzan films, ". . . developed especially to showcase the talents of a new star in the cinema firmament—Count Donatello di Monte Beni."

The spotlight found him, and by his side was not Raffaella but Lili, more radiant than ever in a gown like liquid silver. As the applause swelled, she smiled up at Donatello and stepped back, out of the spotlight.

Donatello grinned and nodded in response to the applause, and strode toward the podium with all his former ease and energy.

"Kendall! His ears!" Hannah cried.

Donatello's hair had been stylishly trimmed, revealing well-formed and perfectly unremarkable ears.

We stared at Donatello as he made his short speech, hardly knowing how to respond to this revelation. When he left the stage, Hannah lamented, "My illusions are shattered. I wanted to believe Donatello is really a faun."

I recalled the Monte Beni legends and frescoes, and Donatello's earlier ability to commune with creatures of nature.

"I'm disappointed, too," I said. "There's little enough magic in the world. I guess I didn't really want to know about the ears, one way or another." It certainly made a better story when the possibility of his mythological lineage existed.

The show was over and those members of the media on deadline hurried out; others remained to mingle and schmooze the celebrities, especially Fabrizia. But Donatello did not make an appearance. We were puzzled until a bellman approached us.

"Are you Mr. Kendall? Please follow me; some friends would like to see you."

He led us to the elevator and up to the fourth floor where he knocked on a door and discreetly retreated. Donatello and Lili were waiting in the suite. I found myself hugging Donatello and telling him how happy I was to see him and how much I liked the film.

Then I greeted Lili and whispered, "You've done wonders for him." She rewarded me with her most captivating smile.

Hannah had told me earlier she had no idea what she would say to Donatello and Lili when she saw them again, and I knew her emotions were in a turmoil. Now I watched with relief as she congratulated Donatello with her usual warmth and enthusiasm.

Then she turned to Lili. The women's eyes met, apprehensive green and tentative brown. Then they, too, were embracing.

"Dear Hannah, I was so afraid you wouldn't speak to me," said Lili. "I'm so sorry about everything . . ."

"I know. So am I." Hannah was weeping, a release from the tension that had been with her for months. She smiled through her tears. "Oh, I'm so glad to see you."

Lili put an arm around Hannah and led her to a sofa where they sat with their heads together and began to repair their friendship.

"It's good to see you and Hannah together again and so happy, Kendall," Donatello said. "I know how you worried about her at Monte Beni. Are you going to get married now?"

"We haven't really talked about it, but yes, now that you mention it, I'm sure we will." I surprised myself with my response; then I realized that I'd made the decision to spend my life with Hannah somewhere on the road through the Appenines. Happily, I had no doubt that she felt the same. We needed to make plans . . .

"And what about you and Lili?" I ventured. I believed that Lili had saved Donatello from his guilt and depression, perhaps even from the ultimate diminishment of the previous Golden Ones. Would she be a part of his future?

Donatello's expression changed from delight to something close to despair. "Ah, no. Come, I will tell you what is happening." We sat down across from the women.

"Lili must leave Italy," Donatello began.

"We saw that the gallery is gone. What happened?" I asked Lili.

"I assume you shared with Hannah all that I told you?" Lili asked me. I nodded. "Well, my . . . investors have asked me to open a new Galleria Castelli in Hong Kong. I will be leaving tomorrow."

"Hong Kong? Isn't that a rather unsettled place right now?" I asked.

"No more so than any other in my line of work. And there are many wealthy buyers there," was her matter-of-fact reply. I saw her then as a valiant figure—beautiful, gifted, and once again, alone. She was leaving behind friendships that warmed her, a love that consumed her.

Hannah protested, "Hong Kong's not the end of the earth, after all. You'll come back to Italy, won't you? We'll see you again?"

Lili did not reply.

"And you know what I will be doing," interjected Donatello. He turned to me. "Are you surprised that I agreed to be Tarzan? I could hide at Monte Beni forever and nothing would change. But Lili helped me find *fortezza*, *coraggio* to make something good." He looked at her with an expression very close to adoration.

"You told me once, Kendall, I will make much money, and I can use it to fix the winery, and the villa. I will help my friends there and make life better for them in many ways." His face was alight and I saw, if not the Faun of old, a new Conte di Monte Beni.

Hannah and I endorsed his plans with enthusiasm, and we talked for a few minutes about the restoration of the estate.

Then Hannah could not help but ask, "Donatello, forgive me, but I'd like to know about your ears. You told us you had unusual ears, but they're just like anybody else's. I'm so disappointed."

Donatello leaned toward Hannah, took her hand, and placed her fingertips on his ear. "Here, you can feel where the stitches were. The company didn't want an actor with ugly ears, so they sent me to a plastic surgeon."

I was overcome. I could only imagine how great a loss the ancient family legacy of "ugly" ears had been for Donatello—a permanent reminder of his lost innocence, his severed bond with nature.

Tears filled Hannah's eyes again. She put her arms around Donatello's neck, pulled his head down and kissed the ear which, I observed as I looked more closely, was still a bit reddish and swollen around the top. "I'm so sorry, Donatello. What a sacrifice! You will always be the Faun to me."

"Thank you, Hannah. You are very sweet, very simpatica, as I told Kendall when I met you the first time."

There was a knock at the door: the bellman. "They're calling for you downstairs, Conte. Signora Bianco asked me to inform you."

"I just can't believe you and Donatello won't be together again sometime," Hannah said to Lili as we returned to the Medici Salon.

"We've had our time," said Lili. She exchanged a glance with Donatello, and I could feel the bond that had been forged between them.

They stopped in the corridor outside the salon, and Donatello kissed her almost reverently.

"*Ti voglio bene,* Lili."

Without another word or touch, he turned away and stepped into the room where Raffaella was waiting.

Lili turned in the opposite direction and rushed away, quickly losing herself in the crowd of people who swarmed the lobby.

We tried to follow Donatello, but he was already mobbed by media people.

"His heart must be breaking," Hannah said.

"Yes. Atonement has been made, penance is being done."

"Don't be mean."

"I thought you wanted the guilty parties called to account."

"But Donatello and Lili . . . perhaps they weren't so very guilty."

I grinned inwardly. Later I would tell her that she was now a moral relativist, too.

"Well, they will always have their enchanted moments to remember," I said. While you and I . . ."

"Yes, what about us?"

"We'll be arguing about Hawthorne and credit card bills and how to discipline the kids."

Hannah's eyes danced. "So you have been giving it some thought."

"Of course I have." I hadn't much, specifically. But the whole adventure, or misadventure, had brought me to the realization that our paths had not merely crossed but merged.

"Well, so have I," she said. "How about this: we'll be a husband-and-wife creative team, words and music. We'll do an opera together, or a musical."

She went on, with increasing animation. "Maybe a very romantic, tragic musical about Lili and Donatello. We'll call it 'Faun.' You can start now by writing down everything you remember . . ."

I recognized her euphoria as a cover for much deeper feelings. "You know we can't use this story, Hannah."

"No, of course not." Her spirits sank visibly. "But write it anyway. I don't want to forget anything."

I agreed, of course.

"Kendall, there's nothing to keep us from seeing Donatello again, is there? Would we make him uneasy, because of what we know?"

"I'm not sure, but tonight felt like goodbye from both of them."

"It felt like that to me, too," she said with a sigh. "Let's go home."

When we reached my apartment, we found two handsomely wrapped packages propped against the door, one addressed to Hannah and one for me. We took them inside and Hannah immediately tore into hers. Nestled within many layers of pastel tissue paper was an exquisite antique music box, with a cameo of couple holding hands on the lid.

"It's the music box I saw at Porta Portese!" Hannah exclaimed. "Lili must have gone back to buy it for me. And I thought she had left me to meet the stalker. I'm so ashamed."

"Don't be. She may well have met him there. It was her assignment, remember."

"The music box makes a perfect engagement gift," Hannah mused. "Do you think Lili had any inkling . . . ?"

"I'm sure of it."

Mine was a larger package. It held a framed painting, obviously Lili's work, a portrait of Donatello at Monte Beni. In her characteristic style, Lili had woven into the background grapes and vines, birds and animals, even the sad-eyed nymph of the fountain.

Hannah ran her fingers lightly, lovingly over Donatello's face, smiling as she touched his smile, sighing as she traced the new lines which troubled his forehead.

Then her fingers went to the hair over his ears. "What do you make of this, Kendall?," she asked.

I peered closely.

Were Lili's masterfully ambiguous brush strokes intended to show us the tips of furry ears, the Monte Beni family hallmark?

Or was she merely teasing Donatello's dark curls—and us—with greenish gold highlights in a pattern established by Praxiteles?

We were never to know.

CHAPTER THIRTY-FIVE

Notes from Lili Castelli

Donatello's face used to evince little more than a genial pleasurable sort of vivacity, and capability of enjoyment. But, here, a soul is being breathed into him; it is the Faun, but advancing towards a state of higher development.

Nathaniel Hawthorne, "The Marble Faun"

Bravo, Kendall! You have given your story a perfect ending.

I must, however, offer a postscript.

I can imagine you and Hannah reading my comments and pausing from time to time to say, "Lili lied to us." And now I must tell you about the final lie.

While you and Hannah were traveling and I was at Monte Beni, the story of the recovery of the Etruscan antiquities and the arrest of the smugglers was released to the media. The identity of the body at the Cavalieri Hilton was revealed, and it was determined that he was the victim of a dispute among thieves. Tozzi tried to protect me, never mentioning me or the Galleria Castelli by name, but my involvement in the affair became known in certain circles (your mentor Cavaluzzi's handiwork, perhaps?). My suppliers as well as my clients no longer trusted me; I could not sustain the gallery; my usefulness to the Carabinieri was at an end.

And the Mafia. Would I now have to fear their reprisals as I had once feared Khol's revenge? Tozzi thought not; in any case, he was not prepared to protect me indefinitely.

It seemed prudent to put a continent between myself and Italy. So I was not "sent" to Hong Kong. I invented that story to end my relationship with

Donatello in the least painful way possible. Because we parted, we will always love one another the way we did at Monte Beni. Our sort of passion could not have long survived in the real world. Any one of the young women who grew up with him in the Tuscan hills would make Donatello a better mate than I. I didn't want to be there when he realized it. So, I left him.

Are you still curious about the shape of Donatello's ears? I could tell you. After that first night in the Boboli Gardens, I became lovingly acquainted with every attribute of the Count of Monte Beni, including the tips of his ears. But does it matter if they were gracefully pointed or less artistically deformed?

We were all mesmerized by the movie, and by Praxiteles' marble faun. Other artists have imagined fauns with differently shaped ears, even tails; did any of them ever see a faun? Did fauns ever really exist?

We are so enamored of the supernatural that we forget all nature is miraculous, and all individuals. Some of us, like Hannah, can create music that moves people to tears or joy. Some write or paint or build bridges or explore space—or communicate with other species, like Donatello. Pointed ears or a legendary pedigree are not required.

I pondered these thoughts frequently in the days at Monte Beni. Donatello worked long hours at the winery, and I occupied myself with painting and exploring the countryside. We would come together at the end of the day like lovers who had been parted for weeks. Even mundane occurrences—a sudden downpour, the breeze in the olive branches, monastery bells, a moonrise—were extraordinary to us when we were together and could forget the past.

I willed Donatello to heal, and rejoiced when I saw him romp with his dogs as naturally as if he were one of them, buoyant, brimming with joy. But in an instant he might become quiet and slip away to brood, breaking my heart.

Raffaella Bianco phoned frequently, but Donatello was not ready to speak with her. I took her calls and tried to explain that he was busy, that he could not make a decision about the contract until after the harvest. I don't think she believed me. Then one day she called and asked for me.

"Lili, please, Donatello must commit himself now. The company wants to introduce him as their new star at the premiere in Rome. And Lili," she paused and took a breath, "they will have to fix his ears first. Do you understand?"

Had Raffaella seen Donatello's ears, I wondered, or did she simply know that they were "ugly," as he would say? "I will see that he calls you back today," I promised her.

I delivered Raffaella's message to Donatello with great apprehension. It was, in a way, his moment of truth. To proceed, he would need not only to conquer his debilitating guilt but also to forfeit the physical link to his former state of innocence. But how else could he live his life?

Donatello listened to me quietly, and nodded. "Let it be so. It is what I must do." I saw a new serenity in his expression and, after he had talked with Raffaella, even a flash of anticipation.

I have followed Donatello's career, as I'm sure you have, with pleasure for his success in the films and with the winery. I'm sorry he has not married but that, too, will come in time.

It's my fond hope that you and Hannah and I can renew our friendship, and that you will visit me here in Paris. I have taken over management of my mother's business, and I'm experiencing real success as an artist at last.

With gratitude and love,
Lili

He is too wise to insist on looking closely at the wrong side of the tapestry, after the right one has been sufficiently displayed to him, woven with the best of the artist's skill, and cunningly arranged with a view to the harmonious exhibition of all its colors.

Nathaniel Hawthorne, "The Marble Faun"